STEM OF EVIL

Book 1

The Bogotá Experiments

Jac Cochran

Printed in the United States of America
Published by Auchans House

This is a work of fiction. Names, characters, businesses, places, events and incidents are either
the products of the author's imagination or used in a fictitious manner. Any resemblance to
actual persons, living or dead, or actual events is purely coincidental.

ISBN 13: 9780615946818
ISBN: 061594681X
Library of Congress Control Number: 2014900091
Auchans House, Champlin, MN

For Debbie and my wonderful family

Acknowledgments

I owe thanks to the many people who provided input, assisted with background material, or otherwise made possible the writing of this book:

Medical professionals:
Dr. R. Michael King; Dr. Mark Dayton; Dr. William Fabian; Dr. Marilyn Thompson

Military professionals:
Colonel John Wilcox, United States Army

Martial Artists:
Sa Bom Nim Scott Ridlon; Kyo Sa Nim Jeff Tyler

Story input, background and readers:
Steve Hubbard; Jean Dayton; Ross Edlund; Edward Cochran
I would also like to acknowledge the contributions of several members of the intelligence community (who shall remain anonymous) for their contributions to this story.

STEM: a fundamental line from which others have arisen.

Prologue

Most people wonder what becomes of them after death. I happen to know the answer to that question—at least in my own case. My name is Andrew de Coueran. I was born in the year of our lord 1214; my earthly flesh died when I was only 39 years old. As it is now the 21st century, I have existed for about 800 years.

I am what some might inappropriately call an apparition, ghost or disembodied spirit. These terms hardly define my true nature...our language is devoid of a name for what I actually am.

I am going to tell you a tale involving extreme evil countered by extraordinary good—hardly an original conflict in a story, but this one is unlike any other. First, though, I am going to briefly tell you about both my earthly life and my unexpected but welcome life after death.

I am also going to impose a bit of my personal philosophy, distilled and refined over several centuries. Kindly bear with me; I believe you will think it worthwhile.

After the end of my human life in battle, I was quite surprised at the continued existence of my consciousness. I quickly realized I was not in the afterlife I had believed in during my existence as a man; I was most definitely still on earth—as evidenced by the multiple manifestations of evil: general incivility, never-ending crime, disease, poverty, hunger and war.

I wondered if all humans shared this enduring consciousness after death, or if I was some how unique in this regard. My father was a Scandinavian sea-warrior who settled in what was, until recently, the county of Renfrew located near Paisley, Scotland. He had explained to me when I was still a child a phenomenon he called "spirit travel"—when, with much concentration and practice, a person's mind could literally separate from the body and travel to any location that person could visualize. While I was skeptical, I experimented and practiced "spirit travel"; this yielded what I thought were extraordinarily thrilling dreams where my consciousness traveled far and wide.

When I was injured in battle, death did not come quickly. I was in great pain, and realized I would likely die. I chose to calm myself as I slowly bled to death with a final journey of my spirit; I visualized myself on a tranquil beach with which I was familiar, and willed my life force to travel there. As the details of the beach and ocean became totally clear—clearer than any of my previous experiences with spirit travel—I understood that my physical body had died.

It had taken nearly two decades since my somewhat premature demise before I realized that I could control the properties of whatever the nature of what my current state is. I had learned I could alter my form: I could transition from being invisible and able to pass unencumbered through solid objects to being completely visible as I was when alive, and able to manipulate physical objects like a living person could, including reading books. I can also speak and be heard whether I have materialized or not. I can transport myself in an instant by visualizing a location with which I am familiar; if it is a new location, I must first travel to it as an ordinary mortal would.

I continue to have the full range of emotions that I had while living, as well as a robust sense of humor; as in life; I still have a fondness for practical jokes. I learned that I could interact with mortals—yet they can not distinguish from my appearance that I am something beyond their limited comprehension.

I was curious about the nature of my being, as I could not come to grips with the idea that my existence is supernatural. I read the works of the philosopher Elbert Hubbard who wrote "The supernatural is the natural not yet understood." This made me incredibly curious.

This curiosity led me to read René Descartes, who wrote "*Je pense donc je suis*" ("I think, therefore I am"); that was sufficient for me.

During my mortal existence I had been a student of warfare and had honed my combat skills; I had mastered swordsmanship and unarmed combat. My sword master stressed three major concepts: Face combat only in justice and with honor; never retreat in battle; always finish what you start. He had also stressed the importance of flexibility and agility in combat; hence, I learned the basics of acrobatics and tumbling.

I still love learning new things…knowledge has grown exponentially since the 13th century. I occasionally "audit" (in my invisible state) a diverse group of college classes…ranging from archaeology to zoology. My fondness for practical jokes is at times quite juvenile. Sometimes I entertained my self in class by materializing just long enough to ask a complicated thoughtful question—and immediately vanishing. I found the confusion this caused to be hilarious! I can be completely childish at times, but I offer no apologies.

I learned in philosophy classes that what my father had called "spirit travel" others had called astral projection or etheric travel; I also learned that there were biblical references to this phenomenon, as well as references by many cultures throughout history.

Late in the 20th century, I had begun invisibly "auditing" advanced physics classes at Oxford University. I learned about quantum mechanics, quantum entanglement and string theory. String theory is an evolving theory in particle physics that attempts to reconcile the differences between quantum mechanics and general relativity. I concluded, albeit without understanding completely, that my existence is consistent with the laws of physics, and would eventually be understood as a natural phenomenon.

Over the course of my long existence, I have sadly observed the savagery and death caused by wars. I marvel at the miracles of modern medicine, but feel compassion and sorrow for the millions of people whose lives are diminished or ended by diseases. I am puzzled by the impassioned contemporary debate over stem cell research—solutions to cure diseases and prolong life seem to be within grasp, but religious and moral objections abound, as do funding limitations.

Ironically, it was only after the death of my body that I became a true student of life. I completely agree with Socrates who wrote: "An unexamined life is not worth living." I pondered on what were the attributes of a truly noble life, versus a mundane existence…or a completely evil one. After great reflection, I concluded that a truly noble life would first and foremost attempt to stop or at least limit conflict, as well as embrace the positive attributes of courage, honesty and humility. Kindness and respect for others are paramount. I also concluded that concentration and endurance are necessary attributes for achieving worthwhile goals in life.

I believe that all human beings are born with the innate capacities for both good and evil behaviors. Genetics may underlie a predisposition one way or the other, but environment and experiences play the larger role; I have concluded that most people are neither completely good nor completely evil; we all have the capacity for both. However, I have noted that the stem of true evil lies in unrestrained sociopathic greed—whether it is for wealth, power or sex. A major catalyst is the inaction of good people who fail to identify evil in its early stages—both in others and within themselves—and act in ways that inhibit or halt its growth.

I do not have any super human powers (aside from being able to alter my form and "teleport" myself to familiar locations); I can not foresee the future nor can I read minds. I have always had nearly perfect memory, and can still learn extraordinarily fast. Unfortunately, the physical nature of my existence prohibits me from using modern electrical devices. Telephones and computers will not function correctly if I attempt to use them. If I need to correspond with some one, I must use an old manual typewriter!

I have learned that some human beings exist who have senses beyond the normal five; only they can sense that I am not a mortal man. I have also learned that my consciousness is inextricably linked to what were my earthly material possessions. During my long existence I have witnessed sociopaths and psychopaths come unchallenged to power and wreak havoc upon the world. It is with shame that I admit that I stood by and watched as an impartial bystander. But now, early in the 21st century, a global evil force has arisen that is so profound and partially based inside my ancestral home that I cannot stand idly by and watch; I will intervene when the time is right. The evil force is growing in power; I will search out a small group of noble warriors to whom I shall lend assistance; I hope it is not too late!

Now begins my tale.

CHAPTER 1

The Red Moon Lounge is an upscale establishment on the top floor of one of Phoenix's best hotels. Stocking the finest and rarest wines and liquor, it attracts an eclectic affluent clientele. Brandon the bartender, who has a nearly photographic memory for names and faces, kept sneaking curious glances at the interesting stranger in a wheelchair. Brandon fancied himself to be an expert at figuring out and categorizing customers; this guy was proving to be virtually inscrutable. For two hours the stranger had been sipping and savoring $20 shots of Johnnie Walker Blue Label, which is a blend of some of the most expensive and rare whiskies. The mystery man was dressed casually, albeit expensively, displaying wonderful taste. He was wearing a light weight blue silk blazer, a white cotton dress shirt that was open at the collar, and dove gray dress slacks. His long black hair, with grey temples, was worn tied back in a pony tail. Every time he took a drink, his Rolex Oyster Perpetual Submariner watch came into view. Brandon thought the ruggedly handsome man looked vaguely familiar, although he wasn't a regular. He was pretty sure he had never met him anywhere else… maybe he had seen his picture in the newspaper or a magazine. The man had a morose look on his face, and the countenance and demeanor of a person who had been to hell and back. But, even though he was in a wheelchair, he also had an air about him—apparent in his voice and emerald green eyes when he'd ordered his first drink—that Brandon was familiar with from his stint in the Marines: in the military, they called it a "command presence." Command presence is when one has the ability to step in front of a group of individuals and they instantly know that person is in charge. The man, who looked to be in his mid-forties, had been drinking heavily, and was visibly drunk; when he tried to order yet one more drink, Brandon politely cut him off, and the man nodded in understanding and wheeled himself towards the exit without argument. Brandon noticed that two Hispanic men, who had been drinking club soda, immediately got up and followed him out the door. Nearly a dozen people were waiting for the elevator. When it arrived, the conscientious folks all let the gentleman in the wheelchair enter first; they all then packed themselves in. The man in the wheelchair audibly cleared his throat, and said (in only slightly slurred speech) to the people in the elevator, "So, I suppose you are all wondering why I called this short meeting." A brief moment of silence was followed by good natured laughter.

Rarely does one see life-changing events coming; they leapt out at the man in the wheelchair unexpectedly on that Tuesday afternoon shortly after he made his drunken departure from the Red Moon Lounge.

Those events began with a dark van the man saw in his rear view mirror (he had no business being behind the wheel, but he no longer cared if he lived or died). He was pretty sure that the van was following him, but could not imagine why. He was an anomaly on Arizona's Interstate 17 that winter day for two reasons: first, he was a paraplegic driving exceedingly fast and erratically using modified hand controls in a classic fully restored 1961 jet black Jaguar XKE; second, his blood-alcohol level was nearly twice the legal limit. Stowed in the space normally occupied by the front passenger seat was his compact wheelchair. Even in his inebriated state, he recognized that the dark van in his rear view mirror had been following him since he left the Red Moon Lounge 20 minutes ago. He tried slowing down to see if the van would pass him, but it just slowed down too. He tried speeding up, but the van stuck with him.

The man's name was Steve R. Moss. Steve was not short for Steven or Stephen. His mother had died during his birth and his alcoholic father (like father, like son) named him. Apparently the father was inebriated when he named Steve, as he couldn't come up with a middle name; his father just gave him the initial "R" which didn't stand for anything. He died in a car wreck before Moss was one year old; the baby was adopted and reared by his father's brother and his wife, who had no children of their own. His Uncle Sumner and Aunt Beth, who both loved him dearly, had given him a wonderful childhood, but it was Uncle Sumner who had the most pronounced influence in his life… he gave young Steve, along with warmth and guidance, extensive training in the relatively arcane Korean martial art of Soo Bahk Do and a thorough grounding in its philosophy. Nearly as important was his love of books, instilled in him by Aunt Beth, who was an elementary school librarian. She had once emphatically advised him, "Stevie, to be a good man, you must be a scholar as well as a warrior!" That truism guided his behavior as he grew up.

Moss…for whom alcoholism was relatively new… was a retired United States Army colonel. He had become an Army Ranger, and had received special operations training. The Rangers are the spearhead of the Army's special operations forces. Ready to deploy by land or air anywhere in the world at a moment's notice, Rangers specialize in rapid infantry assault, night fighting and airfield seizure.

As a child, Moss was a voracious reader of American history; when he read about the legendary Jim Bridger, he became an instant hero and role model for him. Jim Bridger was among the best mountain men, guides, and scouts during the 1800's. His legendary endurance enabled him to survive in the harshest environments…he sounded like one tough son-of-a-bitch to anyone—especially so to a boy in grade school! Moss's decision to join the Army Rangers was motivated in part by his childhood decision to emulate Jim Bridger and his ilk.

Moss was awarded the Distinguished Service Cross for a heroic rescue under fire of wounded comrades, and had been written about in numerous magazines and newspapers (which is why Brandon the bartender thought he looked familiar). The brief time Moss spent in the media spotlight had been uncomfortable for him—it ran contrary to his modest nature and the Soo Bahk Do quality *of Kyum Son* (humility) which had been ingrained in him since childhood. Just prior to becoming disabled, but after retiring from the military, he had been a private investigator and a bail enforcement agent, also called a bounty hunter. This second career was not exactly what one might expect from a retired military officer, but it literally had fallen in his lap. His father's other brother, Uncle Bud, had been the most successful and notorious bounty hunter in the Southwest—Moss inherited his business when Uncle Bud, who had never married, died with Moss as his sole heir. While not getting rich, Moss had been comfortably well-off… he had enjoyed tracking down and bringing in the biggest and meanest bail jumpers, seriously kicking ass only when absolutely necessary. Moss firmly believed in a simple truth expressed by Soo Bahk Do Grandmaster Hwang Kee: "Man is at his best helping others, at his worst—*bettering* others."

Moss had once been happily married. When he and his wife decided it was time to start a family, pregnancy had proved elusive. During an examination to discover the reason for infertility, his wife was found to have a rare form of cancer; despite aggressive treatment, she had died six months later. Although there had been other women in his life (only after his nearly two years of grieving), Moss had not married again.

Steve R. Moss's pre-disability avocations had been teaching part time in a local Soo Bahk Do school (*Do Jang*), playing chess, reading a wide variety of books, traveling and competing in nine-ball billiard tournaments. In his younger days, when he realized he was beating just about all of his competition, he was not above hustling a few games of pool to raise some extra cash—behavior certainly not consistent with the concept of *Chung Jik* (honesty) taught to him by his uncle Sumner as one of the key concepts of the Soo Bahk Do philosophy.

Moss had not adjusted well to the life of a paraplegic. Six months prior, he had been more or less a normal and sober human being. He'd been out for a ride in suburban Phoenix on his nearly new Harley Davidson Fatboy (a present o himself on his 49th birthday) when, at a stoplight, he was rear-ended by a teenage girl who was typing a text message on her cell phone while driving. He had never lost consciousness. He remembered lying on the pavement being mad as hell that his new motorcycle was wrecked, but he hadn't felt any pain. As Moss tried to get up and couldn't, a sick realization hit him and he knew his life was changed forever.

Moss had a small piece of war-time shrapnel embedded in his back near his spine; the accident, which appeared minor to on-lookers, had caused a slight shift in the shrapnel, which doctors previously had told him was inoperable because of the risk of paralysis. A year later, the large insurance settlement had done nothing to make Moss feel better. It had, however, enabled him to tinker with classic cars when he was sober, and to get drunk on only really good liquor.

He pulled off the freeway on Van Buren, and saw that the dark van made the turn behind him. Moss assumed he'd done something with his erratic driving to anger the other motorist, and decided the best thing to do would be to pull over and stop. Maybe the guy would back off when he saw his wheelchair, he thought.

The van pulled up behind him, and an Hispanic man with a black crew cut got out and walked up to his car, leaned over, and got in his face. "Nice XKE, *señor,*" the man said calmly. "It would be a sin to wreck such a fine car. Perhaps you should not drink and drive."

He was happy that the man didn't seem too angry, and began to offer a drunken apology, "Look buddy, I'm not sure what exactly I did to piss you off, but...." Moss never finished the sentence, because the man simply punched him in the eye, then reached over calmly and stabbed a syringe into his neck. Moss started to ask what the hell was going on, but realized that the world was starting to spin even faster than in any drunken stupor he'd ever been in. Recognizing danger when he saw it, and with years of Soo Bahk Do training behind him, Moss pivoted on his butt and surprised his attacker with an explosive open-handed palm strike (*Jang Kwon*); the heel of his palm drove the man's nose upwards and fractured his sphenoid bone, sending a fatal splinter of it into his brain. The dead man falling to the pavement was the last image Moss saw before he passed out.

It didn't take the police long to see the classic Jaguar sitting empty by the side of the road. When the officer walked up to it, he noticed the handicapped license plates, the wheelchair folded in the space normally occupied by the right seat, and quickly surmised that some sorry disabled person had turned into the wrong neighborhood. The officer did a quick check of the area to see if he could find the driver. Nobody had seen anything, there was no evidence of foul play, and the driver had apparently disappeared.

Two days later, a front-page story ran in the Phoenix paper with the headline "**Famous War Hero Steve Moss Missing—Police Baffled**."

Similar kidnappings of other disabled people were happening across the United States; an evil and unscrupulous coalition was gathering subjects for unknown reasons.

CHAPTER 2

Harriet Beecher was depressed—she had now been in the hospital for over two weeks, and her doctor had just recommended to her that she be moved to a hospice called St. Mary's ... she had sadly agreed. Harriet had been on a transplant list for a new liver for nearly three years. Unfortunately, the number of people needing new livers far exceeds the number of donors; like hundreds of other people in the United States, Harriet had been placed on a waiting list. Unfortunately, her time to live was quickly running out.

An hour later, a nice-looking young man dressed like an orderly came to her room with a wheelchair. He smiled at her and said, "Ms. Beecher, my name is Josh... are you ready to go?"

"Young man, I don't think you realize the irony of that question. But yes, I am ready to go," Harriet replied in a subdued voice. Josh helped her in to the wheelchair and headed for the door. Before they had gotten 10 yards down the hall, a nurse spotted them and shouted in a stern voice: "Excuse me, but who are you, and where are you taking my patient?"

Josh explained that he was an employee of St. Mary's Hospice, and that he had been directed by his employer to pick up and transport Harriet Beecher to her new home.

When the nurse challenged him and asked if she could see his identification and order to transport her patient, Josh replied, "Holy cow, I am glad you asked... both are on my clipboard back in Harriet's room... I put them down when I was helping her into the wheelchair and forgot to pick them back up!"

"Well, why don't you leave my patient right there while we go back to her room to check this out," the nurse commanded.

Josh followed the nurse back to the room and closed the door quietly behind him when he entered. In one blistering fast motion, Josh jabbed a syringe in to the nurse's neck and eased her to the floor as she lost consciousness. He then went back out into the hall and calmly wheeled Harriet Beecher out of the hospital. Josh was not an employee of St. Mary's Hospice at all.

When it finally dawned on her that she was being kidnapped, Harriet realized that she was not going to the hospice; however, she did not realize that her health would eventually be restored in a way that she could never have imagined.

***

Dr. Thomas Jefferson Hunt sat out on the deck of his beautifully restored suburban Victorian home trying to drink a cup of coffee without spilling. He noted that his tremors were getting progressively worse. Every day he seemed to be more tired and shakier than the day before. Thomas had recently retired at the relatively young age of 42, as his Parkinson's disease had progressed to the point where he could no longer practice medicine. He was trying to decide what to do with the rest of his life when he heard the doorbell ring. Thomas wondered who it might be, as not too many of his white neighbors came calling on the only black man in the neighborhood. He unsteadily got to his feet and moved slowly to the door. Thomas did not recognize the two well-dressed Hispanic men standing on the front step. Both were dressed in dark suits, and looked like they might be cops.

The taller one flashed a badge and said "We are detectives Hernandez and Banderas. Are you Dr. Thomas Jefferson Hunt?"

"Yes I am. May I ask what this is about?" Thomas responded in a soft voice with slurred words, typical of those afflicted with Parkinson's disease.

"Sir, we have a warrant for your arrest. We need for you to come with us now."

"You have a warrant for my arrest? For what crime am I being arrested?" Thomas asked with alarm and surprise in his voice. "May I see your warrant? There must be some mistake."

"There is no mistake; you are Dr. Thomas Jefferson Hunt and you have stage III Parkinson's disease," Hernandez said while Banderas suddenly jabbed a syringe into the side of Thomas's neck. He reeled back with a stunned look on his face, then Thomas collapsed unconscious on the floor. Both men cursed and strained as they struggled to lift and carry the huge black man down to their waiting van. As Dr. Thomas Jefferson Hunt lived alone, and with no family living in the area, an entire week passed before he was reported as missing. His life too was going to change in a way he could never have imagined.

***

Stanford University philosophy professor Adam DuBois had gotten himself lost again. In spite of his wife's vociferous objections, he had driven himself over to the campus to clean out his office. Adam did not notice the car that began following him as he left his house. He had successfully reached the campus, parked his car, but obviously taken a wrong turn as he walked to his office. He did not notice the two men who were following him discretely.

Because of increasingly worse episodes of forgetfulness, he had, at his wife's urging, gone to his doctor for a checkup; the diagnosis was early-stage Alzheimer's disease. He continued to teach for a while, but would all too often forget in the middle of a lecture what he was talking about. When students began to complain, the head of his department, who was a compassionate understanding woman, did not dismiss him, but required him to take a forced medical leave of absence. Always the optimist, she opined in a Panglossian manner, "Who knows, Adam... a cure may be discovered at any time, at which point you could come back to teaching!" Always the pragmatist, Adam was not hopeful.

He had been walking for nearly 15 minutes when he realized that nothing looked familiar at all. He was too embarrassed to ask any one for directions to his own office. One of the men who had been following Adam walked up beside him and said, "Excuse me sir, but you appear to be lost; may I help you?"

Adam glanced at the pleasant young man and assumed that he was a student. "As a matter of fact, I seem to have taken a wrong turn and could use some assistance getting to my office."

"You really did get yourself turned around, Professor DuBois... you are on the wrong side of campus! It is too far to walk from here, so why don't we give you a ride over there, and then we'll bring you back to your car?"

Adam much appreciated the young man's kindhearted offer and readily accepted. The young man and his friend led him over to their car and opened the back door for him. As he was getting in, the second young man casually jabbed a syringe in Adam's neck.

Four hours later Adam's worried wife called the police to report her husband as missing; the police were not immediately concerned when she told them that her husband had been recently diagnosed with Alzheimer's disease, but notified campus security to keep an eye out for Dr. DuBois who was probably disoriented and wandering around the campus. He was never found.

***

Pete Hubbard had a wonderful life: a loving wife, three beautiful daughters, and a great career as a geologist. The only blotch on his otherwise perfect life was his type I diabetes. While he was extremely careful about his insulin shots, Pete's weight had crept up over the years. His physician warned him that the recurring sores on his feet were taking longer and longer to heal; he was concerned that Pete might end up having to have both feet amputated. Pete was mortified by this thought and had begun an exercise program to lose some weight. He would get up every morning two hours before his wife and daughters arose and go for a 2 mile run through the park adjacent to their home… it had wonderful paved trails. After his run, he would shower and go to work taking care not to wake his wife or his girls. About a month after he'd started doing this, two athletic looking men (who he assumed lived in the area) began running at about the same time each morning as Pete.

One morning, he saw the two men casually chatting with each other as he trotted past. They quickly fell in to step behind Pete. As he did not like having the two men immediately on his heels, Pete sped up; the two men increased their pace to match his. He wasn't really up for any friendly competition, so he slowed to a walk, thinking that men would simply pass him by. Instead, they slowed to a walk just like Pete. He whirled around to confront them. "What's going on… are you guys trying to hassle me?"

This early in the morning, the three men were the only ones in the park. No witnesses were present as he was put in a bear hug by one of the men while the other jabbed a syringe into his neck. When he lost consciousness, the two men quickly carried Pete to a van with a driver in the park's parking lot.

10

Around noon Pete's wife received a phone call from his boss wondering if he was home sick as he had not come into work yet. Fearing that Pete had perhaps fallen and injured himself during his morning run, or worse yet, had a heart attack, she and the girls ran over to the park to see if they could find him. She then called all the local hospitals to see if Pete had been admitted; then she called the police to report his mysterious disappearance. Police quickly came to their home, and then searched the park thoroughly to no avail. Pete had disappeared without a trace.

All the neighbors were interviewed by the police, but no one had seen anything. Three days later Pete Hubbard was officially declared a missing person. Although his wife and boss claimed that Pete did not have an enemy in the world, foul play was suspected.

***

The morning that United States Senator Jake Jackson's disabled younger sister was kidnapped couldn't have been hotter, or the humidity more oppressive under the sweltering Minnesota August sun. The combined heat and humidity was conjured into a "heat index" by the local weathercasters, a number that, like winter's "chill factor," conspired to make everyone as miserable as possible.

Just before noon, Haley Jackson carefully negotiated the wheelchair ramp from her townhouse down to the concrete sidewalk. She wistfully remembered the feeling of hot pavement on bare feet from the days before her accident. Haley, who was an Olympic bronze medalist in gymnastics, had eight months ago been demonstrating a balance beam dismount to her gymnastics class of junior high school girls. What seemed like a minor fall at the time had changed her life forever.

Only 15 seconds out of her air-conditioned home and Haley could feel the first bead of sweat forming on her forehead. Her shoulder-length blonde hair took on golden highlights under the sun, and it framed a face whose beauty was overshadowed by features that radiated both strength and intelligence.

Haley looked up and down the street, and then at her watch. Bill Preston, her driver, had taken the van for gas, and had said he'd pick her up at 11:45. He was ten minutes late; she was going to miss her hair appointment for sure! Haley missed riding in regular cars and on bikes and motorcycles. These days, her transportation was boring vanilla—boxy vans equipped with wheelchair lifts, able to go from zero to 60 miles per hour in, oh, a minute or two.

A black Ford van with government license plates and darkly tinted windows came around the corner. "There she is," the passenger said to the driver, pointing her out. "Pull over slowly, roll down the window and smile."

Haley had a puzzled look on her face as the black van pulled up in to the driveway of her townhouse. The driver's window rolled down and a dark-haired man wearing aviator-style sunglasses and a yellow polo shirt smiled pleasantly at her. "Ms. Jackson? Bill called from the gas station…seems he can't get your van started after putting gas in it. He didn't want you to be late, so he gave us a call to see if we could fill in."

The passenger, a compact block of a man, had gotten out and opened the side door of the van. He was activating a foldout wheelchair lift as Haley asked, "Why didn't Bill call me himself? He has my cell phone number." Her concern over the absence of her regular driver was being mitigated by the thought of the air-conditioned interior of the van. In the small of Haley's back, just above the point where her paralysis began, she could feel her turquoise summer dress begin to cling to her skin.

The driver smiled again and replied, "Ah, but he did try to call. There must be something wrong with your phone. Have you checked it?" Haley slipped the phone out of her bag, and verified that the phone was on. She tried to speed-dial Bill's cell number, but instead of a dial tone, got only a popping and humming sound. "Huh, how about that," she said, "must have dropped it, or the battery is going. Well, let's get moving, we're going to be late as it is." The van was most likely courtesy of the federal government and her older brother Jake, Haley thought. Mainly, being the sister of a United States senator had been a pain in the ass (metaphorically speaking, since she hadn't actually had feeling in her ass since her accident), but there were some perks on occasion.

The driver helped position Haley's chair on the lift, secured it, and closed the door after she was completely in. As she was opening her mouth to ask the driver to hurry a little, her eyes went wide as she felt a hand clamp strongly over her mouth. The man behind her pinned her arms by simply bear hugging her from behind, and Haley's eyes bulged as she saw another hand—an ebony female hand—with a syringe approach her neck. Within moments, the unexpected terror and the heat of the day were replaced by a cold dark heavy fog, and then by a dreamless sleep.

From the back of the van, a female whiskey voice that sounded like it should belong to a jazz singer said, "Don't speed, and turn off the jammer so I can call our pilot at the airport."

CHAPTER 3

S enator Jake Jackson sat waiting for his sister in the restaurant with Sally
Peters, his spokes person and press liaison, who was also his sister Haley's
best friend since high school. Prior to joining Jake's staff, Sally had been
employed by the National Security Agency, or NSA as it was commonly called.
Sally had been a senior intelligence analyst reporting to the NSA director Luke
Jackson, Jake's older brother. Much of what she had done at NSA was classified; Jake knew better than to ask her questions about her intelligence career.
Jake did know that the NSA was the home of America's top code makers and
code breakers. He also knew that his brother Luke was largely responsible for
restoring the NSA's reputation and the public's trust following revelations in
2013 about some of its questionable techniques and data gathering programs.
Luke had given Sally an outstanding recommendation (not telling his brother
the fact that Sally Peters had been the best code-breaking strategist he'd ever
seen). Luke had hated to see her go, but understood Sally's commitment to help
her best friend.

They had planned to meet with Haley for a late lunch after her hair appointment, and before Jake's 3:00 press conference announcing that he would not be
seeking re-election. Haley was uncharacteristically late.

Sally had become his press liaison on a part-time basis, and was public relations "natural" in Jake's eyes. The facts that Sally had been Haley's best friend,
post-accident cheerleader, volunteer live-in personal assistant and persistent
nag to Haley about going to physical therapy, had put Sally's career on hold.
Jake was a big believer in pay-back, and getting Sally back on her career track
was a small step in that direction. That Sally actually looked like a cheerleader

didn't hurt matters. When she was in front of the media, they simply grinned at her and were buoyed by her bubbly personality, often unaware of her keen intelligence.

Jake chuckled to himself as he recalled one male reporter who, after listening to Sally's presentation of Jake's position on the drug war at a press conference, made the mistake of assuming Sally was a stereotypical blonde bimbo. The reporter had asked her if she actually knew where the country of Columbia was. The reporter, to the amusement of his colleagues, was "treated" to an icy ten minutes of extemporaneous analysis of the Colombian drug cartels, the obstacles presented by corrupt officials, and a long list of supporting facts. When she'd finished, she'd asked the reporter, "Did you get all that, or was it hard to hear with your head that far up your personal Central American corridor?" No attending reporter had ever let her voluptuous good looks fool him or her again.

Sally dug out her cell phone and tried Haley's number again. All she got was the standard message indicating that the phone was not currently on.

"Maybe she forgot to take her cell phone along," Sally offered. "Or maybe her appointment ran late, and she's on her way. But if we don't leave now, we'll be late for our own party, and you know how the press hates that. I'll tell Cedric to offer our apologies when Haley arrives."

CHAPTER 4

Haley Jackson awoke groggily to a humming noise that was not unpleasant, but the sound belied what she saw when she opened her eyes. She was lying in a narrow bed, much like a hospital bed, with an IV in her left arm, which was strapped down, as was her right. She could see other similar beds, but also windows like an airliner would have. Strange, she thought. In the bed across from her, she noticed a sleeping man with long dark brown hair streaked with gray at the temples, and a black eye that looked like it would hurt when he was awake. A vague feeling of familiarity briefly entered her consciousness, but quickly drifted away. She was not at all anxious, in spite of not knowing where she was, how she got there, or where she was going. No stranger to hospitals and sedatives, the analytical part of her brain acknowledged that something was very wrong and that she was being heavily sedated. Haley tried to remember the last thing that had happened, and all she could think of was that she'd probably missed lunch with her brother and Sally. She slipped back into a semi-euphoric sleep, thinking about how good the house salad dressing was at Cedric's.

Alicia Jones, former surgical nurse and former cocaine addict, noticed that the Senator's sister had briefly been awake. She stepped over to Haley's IV and slightly increased the drip. She wanted none of the patients awake when the aircraft landed in Bogotá, Colombia that evening, and walked up and down the aisle to check the other men and women. Alicia didn't know precisely why this group had been selected; all she knew for sure was that they all had medical conditions, ranging from Parkinson's disease to diabetes to paralysis. Although she knew none of the details, she knew the group had come from a wide variety of cities in the United States, and that all ranged in age from 19 to 54. Alicia also knew none of these people had volunteered; they all came from well-to-do families and had been afforded the best medical care available. Each had been plucked quickly and without incident (well, except for the longhair ex-soldier who'd actually fought back and killed one of their men) within the last 48 hours. She also knew that not more than two of these people had been taken from a single city, and reasoned correctly that had been done to minimize suspicion.

The Colombian customs officials were expecting a medical flight with patients in comas of variable severity. They would be told they were en route to Dr. Nicolas Falcón's medical center for specialized treatment, and close scrutiny was not expected. The flight crew, including the pilot, was unaware of the actual medical condition of their passengers. They believed the patients were "vegetables" or comatose, and all had conditions that Dr. Falcón would be trying to treat. They knew that rich Americans often sought exotic treatments outside of their own country. Their paperwork for the flight, other than the true identity of their passengers, was all in order.

Alicia remembered the days when she'd carried huge professional responsibilities as a head nurse, and had been in love with her job...it was almost like she was back on her old ward again. Alicia had been engaged to a handsome Jamaican medical student. His only vice was a love of hard partying. At first, she had enjoyed the unbridled fun and experimentation with drugs that she'd previously eschewed during her strict Catholic upbringing. One day she realized that it wasn't so fun anymore, and that she actually needed to get high. Being a nurse didn't provide Alicia with the income she needed to sustain her new habit, but she quickly discovered she could trade legal drugs she smuggled out of the hospital for the illegal ones she craved. This worked well right up to the point where she was, in order, arrested, jailed, fired, convicted and sent to prison for 52 months. Her fiancé had gone back to Jamaica, and Alicia had never heard from him again. When she was released from prison, she was 38, slightly overweight, and depressed because she could no longer work as a nurse in any legitimate medical facility. Alicia had believed that her career was over. That was before she met Pat Dominguez, who introduced her to Dr. Falcón when he was lecturing at a seminar in Los Angeles. Now, Alicia was once again working as a nurse and her drug habit was not only accepted by her employer, but was fed as part of her compensation before she managed to kick her addiction. Knowing Dr. Falcón liked his employees beholden to him, she never told her employer she was no longer addicted; Alicia simply flushed her weekly allotment of cocaine down the toilet.

CHAPTER 5

S ally Peters unlocked the front door of the suburban townhouse she'd shared with Haley and Jake's 19-year-old daughter Katie since Haley had been released from the hospital after her accident. Haley could have gone to live in her brother's mansion on Lake Minnetonka, but she kindly rebuffed his invitation. Finding really nice wheelchair-accessible housing had been a bitch, but Sally knew that Haley would adapt to her disability much faster if her housing fostered independence. She heard Katie's typically loud music playing, and hoped Haley wasn't going to be mad that she and Jake had not waited for her at lunch. "Hey guys, I'm home," she announced.

"Hey Sally," Katie hollered over a blaring radio, "is Aunt Haley with you?"

"No, I was supposed to have lunch with her but she was late. I thought she was home with you by now."

"No way," Katie complained, "it was her turn to cook, and I thought she skipped out and went to dinner with Dad. I tried calling her, but her phone's not on. By the way, how'd the press conference go?"

"Just OK, but not great," Sally admitted. "The big question is why Jake won't run for the Senate again. We both know it's so he can spend more time with Haley. Since your mom passed away, he feels guilty enough having to be in Washington. But he doesn't want Haley to think he's quitting because of her. So we told the press that Jake could no longer align himself philosophically with the president's agenda, even though they're both in the same party. That's true, but Jake would actually like to stay and try to balance the party a little better. So, I'm starving …did you get anything to eat for dinner?"

"No, and I'm hungry too, but we're pretty much screwed as far as groceries go. Maybe we can call Bill, since Haley is too dim to have her phone on, and see if he can stop and get us some tacos when he brings Aunt Haley home."

When Katie dialed Bill's direct number in the van, there was no answer. She then called the van service directly, figuring they'd know where Bill was, since he was required to check in periodically. "Hello, this is Katie Jackson, Haley's niece. I'm trying to contact her driver, Bill Preston, but he's not available by phone. Do you know where he can be reached?"

"I'm sorry, Ms. Jackson," the dispatcher said, "but we haven't heard from Bill since he left to pick up Haley early this afternoon. Frankly, we're a little concerned, and we called the police a little while ago just to make sure he hasn't had an accident."

Katie had an involuntary twitch in her shoulder as she considered the prospect of Haley being in yet another kind of accident. "Would you do me the favor of calling as soon as you hear? We haven't heard from Haley, and she is usually home for dinner."

Katie could hear the hesitation in the voice of the dispatcher. "We'll call you as soon as we hear anything. Perhaps you should call your father as well, since he may know where Haley is. Good night."

Sally could see the growing look of concern on Katie's face, and said, "She's probably with Jake, and Bill is probably sitting in some tittie bar and forgot to call in. Call your Dad, and see if he's planning on getting Haley home."

CHAPTER 6

Moss felt his consciousness slowly surface, like a submarine raising its periscope at the first light of dawn. He recalled a brief struggle... a blow to his face, and then nothing else. He kept his eyes shut and did a slow inventory of his body from the chest up, since he had not had any feeling below his chest since his failed surgery three months ago to remove the shrapnel that had begun shifting even more since his motorcycle accident. He could tell that his arms were stiff, and that his left eye hurt a lot. His breathing seemed to be OK, which was a good sign. Something was not right with his lips, and his tongue felt weird. Moss realized a strand of his own long hair was in his mouth, and he awkwardly spat it out.

Moss was very good at assessing signs of life, as he had observed many dying men during combat. He had been a second lieutenant in the Army back in those days, and had been wounded twice and recovered fully twice, although some shrapnel had been left behind. It was ironic, He sometimes thought, that he should have emerged relatively unscathed from horrific battles only to be crippled by a tiny piece of residual metal many years later. On his darker days, Moss sometimes wished he had died in battle rather than lose the use of his lower body forever. His doctors had been wise enough to recognize his depression, but even Prozac had its limitations. He still grieved for his losses: he would never pick up a woman in his arms again; he would never participate in another Soo Bahk Do tournament; he would never race a motorcycle again; he would never play in a beach volley ball tournament again. Perhaps worst of all, he would never visit his wife's grave again without assistance because the country cemetery was on a steep hill inaccessible to a wheelchair.

His slow return to consciousness was not undetected. "Waking up, are we?" a woman asked softly.

He tried to open his eyes, and realized only the right eye would open. In front of him was a somewhat weathered but attractive black woman who was now leaning down to examine his eye. "Nasty shiner, you got there, buster, but once the swelling goes down you should be able to see fine again. Right now I'm going to put some ice chips in your mouth, and you just suck on them slowly. If you don't puke, I'll give you some water in a little bit and get that IV line out of your arm. My name is Alicia, and I'll be taking care of you for a while." With that, she simply walked out leaving him with many unanswered questions floating up to his increasingly aware brain.

With melting ice in his mouth, Moss took a quick look around. He was in some kind of medical facility, with concrete block walls and shiny white vinyl floors. There was another bed in the room occupied by what appeared to be a bald-headed giant of a black man, still asleep. He was still trying to process the confusing thought he was having about being in an unknown hospital when he noticed the room's single window. While the morning light was streaming in, the stout steel bars embedded in the concrete window frame were casting ominous shadows on the opposing wall. He shut his one good eye and then opened it again only to glumly conclude this was not a dream.

Two men in white coats walked into the room. The older of the two had silver hair, strikingly blue eyes, and a stethoscope around his neck. In lightly accented English he asked Moss how he was feeling.

"Where the hell am I, and who are you?" Moss croaked (his voice sounded more like a frog than a human).

The younger man walked over to the nightstand and poured a glass of water from a blue plastic pitcher, and handed it to him. As he greedily drank, silver-hair spoke again. "I am Doctor Nicolas Falcón, and you are a patient in our hospital. The injury to your eye is minor, and the effects of the drugs will wear off soon. Please try to relax, as we need to examine you more thoroughly."

"Did they catch the bastards who attacked me? And why are there bars on the window?" Moss asked; his normal voice was returning.

"The men to whom you are referring work for us," Dr. Falcón answered. "They kidnapped you on my orders. You are no longer in the United States, none of your friends, family or acquaintances know where you are, and you are going to be here for as long as we choose to have you."

Moss was momentarily stunned. Then he began to laugh. "You kidnapped the wrong guy, you morons. I don't have any serious money, and no one in the world is going to give you a dime for my release. You screwed up, big time."

Dr. Falcón simply smiled, and the younger man with him spoke for the first time. "We do not want you in order to extract a ransom. Tomorrow you will attend an orientation session with the other patients, and Dr. Falcón will then explain to all of you why you are here, and what the coming months have in store for you. Now, shut your fucking Yankee mouth while we examine you. Comprende?"

CHAPTER 7

S enator Jake Jackson, having slept hardly at all, was already on his third cup of strong black coffee of the morning. He, Katie and Sally had called all of Haley's friends with no luck—no one had heard from Haley or had any idea where she might be. Sally had checked with the local hospitals, and there had been no accidents or admissions of any young women in wheelchairs.

Jake, in spite of being 52 years old, was a strong vibrant man. But right now, his knees felt a little weak and the coffee was not helping the growing knot in his stomach. With everything the family had been through since Haley's accident on the balance beam while she was teaching her gymnastics class, Jake couldn't believe that she would take an unannounced trip or stay at an all-night party without letting anyone know.

"I'm calling Don Paulson at the police department," Jake said, "and Scott Wroblewski at the FBI. I'm a United States Senator, for Christ's sake, and these people owe me more than a few favors."

The call to the police revealed that Haley's driver Bill Preston and her van were missing as well. They were immediately concerned that Haley was unaccounted for. The subsequent call to the FBI was quickly routed to the bureau's director, one of Jake's oldest friends.

"Senator Jackson," Scott Wroblewski answered, "how are you, sir, and what can I do for you?"

"Nice to hear your voice again, Scott, but this isn't a social call. My sister Haley, who, as you know, has been in a wheelchair since her accident, didn't come home last night. The St. Paul police tell us that her van and van driver

Bill Preston are also missing. Any help you could give would be appreciated. Do you remember Chief Don Paulson? He's personally overseeing the local effort, but you and I both know that senators always have enemies, and that the local police may not be sufficient. I don't want to assume anything bad has happened, but, damn it Scott, I'm scared for her."

"Senator, you have my assurance that the FBI will immediately coordinate with Chief Paulson, and our agency will help in any way we can. I will call you back within the hour and let you know what's happening. If Haley should call or come home please let me know right away. And, uh, if you get any strange calls please let me know that too."

Scott Wroblewski did not offer his assurance lightly, as he literally owed the Senator his life. Wroblewski had been an enlisted man during the first Persian Gulf War. On what had seemed like an ordinary patrol, his platoon was ambushed by a small group of Iraqis who had peppered the trail ahead with land mines. As the enemy opened fire with automatic weapons, the platoon troops found themselves blown apart by the mines as they tried to run for cover. Scott had taken a round in the thigh, and was trying to return fire as he lay bleeding on the ground. Close to him and also wounded was Captain Jake Jackson, who had left a promising career as a pitcher in the minor leagues to join the war effort. All the other men were down, and the enemy soldiers poured fire in the area where the dead and wounded lay. Scott was sure that he was going to die, and he believed the entire platoon was doomed. As he ran out of ammunition, he could hear that his platoon was no longer returning fire at all, and he could see the enemy troops cautiously starting to move towards them to finish them off.

Scott thought he was seeing things when Captain Jackson suddenly stood up, blood running down the side of his head, with two hand grenades held to his chest with his left arm, and another in his right hand. The advancing troops halted their forward motion, and were in the process of taking aim at the crazy American who was winding up like a pitcher at Fenway. No sooner had the Captain hurled a "fastball" grenade, he yanked the pin on a second and hurled it as well, then dropped quickly to the ground as bullets flew where he'd just been standing. Scott saw the first grenade bounce off the head of an enemy troop, and then explode; the second grenade went off as Scott tried to bury his face into the dirt. With the ringing in his ears, it took a while for him to realize that there was much less gunfire...accompanied by the sound of a helicopter as it landed—and then he passed out.

When Scott awoke what seemed like days later, he was in a field hospital, with Captain Jackson, head bandaged, standing over him. It was some time later that Scott found out that the Captain, a second lieutenant and he were the only survivors of the ambush.

The helicopter pilot, with a shrapnel wound in his back, amid continual gunfire had somehow managed drag all three of them, one at a time while still under enemy fire, back to the helicopter and fly them to safety. A pair of burly Iraqi soldiers had tried to stop the pilot at gunpoint; the pilot, wounded and with an unconscious Wroblewski in his arms, had incredibly disarmed the soldiers with his feet; shattered one of the enemy soldier's kneecaps and kicked the other soldier's teeth out. Both Jake and the pilot had been decorated. The young pilot, Steve Moss, eventually received the Distinguished Service Cross, and had gone on to become a Colonel in the Army Rangers. Much to Moss's chagrin, the media had widely acclaimed his heroism. Scott had not heard from Steve in years, and wondered how his old comrade was doing. After the war, Steve and he often went to baseball games together to watch Jake Jackson pitch for the Minnesota Twins, and had gone to the ceremony together when Jake won the American League Cy Young award.

The FBI was accustomed to collaborating with local police departments. Sometimes things got messy, with a local cowboy thinking the Feds were out to steal his glory; sometimes, though, it was an agency bureaucrat who tried to posture himself as the big dog, pissing off the more-than-capable police officers. In this case, however, the St. Paul police and the FBI had a record of successful cooperation. Together, they had located and captured a serial murderer the year before and Scott had come to respect Chief Don Paulson and the men and women officers under his command.

Just before noon, Haley Jackson's van was found abandoned in a K-Mart parking lot near the uptown area in Minneapolis. Bill Preston, the driver, was found alive and tied up in the back of the van, but unconscious and suffering from heat stroke. An intravenous drip of drugged saline had been placed in his arm, keeping him from dehydrating but also keeping him unconscious. It would be a while before he would be lucid enough to talk. At this point, foul play was a certainty, and Haley's disappearance was now considered a kidnapping. Both the police and the FBI agreed that ransom was the probable motive, and Chief Don Paulson and FBI director Wroblewski placed a conference call to the Senator's home.

"Senator Jackson," Chief Paulson began, "Haley is still missing but we have found the van with Bill Preston tied up inside. He's in bad shape, as the temperature in there likely got up over 110 degrees, but he's expected to recover. The most likely explanation is that professionals pursuing ransom have kidnapped Haley. They took steps to make sure that the driver lived, which is a sign that we're dealing with people who know what they're doing, and not in a hurry to kill anyone."

Jake found himself clenching his jaw, and it took a moment to speak. "Do you think she's still alive?"

Scott Wroblewski fielded this difficult question. "Sir, we are sorry to give you this bad news, but the fact that her driver was found tied up and not dead indicates to us that the kidnappers are not likely killers. The most probable scenario, given your prominence and personal wealth, is that a ransom demand will likely be forthcoming. A less likely scenario is that this is political in nature, with some demand based on your power in the Senate."

Chief Paulson laid out the next steps. "Senator, we have our best people looking for physical evidence in the van. Almost always something is left behind. Professionals would not leave fingerprints, but fibers, hair, and even dirt from shoes can help us. Immediately, though, we'd like your permission to monitor your home phone, your office phone, and Haley's home phone. The kidnappers will likely try to contact you within the next few hours to make demands, and we need to be ready."

Jake's response was instantaneous, "Of course you have my permission. Is there anything else I can do to help?"

Scott made a suggestion, "Senator, we'd like to interview your daughter Katie and Haley's friends as quickly as possible. They may have noticed someone watching Haley, or been aware of other out-of-the-ordinary circumstances. At this point, though, I'd recommend not getting the media involved, although it will be impossible to keep the story quiet for long. With luck, we may find the kidnappers want a rapid resolution, and Haley could be returned quickly."

"All right," Jake said as he thought rapidly, "but you should also talk right away with Sally Peters, who, in addition to being my public relations person, has been with Haley pretty much night and day since she got out of the hospital. She'd likely know if something out of the ordinary has been going on."

The subsequent interviews by the police and FBI of Haley's friends, family and acquaintances failed to reveal anything that could help in the investigation. One neighbor recalled seeing Haley being picked up by a black van on Wednesday morning, noting that it was different than her regular van, but nothing seemed amiss otherwise.

Bill Preston, while recovering from his ordeal recalled nothing except getting grabbed from behind and a jab in the neck. The FBI requested a polygraph exam, and had a portable unit brought into the hospital. Their conclusion was that Mr. Preston had nothing to do with Haley's disappearance, and that he was genuinely concerned about her well-being.

Law enforcement personnel quickly set up round-the-clock monitoring of Jake's and Haley's phones. They were ready to record any calls, and had the capability to trace even calls from cell or satellite phones. Suspecting professionals were the perpetrators, sophisticated tracking technology was brought in by the FBI, technology that the public at large would not be happy about if they were aware how well any phone conversation could be monitored.

The best and the brightest that the St. Paul police and the FBI could bring together began their wait for the ransom call they were sure was coming.

The call never came. Jake, in his anxious, state of mind, realized that he had neglected to call his and Haley's older brother Luke; he immediately gave his big brother a call and gave him all the details about their sister's apparent abduction.

CHAPTER 8

Bogotá—officially named Bogotá, D.C., also called *Santa Fe de Bogotá*—is the capital of Colombia, as well as the largest and most populous city in the country with close to seven million inhabitants. Bogotá is located in the center of Columbia, high up in the Andes Mountains.

On the far southern outskirts of the city lies an extremely modern stucco and glass multi-story medical facility, complete with a helipad on the roof. The facility was named Falcón Hospital and Research Institute (FHRI). It contains not only a conventional hospital, but a world-class genetics research facility, as well as the world's leading edge biomedical engineering center (a carefully guarded secret). Two helicopters were kept on the helipad at FHRI: one for transporting emergency patients to the hospital's world-class trauma unit, and another for the personal transportation of the hospital's founder and medical director, Dr. Nicolas Falcón.

He had staffed FHRI with scientists and engineers who chaffed under the restrictions imposed on their research by government funding agencies. Convinced of the good they could do if only the government's "interference" disappeared, they had no qualms about the ethics of their bypassing human subjects research review.

The researchers at the FHRI biomedical engineering center had made tremendous advances in growing and engineering human tissue, including entire organs. They strategically placed different growth factors and physical cues within biodegradable polymer porous scaffolds—designed with the latest computer-aided-design (CAD) software and "printed" layer by layer with a 3-D rapid prototyping machine—to influence how and where cells would differentiate and grow. The scaffold provided physical cues for cell orientation and spreading, and pores provided space for the growth of tissue structures.

The FHRI biomedical engineers then seeded the scaffolds with human embryonic stem cells, which multiplied and lined the scaffolds' inner and outer surfaces... enabling them to grow tissue and organs which would not be rejected by the recipients. The seeded scaffolds were then placed in an enhanced 'bioreactor'—a piece of electrical equipment originally developed by NASA, but greatly improved at FHRI—to mimic the effects of weightlessness. Inside the bioreactor, the freedom from the force of gravity allows the embryonic stem cells to proliferate more quickly.

Then, various hormones and chemicals are added to coax the stem cells into turning into the tissue of which ever tissue or organ they chose to engineer.

A dark short fat woman who smiled constantly, but spoke not a word of English, was wheeling Haley Jackson down the hall of the hospital. At least it looked like a hospital, but she didn't have a clue where she actually was, and Haley had only a vague recollection of some time having passed while she was sedated.

While the woman pushing her chattered away in Spanish, Haley understood not a word and lamented having taken four years of German. She'd discovered on a trip to Europe—a graduation present from her father—that the Germans spoke far better English than she spoke German. She had a million questions to ask, and no one seemed to speak English here...if only she'd taken Spanish instead of German! That changed quickly as she was wheeled into a large conference room, more like a small auditorium, and all Haley could hear were questions being shouted in English by 100 to 200 obviously distressed people in hospital gowns. Some were in wheelchairs, some were amputees, some appeared normal—their diseases and/or disabilities not apparent.

Haley noted that there were some twenty-something's, and a few people in their thirties and forties, but none much over fifty. About half women, she thought, and a few Asian and black people. Haley saw that there was a podium at the front of the room, and a young stocky man with a crew cut tapped twice on the microphone to make sure it was working.

"Ladies and Gentlemen, could I have your attention please. We know you all have a lot of questions, and we plan to answer them all, but first I want to introduce your distinguished host, Dr. Nicolas Falcón, who will begin your orientation here with a brief address."

Haley was nervous, and could tell the other patients were too. Orientation? Brief address? What the hell was going on here? A distinguished looking man with silver hair wearing a tailored tropical beige suit strode to the podium, and stepped up to the microphone.

"Welcome to the Falcón Hospital and Research Institute, or FHRI," Dr. Falcón began. "Let me begin by telling you that all of you patients arrived at roughly the same time from North America. No one, not your families, your friends, or the authorities, have any idea where you are." The group instantaneously erupted, with shouts and questions flying left and right. Dr. Falcón simply stood silently until the group quieted, realizing he was not going to speak at all until he had their full attention.

"In short, you have all been abducted," Dr. Falcón continued. "You have been abducted not for ransom, not as hostages, and not for any political reason. Listen to me very carefully," he said, as his voice grew softer, with the group now so quiet that Haley could hear the man breathing behind her.

"The reason you are here," the doctor began again in a low soothing voice, "is to explore the opportunity—for each and every one of you—of once again having full use of your bodies, such that you shall each walk again, or, for those of you who are ambulatory but suffering from disease…we shall attempt to fully restore your health."

The group was stunned, with many mouths agape, but a solitary baritone voice broke the silence.

"What kind of sick bastard are you? Kidnapping disabled and sick people, injuring some in the process, and now telling us it was done so you can help us? What are you really doing, working on new ways to torture people?" Everyone in the room had turned to the voice. It came from a longhaired man in a wheelchair near the back of the room. Steve Moss would have been extremely handsome except for a black eye that looked recent. Haley did a double take, realizing that she had met this man before. His strong handsome features and emerald green eyes were not easily forgotten. She recalled he was a bit over six feet tall, and had been powerfully built (he now looked a bit beaten down and out of shape).

Dr. Falcón smiled patronizingly, and spoke again in reassuring tones, "Let me introduce to you to our skeptic, Colonel Steve Moss, a genuine American war hero. The colonel has not been in a wheelchair for long, like many of you

35

in wheelchairs. A piece of metal in his back, from an old war wound, began shifting subsequent to a motorcycle accident, and threatened his spinal cord. Surgery was performed to remove the metal, but in the process damaged his spinal cord, although his life was saved." There was a puzzled look on Steve Moss's face as he realized this man knew the details of his personal medical history.

"We have medical histories for all of you. We know how each of you was paralyzed or became ill, what treatments you've had, who your doctors were, and here is what you all have in common: Given the most modern accepted medical treatments, the prognosis for each of you is permanent paralysis, debilitation from disease, or death from organ failure."

"Let me underscore the phrase 'accepted medical treatments' because what I am going to propose to you falls outside the bounds of conventional medical practice. In fact, the treatment we have in mind for you is completely illegal at the current time. I'm sure all of you have heard or read stories about the promise of stem cell research. You have heard that the United States president and congress have put severe restrictions on the funding for such research. You may have also heard that the supply of stem cells for research is limited to a little over 60 existing lines, with a number of legal issues surrounding the access to those cells."

"In the coming days, you will be getting an in-depth explanation of the progress we have made at our facility here, none of which has ever been made public. We do not suffer from lack of funding or from laws and policies defined by politicians seeking to placate their constituencies. We are now at the point of trying some of our newest discoveries on human subjects. Each of you will have the opportunity to decide whether you wish to be in an experimental group, or a control group. In short, the choice whether to take the risk to feel again, to walk again, to have your prosthetic limbs replaced by real flesh and blood limbs, or to be cured of your disease, will be yours. However, none of you will be permitted to leave the facility or contact anyone outside the facility for the duration of the experiments."

Haley could barely believe what she was hearing. This doctor was telling them they were to be used as human guinea pigs! She couldn't restrain herself, and spoke up loudly in a tone dripping with sarcasm, "You wouldn't be related to a certain World War II Nazi Dr. Mengele who was a close personal friend of Adolf Hitler, would?" Haley knew that Dr. Josef Mengele was a Nazi doctor who performed experiments on prisoners in Auschwitz which were widely condemned as cruel and sadistic.

Some of the warmth left the voice of Dr. Falcón as he responded to Haley's confrontation, "While your question was mean-spirited, the truth is that I actually am a grandson of the much maligned and misunderstood Dr. Mengele. My brother Eduard and I are the children of Dr. Mengele's illegitimate son. While neither Eduard nor I apologize for our grandfather's research and experiments, we do not condone the Nazi's role in the holocaust. The knowledge gained through our grandfather's research contributed to the development of several modern medical treatments...a fact largely ignored by historians!"

"The inquisitive and sarcastic lady who asked this question is Miss Haley Jackson, sister of the famous baseball legend and U.S. Senator Jake Jackson. Ms. Jackson is somewhat famous in her own right, as she won an Olympic bronze medal in gymnastics. The Senator has been a part of the debate on extended funding for stem cell research, and has questioned the 'sanctity of life' arguments regarding the unborn embryos from which we harvest stem cells."

Haley was about to offer an angry retort when another woman spoke up, "Are you serious about there being a chance of us walking again...a chance of having feeling again?"

Dr. Falcón spoke quickly, and with apparent sincerity, "We would not have broken a multitude of laws and taken the risks to bring you here if we did not believe we could do what I have said. Believe me, this was the only way possible to make progress now rather than decades from now. If we had openly asked for volunteers, we would have had to reveal that we have unlimited supplies of embryonic stem cells available, that we have extensive funding, and that our progress on animals has been nothing short of miraculous, not to mention that we have ignored many laws and policies.

"I regret that you have been taken from your families, from your homes and jobs and friends, but consider yourselves the first prisoners of a scientific war. Unlike most prisoners of war, though, our intent is to return you one day to your homes with your functioning restored, your paralyses gone, your missing limbs replaced, your diseases cured... virtually as good as new." That statement was a pure fabrication intended to placate this group of human guinea pigs. Even if they survived the experiments, and even if they were totally cured, none of them would ever be released.

Dr. Falcón picked up a bound blue book from the table behind him and said, "Each of you will receive a copy of this unpublished book today. It contains a broad background of our research, and it has been written for the lay person. From this book you will have sufficient information to decide whether you want to participate in the experimental group or the control group. We will meet again next Monday, and you will then have an opportunity to ask questions about what you have read."

As the books were passed out to men and women who looked completely confused, Dr. Falcón smiled once again, and began to explain the "house rules" of their stay at the hospital. "You will, of course, have no access to telephones or computers, and you will not be permitted to send letters or communications of any kind to anyone outside of this facility. However, we recognize that your health, which we will monitor closely, would suffer without some regular human interaction. You will, therefore, be permitted to visit one another in your rooms and common areas. Your meals will all be served in a communal cafeteria, with your special dietary needs addressed and monitored. You may have noticed already that there are video cameras in all areas, including restrooms. In addition, there are microphones scattered throughout the facility, and you will be monitored 24 hours every day of the week. Movies, music and books can be checked out of our modest library, and your rooms all have basic television, DVD and CD players. Your televisions will not receive any broadcast stations; you will occasionally receive closed circuit messages from the staff, as well as communications from me. Also, the staff is under strict orders not to answer any questions regarding our geographic location, so don't bother asking them.

"We have an impressive physical therapy area," Dr. Falcón continued, "that includes a gymnasium and a range of physical therapy apparatus, weight machines and sports equipment."

Haley could tell that the others were having as much trouble absorbing all this as she was. The doctor was making the hospital sound more like a spa and the patients more like guests than the kidnap victims they were. She glanced over at Steve Moss, and noticed he was looking directly at her, recognition clearly in his eyes. It had been a few years, but as a long-time friend of her brother Jake, Steve had visited their home many times.

Doctor Falcón spoke again, "You are now free to explore the facility and visit with each other. I encourage you to read the material you've been given, and to write down questions for Monday. I hope your stay with us will be fruitful, and that in time you may forgive us for the unfortunate but necessary steps we took to bring you here."

Many of the other kidnapped men and women had looks of guarded optimism on their faces. Those looks dissolved as Dr. Falcón spoke one last time.

"Oh, one final detail about your stay here: Any attempt to escape, or any attempt to bribe or otherwise engage a staff member to help you escape, will result in your becoming an organ donor…a donor of ALL your organs. This is, after all, a for-profit institution."

With that, Dr. Nicolas Falcón strode out of the room, smiling from ear to ear.

The group of patients sat in momentary silence, with no one seeming to know what to say or do next. Moss spoke up, in slow measured sentences. "It seems that, like it or not, we are all here to stay for a while. I would warn all of you against getting your hopes up based on that crazy bastard's pipe dream of getting paralyzed people to walk again. I am fortunate to have as friends two of the best researchers in the world in the area of spinal cord injuries, and both of them have told me any solution to paralysis is likely a decade or more away."

The ebony giant that was Moss's room-mate was now very much awake, and with a deep melodic bass voice he interrupted, "My name is Dr. Thomas Jefferson Hunt, and I am, or was before my Parkinson's disease got worse, a physiatrist—a doctor of physical medicine and rehabilitation—at Walter Reed. Mr. Moss is correct in what he is saying, but with some restrictions. The progress in this area has been greatly slowed by three factors. First, federal funding has been limited, and has many restrictions tied to it. Second, most of the promising potential therapies involve the use of stem cells, and access to them is limited by a number of legal and ethical factors. Third, our government has many restrictions on human experimentation, which makes rapid testing of possible solutions impossible."

"So what's your point, Dr. Hunt?" Moss asked, "And what exactly does a physiatrist do?"

"A physiatrist is a specialist in physical medicine and rehabilitation. We evaluate disabilities and plan specific activities, therapies and treatments aimed at maximizing patients' recoveries. My point is that none of these restrictions

I mentioned seem to bother Dr. Falcón. How do you all feel about this? We know this doctor—the grandson of the infamous Dr. Mengele—is planning to experiment on us, in spite of the illegality of doing that. What we don't know is what kind of funding he has, where it comes from, and what kind of stem cell expertise he has access to. Whether he is sane or not is an issue also. My fear is that he is not. Also, the growing of new cells is only the beginning of curing paralysis or disease. There are many other complex and difficult problems to be addressed. I should also point out that our captors could not realistically be expected to ever let any of us get out of here alive."

There was a look of palpable fear on the faces of many of the patients. They all sat for a moment, a strange collection of people all trying to process what had happened to them in a highly stressful situation.

Haley spoke up in a quiet voice, "What is certain is that we'll be together for a while, and that we must all be worried about our families and friends, not to mention our personal safety. There is a very real possibility that the authorities will discover that a large number of people were kidnapped, and be able to rescue us. Until that happens, the best thing to do right now is introduce ourselves to each other and then explore our prison."

After each patient had explained who he or she was, where they were from, and how they'd been kidnapped, they broke up into smaller conversations, and finally wheeled or ambled out of the room to explore.

They had learned that all their kidnappings had been fast and professional, with virtually no witnesses. A few had lashed out in self-defense, but had been quickly subdued, sometimes incurring minor injuries. No one expressed much faith in being found quickly, and most expressed their fears about what would happen to them next.

CHAPTER 9

Haley and Moss had taken some time to renew their acquaintance. Haley had been unaware that Moss, who had been a muscular but trim 6-footer, had suffered an accident and surgical failure putting him in a chair. He was trying to come to grips with his growing attraction to this woman he'd known mostly as his friend Jake's younger sister. He recalled that she had won an Olympic bronze medal in gymnastics. Haley had matured gracefully into a beautiful woman, with shining blonde hair down to her shoulders and blue eyes that were truly lovely. A part of his brain registered the attraction, but another part cursed it since he'd never be able to do anything about it.

Haley had been aware that his wife had died of cancer four years ago, just one month after her sister-in-law—Jake's wife—had committed suicide; she had struggled with depression, and was not well suited to being the wife of a Senator who was often traveling and in the public eye. She knew her brother must be worried sick, as Sally and Katie would be, too. She was glad to see a friend of her brother's, especially one who was a courageous war hero. Haley knew that she would need some additional strength to get through this ordeal; Steve Moss, in spite of being in a wheelchair himself, was the strongest man she'd ever known next to her brother; she'd heard Jake tell the tale many times about Steve's wartime heroics.

Moss was highly skeptical of everything he'd heard in the hospital conference room, and expressed his concerns as he sat with Haley and Dr. Hunt in the cafeteria. "I believe that the group of patients is going to be subjected to illegal human medical experiments, and I have no faith whatsoever in Dr. Falcón's claim that paralyzed people could be made fully functional again, or various diseases cured. I am curious why Dr. Falcón had passed out the research book for us to read...probably some kind of propaganda to get us to be more cooperative."

Dr. Hunt countered, "I want to reserve judgment until I've read some of this book. I think I'm going to go back to our room and read for a while. Perhaps tomorrow we can explore our new 'home' together after breakfast?"

Haley and Moss agreed, and went off to their rooms to rest and take an initial look at the book Dr. Falcón seemed eager for them to read.

After getting himself out of his wheelchair and in to his bed (a cumbersome process), Moss opened Dr. Falcón's book and began to read.

The Bogotá Experiments

Human Paralysis, Disease, and Stem Cell Research
At the Falcón Hospital and Research Institute (FHRI)
By Dr. Nicolas Fernando Falcón

Introduction

*A*t *FHRI we are committed to innovative and leading-edge research regarding diseases and maladies affecting human beings.*

The complexity of the human body is incredible. It is made up of approximately 222 kinds of cells, which form tissues, organs and systems that are amazingly flexible.

The body has a stupendous capability to heal itself when injured, and to fight off infections from bacteria and viruses. However, the body can't heal itself from all injuries or diseases; the assistance of medical science is often required in the form of drugs, surgeries, and highly specialized procedures. Unfortunately, some types of injuries and diseases currently have no cure. Examples include diabetes, Parkinson's disease, Alzheimer's, loss of limbs, organ failure and injuries to the central nervous system.

The body begins as just two cells, a sperm and an egg; the united two-cell organism is called a zygote, but not for long as the cells divide, effectively reproducing themselves. The cells reproduce quickly, forming a small embryo whose cells are not yet specialized. These unspecialized cells will eventually specialize, and form the bones, muscles, heart, lungs, brain, and all the other organs, systems and tissues of the body. But in the early stages of an embryo's development, all of its cells have the potential to become any of the specialized cells (pluripotency), including blood, bone, nerve, muscle and skin cells; hence, these are the cells from which all others stem, resulting in the term "stem cell."

Moss paused to rub his good eye and think. He recalled all the debates going on in the media about stem cell research. Federal funding had been severely restricted because the whole topic was a political hot potato. None-the-less, research was going on and progress was being made. What was so different or special about Dr. Falcón' research? He settled back, and resumed reading.

Embryonic stem cells are initially unlike any specialized cell; they have the ability to form any kind of adult cell. Because undifferentiated embryonic stem cells can reproduce indefinitely in culture, they could potentially provide an unlimited source of specific, adult cells such as bone, muscle, liver, nerve or blood cells.

In our research at FHRI, embryonic stem cells are harvested from fertilized embryos. In the late 20th century, a group of University of Wisconsin developmental biologists led by James Thomson established five independent stem cell lines. This was the first time human embryonic stem cells had been successfully isolated and cultured.

The cell lines were capable of prolonged, undifferentiated proliferation in culture and yet maintained the ability to develop into a variety of specific cell types. Examples include neurons, muscle, bone and cartilage cells.

The embryos used in the University of Wisconsin research were originally produced to treat infertility and were donated specially for that project with the informed consent of donor couples who no longer wanted the embryos for implantation.

In virtually every in vitro fertilization clinic in the world, surplus embryos are discarded if they are not donated to help other infertile couples or for research. The research protocols were reviewed and approved by a University of Wisconsin Institutional Review Board, a panel of scientists and medical ethicists who oversee such work.

Why embryonic stem cells are important

Embryonic stem cells are of great interest to us here at FHRI because of their ability to develop into virtually any other cell made by the human body. In theory, if stem cells can be grown and their development directed in culture, it would be possible to grow cells of medical importance such as bone marrow, neural tissue or muscle. Even entire structures, such as human bladders and heart valves have been grown from stem cells; at FHRI, we have gone even further…we can create entire organs from embryonic stem cells!

The ability to grow pure populations of specific cell types offers a proving ground for chemical compounds that may have medical importance. Treating specific cell types with chemicals and measuring their response offers a short cut to sort out chemicals that can be used to treat the diseases that involve those specific cell types. Stem cell technology permits the researchers at FHRI to engage in the rapid screening of hundreds of thousands of chemicals that must now be tested through much more time-consuming processes.

Moss rubbed his good eye again and closed the book. With all he'd been through, it wasn't long before he nodded off to sleep.

CHAPTER 10

Dr. Nicolas Falcón was stirring a teaspoon of heavy cream into his strong Columbian coffee as his older brother Eduard entered his office, with an attractive young woman pushing his wheelchair. Both Eduard and Nicolas Falcón were strongly built men, but most people who did not know them well did not realize they were brothers. Eduard was what women called "ruggedly handsome"; Nicolas had more classic good looks. While Nicolas looked urbane and erudite in his summer-weight tropical suits and Egyptian cotton dress shirts, Eduard simply looked mean as hell. His all-black wardrobe of raw silk shirts and slacks was accented by pastel sport coats and heavy gold jewelry. The difference between brothers was striking, and any of the family resemblance was difficult to see unless one looked carefully at the brothers' eyes. Both men had eyes that were so blue that they appeared as sapphires from a distance, but on closer examination, intelligence, strength and cunning radiated strongly. They had survived a dangerous childhood through their wits and unwavering dedication to each other.

There was also a hidden difference between the brothers. Eduard's left arm—from just below the elbow—was artificial. The prosthesis was custom made, with lifelike "skin" and manicured fingernails. The covering of the prosthesis had been fashioned by an artist, a student of Duane Hanson's lifelike sculpture. It had individual hairs, and the pores and texture of real skin. The hand was "touched up" weekly. Most people were unaware of Eduard's missing limb, believing the useless hand was the result of a childhood accident.

Nicolas had been named after an ersatz ancestor ("Falcón" was simply a phony name given to their father by the Nazi document forgers) Nikolaus Falcón who was a German adventurer in the colonies of Venezuela and Colombia. As kids, Eduard and Nicolas Falcón had been among Bogotá's horde of orphaned street children who lived through begging, stealing and picking pockets. Their father, who had become a judge after emigrating from Germany to Columbia (using forged identity documents provided by the Odessa Network), had been assassinated by a Columbian drug cartel that had vowed to wipe out his entire family in retribution for sentencing their leader to life in prison. Their mother, a member of the Scottish aristocracy (their father had met her while attending Oxford University), feared for her life. She fled the country, leaving her children in the care of their uncle, who unbeknownst to her, was murdered shortly after her departure. With no means of contacting their mother, and no other family in Columbia, the brothers were left homeless and had to fend for themselves.

Eduard was older by four years, and would fight even the biggest aggressor when his younger brother was threatened. One day, when Nicolas was 10 and Eduard 14, Nicolas had stolen two apples from a street vendor who chased the boys down the street with a large machete he pulled from behind his stand. The man, who had probably been stolen from once too often, chased the boys into a dark alley, which had no exit and no witnesses. The angry man had grabbed Nicolas by the hair, and informed him that he'd been a thief for the last time. As he swung the machete back, preparing to behead the boy, Eduard raised his arm at the last moment, saving Nicolas's head at the expense of his own hand. The man, with blood spurting in his face from the stump of Eduard's severed hand, dropped the machete and ran.

Eduard screamed at the running man, "I promise you, one day I'll find you and kill you!"

Two years later, the same man lost, over an excruciating 5 minutes, both of his hands, his penis, and finally his head to the same machete. Eduard always tried to keep his promises, and Eduard always tried to get even.

To ensure his physical superiority, Eduard had, over the years, become a student of multiple martial arts as he grew his increasingly successful drug business. He sampled a wide variety of them, from Kung Fu to Tae Kwon Do. Eduard would study each martial art long enough to extract its most impressive and deadliest techniques; he was content with proficiency, but never strived for mastery. Eduard was totally unconcerned with any martial arts underlying philosophies.

While Nicolas had gone to medical school, Eduard had earned first a Masters of Business Administration degree followed by a doctorate in behavioral psychology, both of which he put to good use. He understood human motivators extremely well, including positive and negative reinforcement, punishment, or well crafted combinations of all of those. Eduard became a master manipulator.

Very carefully and slowly, drawing heavily from techniques he had gleaned from The Art of War by Sun Tzu and Machiavelli's The Prince, Eduard built a huge drug cartel and then forged strategic alliances with other drug cartels around the world; he had eventually become the wealthiest and most powerful of them all. Eduard had people on his payroll within every major law enforcement agency in the world. He had become, for all intents and purposes, legally untouchable.

As powerful as the Falcón organization had become, it was not without rivals and competition. The fiercest competitor was a terrorist organization called "Brotherhood of Allah" which was funded by narcotics, prostitution, and a variety of other criminal activities. It was led by a brilliant but fanatical Saudi scientist named Fahim Al-Firaih; he was Eduard's arch enemy and lusted after control of the Falcón fortune and empire. Al-Firaih had vowed to one day take down the infidel Eduard Falcón…he was a patient man who would strike only when the time was right.

CHAPTER 11

"**G**ood morning, Eduard," Dr. Falcón began, "Did you sleep better last night?"

"I slept much better, Nicolas. The new medication you gave me seems to have relieved the muscle spasms in my back. Have our new 'guests' arrived at the hospital yet?"

"Yes, all of them are here. We were quite careful in their selection. Our friends from PraxMed Pharmaceuticals definitely succeeded in matching my needs to patient records in hospitals all across America (their hackers' success in secretly penetrating every major hospital and medical facilities computer systems gave PraxMed unlimited access to patient records). The group will suit my experiments' needs quite well."

PraxMed Pharmaceuticals, Inc. was not the largest drug company in the world, in spite of their $30 billion in annual revenues. PraxMed, however, was possibly the most ambitious and unscrupulous drug company ever. They were not only helping Dr. Falcón surreptitiously find patients suitable for experimentation, but they had paid the best professionals available to arrange for their kidnapping without significant injury to any of the patients. PraxMed had also been financing the FHRI's secret stem cell research, perfectly aware that all legal restrictions and codes of ethics from their own countries were being ignored. Their hope was, with extensive human experimentation, to be able to find marketable cures before any of their competitors. The cures would be presented to the world as having come from research in their legitimate facilities, but those facilities would know the answers in advance as a result of the Bogotá experiments led by Dr. Falcón. While cures for diseases like diabetes and Alzheimer's could eventually earn them much more money, making paralyzed people able to walk again would be such a spectacular story that their stock price would likely double. The fact that Eduard Falcón would benefit personally had not escaped their attention; the drug-lord had proved valuable in the past at helping them eliminate employees who had stumbled across PraxMed's shady underbelly.

Despite an impoverished childhood, Eduard Falcón had built one of the world's largest multi-national drug cartels. His funding, along with that from PraxMed, had built one of the most sophisticated stem cell research facilities in the world.

An ambitious "lieutenant" in Eduard's organization had nearly assassinated him. As a rule, no one was allowed to carry weapons in Eduard's palatial home, but the trusted lieutenant had shot him in the back with a tiny Kel-tec P32 he had carried inside the shank of his boot. As Eduard fell to the floor, he pointed his prosthetic hand at his attacker. He flexed the remaining muscles of his severed forearm, which triggered a modified Ruger Super Redhawk Alaskan revolver concealed within his prosthesis. Eduard had gotten the idea for this innovation from a television show he'd seen about private investigator named Jay J. Armes, who had lost both his arms as a child. When he pulled the trigger, a bullet left the muzzle of the gun with a velocity of 1350 ft. per second—sufficient for killing big game. The bullet exited the prosthesis through the middle finger, a symbolic design feature Eduard had insisted upon with the gunsmith. The lieutenant's head had virtually exploded as the bullet struck.

Even though Eduard was a hard man to kill, the would-be assassin's bullet had struck him in the spine, and he was now a paraplegic, confined to a wheelchair. Killing the traitor had not been sufficient to assuage Eduard's anger; he was happy to think on occasion about how the man's heart had been sold to an ailing but rich Hong Kong business man, and his liver and kidneys sold to the highest bidders in Europe. There were many benefits to having a doctor for a brother.

"Nicolas, I have asked you before, and I do not wish to seem impatient, but how long do you think it will be before you can get me out of this damnable wheelchair?"

Dr. Falcón was careful always in setting expectations for his brother. He was keenly aware of Eduard's temper and disdain for those who did not "measure up" in his eyes. "Eduard, as I have told you before, there is no guarantee that we will succeed. The stem cell research has been promising, but it is only part of the solution. Growing new neurons is not the only problem. Getting the new neurons to repair the damage will require a giant leap forward in stimulation of axon growth, re-myelination of existing neurons, and a host of other problems, including the possibility of rejection."

Eduard looked quizzically at his brother, and then broke into laughter. "Nicolas, you speak in tongues to me, and it makes no sense at all. I know how smart you are, and I know how expensive your education was, because I paid for it. Like I told you before, whatever you need, you will get. Who ever gets in your way, I will have removed. You will succeed."

CHAPTER 12

Sally Peters had insisted on accompanying Senator Jake Jackson to a joint meeting of the St. Paul police and the FBI. All she knew for sure was that there was new information in Haley's case, and that Jake and she were going to be part of the briefing. In the short time since the kidnapping, Jake had been sure that every ringing of the phone would be the kidnappers with a ransom demand, or maybe some weird political demand. Not only had there been no contact from the kidnappers, but no witnesses or evidence had been found thus far.

Sally had been unable to sleep more than a few hours at a time since Haley disappeared. Not only had they been best friends for years, but also Sally had played a large role in Haley's recovery—both physical and emotional—after Haley's fall from the balance beam. Sally recalled Haley's deep depression after learning that her lower-body paralysis would be permanent, followed by her acceptance and resolve to rehabilitate as far as humanly possible. Haley was one of the strongest people Sally had ever known, but she worried that the trauma of the kidnapping might (assuming Haley was otherwise unharmed) take her back into the depths of depression.

Sally and Jake were shown into a large conference room which had a large screen with a map of the United States projected upon it. St. Paul's Chief Don Paulson and the FBI's Scott Wroblewski entered the conference room together, and quickly came over to greet Jake and Sally. Neither man looked like he'd slept much over the weekend. The room quickly filled with men and women from both the police department and the FBI, and Chief Paulson stepped up to the podium.

Chief Paulson was a friendly and gregarious gentleman, and was well respected in the community. But his police department knew him to be pure bulldog, one who did not accept second-rate performance from any of his team.

"I'd like to begin by introducing Senator Jake Jackson, and Sally Peters, who is both a family friend of the Jacksons and the Senator's press liaison here in Minnesota. Senator, I want to assure you that we are doing everything possible to find your sister, and that the FBI is collaborating fully in this investigation. This meeting is going to be a combination of information sharing and brainstorming, because, quite frankly, we have discovered some new and disturbing information."

Sally saw Jake immediately tense up and brace himself.

The chief had a strained look on his face, and began to explain, "The FBI has learned that, in the past few days, there have been a number of kidnappings across the United States—all of them involving men and women with some degree of paralysis or disease, some of them, like Haley, confined to wheelchairs. Some of the kidnap victims are ambulatory, but with diseases and all of them were snatched cleanly and professionally, with no witnesses. I am now going to turn the meeting over to FBI Director Scott Wroblewski who will provide you all with the details."

Scott Wroblewski stood up and walked over to a laptop computer, which was driving the projector. He typed a few commands, and the screen transitioned to another map, which had several U.S. cities, circled in red.

"These are the cities that have reported kidnappings of victims in the last week. You'll note that they are major cities, Boston, Phoenix, Chicago, Los Angeles, Denver, Cleveland, and San Francisco…cities that all have major medical facilities. So far, we know of no ransom demands, or of any contact at all between the kidnappers and the victims' families. At last count, over 100 separate kidnappings of this type have been reported."

"Why in the world would someone kidnap people in wheelchairs, or with diseases?" Jake interrupted.

Wroblewski shoulders did a barely visible slump, and he answered, "Senator, we don't have any good theories right now. And we're hoping this meeting will help generate some. We've discussed everything from insurance-related motivations to sick euthanasia plots, but no one has come up with anything very convincing."

Sally didn't like what she was hearing. "What kind of insurance-related motivation could there be?"

A young FBI agent, a woman who looked more like a bookkeeper than a law enforcement officer, ventured a response. "People with paralysis or chronic disease often have long-term medical needs that can be very expensive. If the person disappears, there simply won't be any insurance claims. However, our early investigation does not show a single insurer or group of insurers correlating across victims, but we will continue to look at who might benefit financially if these people disappeared."

Jake spoke, sounding as though he didn't really want to hear the answer to his question, "What did you mean about euthanasia relating to a motivation for kidnapping?"

Scott Wroblewski deferred the question to Dr. Ian Whitely, an older man with a trimmed gray goatee, who he identified as one of the FBI's forensic psychologists.

Dr. Whitely looked directly into Jake's eyes as kindly as he could. "There are people who believe that the handicapped are an unreasonable drain on medical resources. Further, they are uncomfortable around disabled people, and view them with disdain. It is possible that a small group of people may have kidnapped the victims to make a point at a later date, or to simply eliminate them. I do see this as a very remote possibility, but one we need to consider."

As the meeting went on, a number of theories were offered, from the reasonable to the outlandish. The events were so far out of everyone's law enforcement experience that they found themselves stretching for an explanation. The idea that someone might be gathering human guinea pigs for medical experimentation never came up.

As the meeting concluded, many of the participants tried hard to reassure the senator that they would work tirelessly to find his sister and the other victims. Plans were coordinated for establishing command, control and communications across all the kidnapping cases. Just as everyone was getting up to leave, Scott Wroblewski asked them to sit back down for a moment as he clicked his cell phone shut.

"Ladies and Gentlemen, please take your seats. We are about to receive a telephone call from the President of the United States."

President James Paxton was an interesting and colorful man. People tended to be either love him or hate him. The president had two prior careers: he had served in the United States Navy where he had risen to the rank of admiral before retiring; he had then been elected to the United States House of Representatives, where he had been Speaker of the House prior to being elected president.

President Paxton, while having a big heart, was used to getting his own way and believed himself to be a morally superior man. This self perception was fueled by the president's younger brother, the Reverend Mason Paxton, an internationally known evangelist who preached a unique variant of the gospel of prosperity. While capable of extraordinary politeness and diplomacy, the president could also be bellicose and belligerent, particularly to his political adversaries. He loved all things military, and ran the executive branch of government as though it were a fleet under his command. And detractors referred to Paxton as "that naval martinet ramrod in the oval office."

The incoming phone call was answered via a special speaker phone mounted on the conference table, and the voice of a White House operator came on line: "Senator Jackson, Director Wroblewski and Chief Paulson, are you all there?"

The volume of the phone was adjusted, a brief roll call of all attending was taken, and then the president's voice came on the speaker: "Senator Jackson, my feelings go out to you and your family in this difficult time."

"Thank you, Mr. President," Jake replied. Jake was not particularly fond of this president, but appreciated his personal involvement.

"I have been briefed by my chief of staff," the president continued, "and I understand there have been many similar kidnappings across the country. I want to reassure you, Senator Jackson, that the federal government will do whatever it takes to find your sister and the other victims. For the rest of you, let me stress that this investigation needs to be a model of cooperation and collaboration between federal, state and local law enforcement agencies. I do not want to hear about anyone sitting on information, or failing to enter reports, or missing computer entries."

The phone call only lasted five minutes, but certainly gained the attention of all present. Sally knew that the media would have a field day with this story, and also knew the president was beginning to position himself relative to the criticism the FBI would surely get if the cases were not solved quickly. The FBI had suffered a string of miscommunications, non-communications, and botched field operations in recent years; Sally was not at all confident in their ability to find Haley and the others.

CHAPTER 13

Eduard Falcón sat by his kidney-shaped swimming pool and sipped on a very old and very expensive single-malt whiskey. Being confined to a wheelchair was greatly at odds with his self-image. Eduard still envisioned himself as agile and athletic, and while he didn't quite see himself as a ladies' man, he knew that his power and wealth had acted as an aphrodisiac with many women. His mind could not reconcile the reality of his confinement to a wheelchair with how he planned to live the rest of his life. Either a cure would be found for his paralysis, or he would end his own life. In the mean time, Eduard would make sure his brother the doctor would have all of the equipment, staff and money—and human subjects for experimentation—necessary to cure his condition. He looked down at his lap, knowing he now had no feeling whatsoever, and imagined himself once again poised over a naked woman bound spread-eagle beneath him, cowering as she saw the size of his swollen manhood.

A young woman emerged from the palatial house and approached Eduard with a tray of before-dinner appetizers. "Set them on the table and come over here please," Eduard commanded. The woman wore a simple white uniform, much like the rest of the household staff. As the woman placed the tray and stepped in front of Eduard, she noticed his dark mood radiating from his eyes, and swallowed hard. She was an attractive woman, with long black hair worn with a single braid down her back. She was quite trim, unusually so for a woman so busty. "Show me your breasts," Eduard said matter-of-factly. The woman looked at him and hesitated only a moment before reaching to the zipper beneath her chin. After she unzipped the starched cotton uniform to her waist, she slid her white brassiere up over her breasts, and then lowered her arms to her sides.

Eduard simply looked for a while, letting old tapes of virility play through his mind. He then reached up with his good hand and pinched his servant's nipple hard. She opened her mouth as though to scream, but then closed it again without a sound having escaped. Eduard then gave the nipple a cruel twist, and although the woman remained silent, a tear escaped from the corner of her eye. Eduard eyed the tear as the harshness of his face transformed to a smile. He released the nipple and said, as though the last few seconds had not existed, "I will dine at 8:30, and make sure the soup is not too hot."

Eduard was not simply a sadist. He was a student of pain. He had discovered long ago things far beyond the realm of what he had learned while pursuing his PhD in behavioral psychology: that he could bend others to his will through simple rewards, such as money, drugs and women. But he had found that developing absolute obedience among the many that worked for him had arisen not from rewards, but from fear of what Eduard would do to those who failed in their missions, or otherwise displeased him.

CHAPTER 14

The PraxMed Pharmaceutical secret strategy meeting was about to begin. The location of the meeting was no where near any of the company's real offices. The location was in a secure meeting room at a non-descript office building owned by a shell corporation, controlled by PraxMed but untraceable to it. Just before the meeting was to begin, security staff electronically swept the room to ensure that no one would be eavesdropping or recording. As a final precaution, all the meeting attendees were frisked for bugs or recording devices. The one exception was the person who had called the meeting—he recorded all of the meetings he attended via a state-of-the-art hidden camcorder. Having learned the lessons provided by Enron and other corporate scandals, he was making sure he had his own "insurance policy" to bargain his way out of trouble if things should ever go wrong.

Ted Mallick, whose title was "Vice-president, Special Marketing Operations" planned to kick the meeting off once everyone was seated. Mallick's appearance was not quite stereotypical of the large corporate executive. He was tall—slightly over 6'2"—and attractive in a slightly oily sort of way. His haircut was expensive, his suit tailor-made, and his tie was done in a carefully fashioned half-Windsor knot. The only thing that was out-of-place was a ragged scar above Mallick's right eye-brow, which gave his smile a "don't-fuck-with-me" overtone. Mallick would tell the curious that the scar was from his boxing days in college; in fact, the scar was the reminder his drug dealer had administered when Mallick had "forgotten" to pay the dealer when promised.

The 14 other meeting attendees included several highly paid executives whose names did not appear on PraxMed's organizational charts. These were all highly capable professionals who, like Mallick, had been recruited by PraxMed in spite of black marks on their records. Not that PraxMed was lenient in its hiring; these people had been recruited because things had been discovered about their backgrounds that would allow PraxMed to exert tremendous control over their employment. Do what is asked, watch your career blossom. Screw up, you will not get fired, but you will get punished in ways that will guarantee you will not do so again. Quitting was unheard of for this group, since no one would ever pay them as much as PraxMed...nor would anyone ever hire them if the secrets of their past were revealed.

Ted Mallick's resume was an unusual one for an executive. While he had been working on his MBA at Wharton, he had been supporting his fairly expensive cocaine habit by selling "legitimate" drugs like Valium, Oxycodone and Vicodin that he had stolen from his father's pharmacy. When his father caught him in the act, and immediately cut off his access, Mallick was left with no means of paying his cocaine supplier. He had feared for his life, but after a perfunctory beating, Mallick was surprised when the drug dealer told him he would forgive his debt if he'd agree to interview for a job with one of the drug dealer's "legitimate businessman" friends. Upon graduation, he accepted a generous offer from PraxMed, who off-the-record, agreed to overlook his "little cocaine problem" in return for absolute allegiance and unusual assignments.

"Good morning," Mallick said perfunctorily, "and welcome to the quarterly review of our special marketing projects. I remind you that all content presented today is confidential and proprietary, and anything you hear today is not to be shared with anyone outside of this room." The attendees took this admonition seriously, as the last person who had not been discreet was now a "missing person."

"As you know," Mallick continued, "we have a number of research projects underway aimed at leap-frogging the competition, especially in the area of pharmaceuticals that enable and support stem cell therapies we expect to emerge in the next few years. Stem cells all by themselves are worthless. However, developing treatments that employ stem cells along with specific pharmaceuticals and treatment protocols are priceless. The trick is developing these far faster than the competition. This can be made easier if we know in advance exactly what treatments and drugs work on humans and which ones don't."

A bespectacled older woman interrupted, "How can animal trials do that? Even on the animals most similar to humans, regardless of the most successful outcomes, don't guarantee the same results for humans."

Mallick smiled patronizingly at the woman, "You are entirely correct. Only human trials will tell us what works and what doesn't."

The woman, clearly puzzled, replied "But experimenting on humans in the United States without FDA approvals is illegal and, even in other countries, international standards apply to the use of human subjects in medical research. So how can we know in advance of PraxMed's competition what products and treatments will work?"

Mallick didn't answer. Instead, He passed out small folders to all of the meeting attendees and said, "You'll find the answers to your questions in these folders. You will spend the rest of the meeting reading, and I'll collect them when you leave. Let me remind you again that this is highly confidential, and anyone disclosing this information outside of this room will be subject to the ultimate level of discipline."

Mallick certainly had their attention. Everyone in the group eagerly began to open the folders.

Praxmed

Confidential And Proprietary

How might embryonic stem cells be used to treat disease?

The ability to grow all kinds of human tissue facilitates the potential to treat a wide range of cell-based diseases and to produce tissues that can use for transplantation.

Diseases like Parkinson's disease and juvenile onset diabetes occur because of defects in one of just a few cells types. By replacing faulty cells with healthy ones, a cure may be realized. Failing organs, such as a heart, pancreas and liver failing hearts could potentially be healed by injecting healthy cells to replace damaged or diseased cells. Although difficult, growing replacement organs is possible.

What are the benefits of studying embryonic stem cells?

Embryonic stem cell research offers hope to people worldwide. They have the potential to treat or cure a wide range of diseases, including Parkinson's, Alzheimer's, diabetes, heart disease, stroke, spinal cord injuries and burns.

This research is still in its infancy; real-world applications will only be possible with additional funding and study. Scientists need to better understand the mechanisms and processes that lead to cell specialization in order to direct cells to become particular types of tissue. For example, islet cells control insulin production in the pancreas, which is disrupted in people with diabetes. If an individual with diabetes is to be cured, the stem cells used for treatment must develop into new insulin-producing islet cells, not heart tissue or other cells. Research is required to determine how to control the differentiation of stem cells so they will be therapeutically effective. Research is also necessary to study the potential of immune rejection of the cells, and how to overcome that problem.

In late 1998, a group of scientists led by University of Wisconsin-Madison developmental biologist James Thomson became the first in the world to successfully isolate and culture human embryonic stem cells.

Because embryonic stem cells are the originators of all other human cell types, this accomplishment has set the stage for giant steps forward in medicine and cellular biology.

The promise of stem cells lies in their ability to be cultured in the laboratory and, ultimately, directed to become specific types of cells or tissue that can be used to treat a host of cell-based diseases such as juvenile diabetes, Parkinson's and heart disease.

Stem cells arise early in development, when embryos are less than a week old, and exist there in an undifferentiated state for a very short time before going off to become other types of cells. This means that we can't rely entirely on aborted fetuses, as they are already too old. Instead, we use embryos obtained from in vitro fertilization. In the course of development, they ultimately become skin cells, neurons, muscle, blood cells and every other of the 220 cell types that make up the tissues and organs in the body.

In their undifferentiated state in the laboratory, stem cells show an ability to divide indefinitely.

While stem cells hold significant clinical and technological potential, scientists are only beginning to understand their basic biology. For example, the cellular events that lead to cell specialization are not well understood and much work needs to be done before scientists are able to direct undifferentiated stem cells to become specific types of cells. There is also the potential that cultured human stem cells used in transplant medicine could face rejection by the body's immune system.

What is PraxMed Doing?

PraxMed has formed a silent partnership with a foreign company that is conducting research in stem cell therapies for a wide range of diseases and disorders using human subjects. This company has a virtually unlimited supply of embryonic stem cells and very deep pockets for research and biomedical engineering; they now have the capability to grow human organs!

Their government has nothing like the United States' Federal Drug Administration and no laws regarding human experimentation that are well enforced. PraxMed has entered into a relationship with this company where we, with our extensive access to hospital records, provide them with a list of medically ideal candidates for stem cell experimentation. Exactly how these candidates are convinced to participate is not PraxMed's concern. Monthly, PraxMed receives a report on the efficacy of the drugs, hormones and chemicals we have been supplying them, along with their recommendations for new drugs PraxMed should be developing to support stem cell therapies. This is proving, thus far, to be a very fruitful arrangement.

CHAPTER 15

After a long morning with her three young children, Louisa arose from her badly worn couch to answer her door. Her sister had arrived to watch the children while Louisa would be at the clinic, where she was going for the third abortion of her life. As she boarded the bus for the long ride to the clinic, sadness nearly overwhelmed her. Not only had she endured many hardships growing up, but her poverty would simply not allow for another mouth to feed. Thank God she wouldn't have to pay for the abortion. Not only was it free, but it would be performed in a clean clinic by a real doctor. Surely, Dr. Nicolas Falcón was a saint to provide this service free for the poor women of Bogotá!

Once the bus had arrived, Louisa entered through the impressive lobby of the clinic. Any visitor to the city would have been amazed at the contrast between the city's manifest poverty and filth, and the opulence and sterility of the clinic. Walking up to the check-in counter, Louisa was greeted by a nurse with a warm understanding smile. "Name please?" the nurse asked in Spanish.

"Louisa Alverez." Her voice quivered, even though she was trying to be brave. "I have a 2:00 appointment for a procedure."

Throughout Louisa's ordeal, she was treated with the utmost courtesy and respect. It's almost, she thought, like I'm bringing them gold rather than an unwanted baby. Little did she know that "gold" in the form of future embryonic stem cells was exactly what she had brought them. Not from the fetus she was carrying, but from her eggs they would steal via a stealthy harvesting through transvaginal ultrasound aspiration. These would later be used to grow embryos via in vitro fertilization.

CHAPTER 16

D r. Thomas Jefferson Hunt awoke somewhat disoriented. After a bit, the knowledge of his kidnapping and the events of the last few days came rushing back. He was in a hospital bed in a room shared with the ex-military officer Steve Moss. Dr. Hunt had been a Walter Reed specialist in rehabilitation medicine before he was diagnosed with Parkinson's disease. Knowing all too well the long-term prognosis for the disease, and knowing there was no cure, he had taken an early retirement in order to do some traveling while he could still do so comfortably. Now, apparently, his ability to control any of his future was in doubt. Realizing he and all the rest of the "patients" were literally prisoners of a criminal organization, Dr. Hunt questioned whether any of them would ever be released, or even allowed to live once their usefulness as human guinea pigs had ended.

"Good morning, Sleeping Beauty," Moss said. "Sleep well in our swell cell, Dr. Hunt?" Moss added sarcastically.

"I'm not a doctor in here, so please call me Thomas, and good morning to you, too. Your eye is looking a little better today, I see. Bastard must have hit you awfully hard, given how swollen it was yesterday." Moss noticed Dr. Hunt exhibited fairly severe tremors.

"Asshole hit like a girl, Tom. God, I really need a drink," Moss grumbled as he saw his hands shaking.

"First, please call me Thomas, and never call me Tom. Second, when you say you need a drink, are you just bitching, or are you an alcoholic?"

"I thought I was just a drunk, but I'm now thinking I'm an alcoholic based on the way my hands are shaking."

Thomas told Moss that he, too, had suffered from a drinking problem. He revealed that he had served two times in the United States Marine Corps. The first time was when he had enlisted right out of high school. His drinking began when his best friend was killed before his eyes in combat. Once he realized how self-destructive his behavior was (he'd hit an officer, who fortunately didn't bring charges), he sobered up. He had gone to college and then medical school, after which he'd accepted a commission as a Marine Corps officer.

The men's conversation was interrupted by the sound of their door being unlocked. In came a somewhat weathered but attractive nurse pushing a cart with two covered meals on it. "Good morning, gentlemen. My name is Alicia, and I'll be your server today," she smirked.

"Good morning and we'll be your prisoners today," Moss retorted in a flat tone. "Come with some gruel to slop the detainees?"

"Well, before you get all smart-assed with me, why don't you look at what I've brought you first? What's up with those shaking hands? It's your room mate who has Parkinson's, not you," she said as she placed a tray in front of each of the men.

"Well, I'm an alcoholic…I don't suppose a guy could order a scotch in here?"

"Sorry honey, but drinks are not on the menu. You're going to have to go cold turkey and dry out by yourself."

Expecting something akin to prison fare, Thomas and Moss were amazed as Alicia uncovered their food. Each of them was looking at a tray containing Eggs Benedict next to a plate of buttermilk pancakes smothered in blueberry compote. This was accompanied by fresh-squeezed orange juice and a cup of steaming coffee that smelled like that served in a fine restaurant.

"Not exactly the bread and water I was expecting," Thomas said with surprise still on his face.

"It will get even better," Alicia replied. "Each day you'll select your meals from a restaurant-type menu, and be given the option to make special requests. Even though you're our involuntary "guests" we plan to treat you very well. Dr. Falcón believes happy patients are cooperative patients."

"If you really want to make us happy, why don't you let us go right now?" Thomas queried.

"You are a silly boy. We don't let you go right now because we're not done with you yet! And if either of you thinks you'll 'check out' on your own, take a look up there," Alicia said pointing up at the center of the ceiling. Moss and Thomas looked where she was pointing, and saw a video camera on a motorized mount. Our security team will have all of you under constant surveillance. There are many hidden cameras as well. Any of you patients attempting escape will become participants in one of our doctor's favorite pastimes—vivisection without benefit of anesthesia."

As Moss opened his mouth to ask another question, Alicia Jones pivoted to make her exit.

Just before she left, over her shoulder she added, "oh yeah, your physical exams are this afternoon. Eat hearty, my boys."

CHAPTER 17

Eric Rasmussen was a TV political talk show host who had gained a reputation for addressing the most controversial topics in politics, from vote rigging in Florida to corruption in government. Today his topic was the proposed federal regulations on the use of embryonic stem cells in medical research. Today's guests were Sally Peters, who was Minnesota Senator Jake Jackson's spokes person and press liaison, and Arizona's Senator Anthony Brown. After brief introductions, the show began.

Rasmussen: Good morning Ms. Peters and Senator Brown. As you know, Minnesota Senator Jake Jackson was to join Senator Brown in a discussion here about the proposed federal regulations on the use of embryonic stem cells in medical research. As you've probably heard by now, the senator's sister, Haley Jackson has been missing for two weeks, the apparent victim of a kidnapping. Rather than cancel, the senator inquired if he could send his spokes person, Ms. Peters, and Senator Brown graciously agreed. Ms. Peters, any new developments in the Haley Jackson case?

Sally Peters: Unfortunately not, Eric—in spite of the best efforts of the FBI and the St. Paul police department, Haley's disappearance remains a total mystery. But, while I thank you for asking, that's not what we're here to discuss. Senator Jackson, while extremely concerned for the safety of his sister, very much wants known his reasons for opposition to the proposed federal regulations on the use of embryonic stem cells in medical research.

Rasmussen: Please convey to the senator that we are all praying for his sister and her safe return. Now, Senator Brown, as author of the new legislation, perhaps you can briefly outline your opposition to embryonic stem cell research?

Senator Brown: Eric, The regulations I've proposed would make illegal any research employing the use of embryonic stem cells in medical research. Even use of existing lines of embryonic stem cells because their use, quite simply, defiles the sanctity of human life. We believe stem cell research has some promise, but that promise can be achieved using adult stem cells.

Sally Peters: Senator, what you say about adult stem cells ignores some very important facts.

Rasmussen: And what would those facts be, Ms. Peters?

Sally Peters: Why not derive stem cells from adults? There are several approaches now in human clinical trials that utilize mature stem cells (such as blood-forming cells, neuron-forming cells and cartilage-forming cells). However, because adult cells are already specialized, their potential to regenerate damaged tissue is very limited: skin cells will only become skin and cartilage cells will only become cartilage. Adults do not have stem cells in many vital organs, so when those tissues are damaged, scar tissue develops. Only embryonic stem cells, which have the capacity to become any kind of human tissue, have the potential to repair vital organs.

Another limitation of adult stem cells is their inability to proliferate in culture. Unlike embryonic stem cells, which have a capacity to reproduce indefinitely in the laboratory, adult stem cells are difficult to grow in the lab and their potential to reproduce diminishes with age. Therefore, obtaining clinically significant amounts of adult stem cells may prove to be difficult.

Senator Brown: So you're saying what…that adult stem cells have no value for research?

Sally Peters: I didn't say that. Studies of adult stem cells are important and will provide valuable insights into the use of stem cell in transplantation procedures. However, only through exploration of all types of stem cell research will scientists find the most efficient and effective ways to treat diseases.

Senator Brown: If God had intended man to be a monster…

Sally Peters: Rather than talking about God's intentions let me tell you this: we have all seen suffering beyond measure among the living, which could be eliminated, or ameliorated by the treatments we believe possible. So who are the monsters among us? Those who dare to envision a future with less suffering for those already born, or those who pontificate from their high horses to protect a cluster of less than 64 cells we call an embryo destined to be discarded? They would be just as dead…and useless. I would suggest that the monsters among us are those who block progress in the name of their holier-than-thou religions, not the scientists charging into new frontiers!

Rasmussen: Here is the problem as I see it. On the one hand, we have people who believe the embryo is human life and as such, should not be exploited regardless of how much good could come from it. On the other hand, we have scientists who offer hope that many of man's afflictions can be cured. Basically we have two viewpoints, one religious and one scientific. Senator Brown, is there any room for compromise?

Senator Brown: When it comes to protecting the unborn, I believe the answer is no.

Sally Peters: That is unfortunate, since Senator Jackson firmly believes that, if the United States adopts these restrictions, it will lose initiative and control to foreign competitors! It doesn't mean embryonic stem cell research is going away; it does mean we will, perhaps drive it into unscrupulous hands.

Rasmussen: I'm afraid we have to break for this commercial message. We'll be right back.

The show lasted an hour and, of course, nothing got resolved.

CHAPTER 18

Once again, the "patients" sat before Dr. Falcón as he explained the differences between a control group and an experimental group. "As I told you during the orientation session, each of you will get to say whether you prefer to be in the control group or the experimental group. Your preferences will be noted, but do not guarantee to which of the groups you'll be assigned. You will all appear to be receiving treatments, but about half of you will be getting placebos rather than actual therapeutic treatments. We need to do this in order to determine if the treatments are truly effective (this was not exactly true, but he said it for the patients' benefit).

A man in the back of the room said plaintively, "So there is no way we'll know if you're experimenting on us or not?"

"Not at first. However, later on you will likely find out," replied Dr. Falcón.

"And how exactly would that be?" the same man asked.

"There are three ways. First, you'll know if your condition is greatly improved. Second, you'll know if your condition worsens significantly." Dr. Falcón paused for dramatic effect and then continued, "Third, we'd know because you died."

The room became instantly silent until Haley piped up in a synthetically cheerful voice, "Any chance we could just go to Disneyland instead?"

A few people laughed nervously, everyone keenly aware for the first time that some of them might actually die in this place without any of their family or friends knowing.

Dr. Falcón smiled as though he saw great humor in the situation. He glanced at all the stricken faces, and he said cavalierly. "Oh cheer up! A lot of you are going to walk out of here cured! We will be making our selections for control versus experimental group this evening, so please make your nurses aware of your preferences this afternoon. But right now, just out of curiosity, could I see a show of hands for those who would prefer to be assigned to the experimental group?"

Only two people raised their hands, and Moss and Haley both noted that those two people had told them previously that they were already terminally ill.

"How terribly disappointing this is. It appears we will have some draftees! Your treatments shall begin tomorrow." Dr. Falcón admonished, after which he stomped out of the room.

If ever Moss actually needed a stiff drink, it was now.

CHAPTER 19

T homas, Haley and Moss had just finished lunch in the cafeteria. Haley had ordered a chef's salad, Thomas the chicken Kiev, and Moss a rib eye steak with a baked potato. After having caught up on each others pasts, they were discussing their current predicament.

"Do either of you think we'll ever get rescued? You can't kidnap a room full of people without leaving some kind of trail, can you?" Haley asked.

"The problem" Moss replied, "is that these were not typical kidnappings. No requests for ransom, no demands of any kind. We just disappeared one day into thin air, leaving the authorities little or nothing to go on. So, unless these people did something stupid—and they don't impress me as being stupid—I don't have much hope for a rescue."

"Unfortunately, I agree with Steve," Thomas added. "I believe an escape is our only hope."

"Oh, like that's going to happen," laughed Haley derisively. "You forget that we are all either very ill or in wheelchairs, and did they tell you what they'd do to you if you got caught? Vivisection—getting filleted while alive! Plus, we are under constant surveillance; they even have hidden cameras and microphones throughout this place. I'm sorry, but I think the situation is hopeless!"

"Not necessarily hopeless," Moss said after reflecting for a while, "just extremely difficult. One thing is very clear."

"What is extremely clear?" asked Thomas, looking puzzled.

"In order to escape, we're going to have help from someone on the staff," Haley deduced.

"Yes," Moss nodded. "They can't all be madmen. Some of the staff must be sympathetic to our plight."

"Our job, then," reasoned Thomas, "is to find one or more willing and able staff people to recruit for an escape plan." Haley and Moss both shook their heads in agreement. "The big question is, other than sympathy, why would any of them be willing to risk helping us? Even if we escaped, they'd likely be killed if it were ever found out they helped us."

"Well, how about money, immunity from prosecution and guaranteed U.S. citizenship? My brother is wealthy and a Senator; I'm positive our government would guarantee the safety of anyone who helped us," Haley offered. Moss looked into Haley's eyes and saw intelligence and fierce determination. Under better circumstances, this would be a woman he could fall for. Moss quickly put that thought to rest.

"That just might work," Moss said.

That afternoon, Dr. Falcón's experiments began. All of the captives received multiple injections; some, like Haley and Moss, were wheeled into surgeries and others, like Thomas, got stem cells implanted in various parts of their bodies.

CHAPTER 20

Three months had passed since Haley Jackson's mysterious disappearance, and Jake was beginning to lose hope of ever seeing his sister alive again. As he sat in his mansion's study, richly furnished in leather and oak, he was reflecting on his family's better times. Jake's two dogs and two cats were keeping him company. His thoughts were interrupted by a knock on his door.

"Come in, Chris," Jake said to his majordomo.

"Ms. Peters is here to see you sir, shall I show her in?" Jake nodded, and moments later Sally walked in carrying a full grocery bag.

"You haven't been eating well these past few weeks. If you don't mind, I'd like to fix us an old-fashioned country breakfast. How do omelets, waffles and cranberry muffins sound?" Sally asked, knowing these were some of Jake's favorites. While Sally was saddened by the disappearance of her best friend, she was concerned that Jake was slipping into a full-fledged depression. Jake just blinked and didn't speak at first. It had been a long time since a woman other than household staff or his daughter had cooked for him.

"That would be nice … would you mind if I help?" Jake followed Sally into the kitchen and began setting the table while Sally unpacked her grocery bag.

"Does the FBI have any new leads, or any new theories on why Haley and the others were taken?" Sally asked.

"Unfortunately, the answer is no." Jake replied. "All of the cases seem to be the same in that there are no witnesses, no physical evidence, no ransom requests nor any other kind of demands. Other than alien abduction, nothing else makes sense."

With a deadpan tone, Sally said, "I wonder what Martians have for breakfast?" For the first time in weeks, Jake allowed himself a small smile. He was a man of action, a solutions provider, but Haley's disappearance had him flummoxed.

"You know what gets to me the most, Sally? A man's job is to protect his family and I've failed miserably. I lie awake at night wondering where Haley is, or if she's even alive. I pray that she is, but then I worry about what the sick bastards who took her are doing to her." As Sally looked over the counter at Jake, she could see tears welling up in his eyes. She left the eggs she was stirring and walked behind the chair where Jake was sitting. Sally began to massage Jake's shoulders, feeling the tension in them.

"Don't be so hard on yourself, Jake. There is nothing you or anyone else could have done to prevent Haley from being taken. You're the best dad Katie and brother that Haley could ever wish for." Sally thought she could feel a little of the tension abate in Jake's strong shoulders as she continued kneading them.

Along with sadness, Jake was feeling gratitude for this wonderful woman whose heart was so obviously full of warmth and caring. "I don't know what I've done to deserve such a wonderful friend," Jake said, reaching up to pat her hand.

Sally responded by gently kissing the top of Jake's head. "After all our years of working together, Jake, I've come to respect you more than any man I've ever known. In the last few months I've realized how unpredictable life can be. One day you're here—the next day you might be gone. I think you have to grab happiness when you can, otherwise life might just pass you by."

"What exactly are you trying to say?" Jake asked. Sally stopped the massage and walked around the chair so she was facing Jake.

"What I'm trying to say," Sally replied tenderly, "is that we could be much more than just friends." She knelt down until she was looking directly into his eyes and kissed him deeply, her passion apparent. Jake was taken by surprise and at first he didn't respond. Sally pulled back, fearing she'd been too forward. "I'm sorry," she mumbled, "but I was hoping the feelings were mutual."

Jake paused for a moment before speaking. "Don't apologize, Sally. As your boss, it would have been inappropriate for me to imply that I had feelings for you. But the truth is I've been in love with you for a very long time." Jake reached out, and with his index finger traced the soft curve that ran from

Sally's chin up to her ear lobe. He then cupped her face in both of his hands, and slowly kissed Sally like she'd never been kissed before. "Would you mind if we ate breakfast later?" Jake asked as he stood up, taking Sally in his arms, and leading her by the hand, took her upstairs to his bedroom.

CHAPTER 21

S everal months had passed since Dr. Falcón's experiments began. One woman had been cured of diabetes and three of the Parkinson's patients were showing marked improvement, including Thomas. Five patient's conditions had worsened and two had died. All of the remaining patients showed little or no improvement. Most of the patients with spinal cord injuries were showing no change in their conditions at all, despite having been subjected to a variety of experimental techniques.

Haley, Thomas and Moss had devised a secret way to communicate using notes written in code, and passed surreptitiously. Moss had a strong background in cryptography and had provided the others with a cipher that made the notes look innocent. The notes were, in fact, communications about their attempts to convince someone on the staff to help them.

Their progress was impeded by the need to "fish" as they interacted with the staff, since they never knew for sure when they were being watched or listened to. During breakfast, Haley had passed a note to Thomas that, when deciphered, said:

Last night, just before nodding off to sleep, I had the oddest feeling, like my toes were twitching. At first I just thought it was a side effect of one of the drugs they've been making me take, but when I looked down at the blanket over my feet, I saw movement! What should I do now? I don't want any of those bastards to know I am making any kind of improvement.

Thomas rechecked his deciphering to make sure he'd read it correctly and later found a way to pass the note to Moss back in their shared room. As he watched Moss decipher and read the note, which he'd placed in a magazine to avoid the camera, Thomas could see the look of puzzlement change to amazement on Moss's face. Moss put down the magazine and opened his mouth to speak, then closed it. He wanted Thomas's medical opinion, but couldn't figure out an "innocent" way to ask. Finally, he waited until he was sure Thomas was watching him, and then said, looking down at his own feet, "Thomas, you know that ancient Chinese saying?"

"Which one do you mean?"

"Even the longest journey begins with a single step." Thomas followed Moss's gaze down to his feet beneath the blanket on his lap, and was stunned to see that his feet were shifting around slightly!

Thomas smiled almost imperceptivity and countered with "There is another old saying: 'You have to walk before you can run.'"

Moss grinned, "Very true, oh wise one, how very true."

CHAPTER 22

Alicia Jones walked into their room with a cheerful smile on her face. Over the past few months, Haley, Thomas, and Moss had agreed that Alicia was the most likely member of the staff to come to their aid, although they were still a long way from broaching the subject with her. Three things made Alicia a likely candidate to assist them in escaping: first, they had learned from Alicia that she had a teenage son living in America whom she hadn't seen since she'd left for prison. The boy had been adopted by his foster parents, but Alicia longed to see him; second, she had struck up a genuine friendship with them; last, but far from least, she appeared to have a huge crush on Thomas.

"So how're my bad boys doing this morning? You both are lookin' mighty fine." Alicia said.

"'Aight," Thomas answered, smiling brightly. "You lookin' mighty phat today," Alicia grinned because she knew Thomas spoke the King's English, and because she knew he was flirting with her. ("Phat" was not "fat"... it was an old slang term he had used in implying she was a sexy woman). "Thomas," Alicia said, "Since you've had what appears to be a full recovery from Parkinson's disease, Dr. Falcón was wondering if you'd be interested in helping with the rehab program?" Thomas looked thoughtful before he answered.

"Please understand that I in no way excuse how these patients were obtained, nor do I condone the involuntary human experimentation going on here. However, now that I have completely recovered, I do "itch" to practice medicine again. Tell Dr. Falcón I am willing to help with one stipulation."

"And what would that stipulation be, sugar?" Alicia asked.

Thomas winked when he answered, "My condition is that Alicia Jones be my assistant."

Alicia grinned from ear to ear, and replied, "I'll give him the message, and we'll see what he says."

Once he'd left the room, Moss rolled his eyes and said, "Move over, Casanova."

CHAPTER 23

As Thomas and Moss were watching a TV show about whales, the screen suddenly went blank, and then a message began to scroll across the screen. Simultaneously, the loud speaker in the hallway blared:

"ALL PATIENTS MUST REPORT TO THE GYMNASIUM AT 4:00 PM. THIS IS A MANDATORY MEETING."

That was in just ten minutes. Both Thomas and Moss registered their surprise...the voice on the public address system was an angry one. Without hesitation, Thomas walked over to Moss's wheelchair and said, "I don't think we want to miss this."

When they entered the gymnasium they saw that the rest of the patients looked as perplexed as they were. A big screen TV was at the front of the room. One of the armed guards came up and turned the TV on. The screen was filled with a somber-faced Dr. Falcón where he appeared to be standing in an operating room.

"Good Afternoon. As you recall, when we first met, I warned you about trying to escape. Unfortunately, Mr. Richards here," the camera panned over to a terrified man strapped to an operating table, "didn't take me seriously. Last night we had verified that his diabetes was cured. Mr. Richards 'rewarded' us by attempting to overpower a guard and seize his weapon. As you can see, he wasn't successful, and now I want you to all watch as Mr. Richards pays for his foolishness. Watch and learn." The camera panned over to Richards' face, which had a look of sheer terror on it. The shot was then zoomed out to show a surgeon in full operating garb standing over him

Dr. Falcón began narrating as the surgeon selected a scalpel. "As you probably know, burn victims often require skin grafts. An autograft, where the skin comes from the patient's own body is best, since the body won't reject it. However, autografts aren't always possible, so cadaver skin is sometimes used. But a better solution is to graft skin from a live donor." Dr. Falcón paused while the surgeon made a quick shallow incision from the clavicle down to the pubic bone. Richard's scream made it clear that no anesthetic was being used. All the patients in the gymnasium gasped as the realized what was happening. Several stood up or shouted to turn the TV off. Two women were out of their seats, heading toward the exit. A guard blocked their way, and shouted, "All you gringos sit down and watch. I'll shoot the next person who tries to leave." On the TV screen, the surgeon was making more incisions—this time circular—around the face, as Richard's screaming was in an increasing crescendo.

The surgeon began peeling off the skin on the face;—the abrupt cessation of screams made it clear Richards had passed out. The surgeon adjusted an IV line and speeding up a continuous drip. Richard's eyes opened and the screaming resumed.

"You might be under the false impression a man can't live with his skin removed. However, if fluids are immediately replaced, one can live for several hours, and drugs can be administered to keep the patient fully conscious. Recently, the world saw the first face transplant…from a cadaver of course. Imagine how much a face taken from a live donor will be worth!"

The surgeon then made a long incision in Richard's abdomen. "Before mankind invented more modern forms of torture, disembowelment was a real crowd pleaser," continued Dr. Falcón as the surgeon began slowly removing the intestines, coiling them up in his hands before Richards' horrified eyes. The camera moved back onto Dr. Falcón's face as he summarized what was going to happen next. "The surgeon will now remove all of the major organs and the eyes, which will be sold on the medical black market. Your lesson for today is now over. I hope none of you will be as foolish as Mr. Richards was. After all, as the Japanese say, 'it is important to save face.'" He smirked at his own dark humor, and then walked out of the operating room.

The guard walked up and turned off the TV, saying, "Show's over, now go back to your rooms."

The patients sat in mortified silence for a moment, then the fear of being seen as disobedient set in, and they slowly left the gymnasium.

CHAPTER 24

At both breakfast and lunch, the patients had guardedly discussed yesterday's events in hushed voices. There was no doubt left in any of their minds about the true nature of their captors. Even the few battle-hardened veterans like Moss found Dr. Falcón's retaliation for Richard's escape attempt grisly and macabre beyond belief. Thomas, who had witnessed human dissections—albeit never on a living person—in medical school found Dr. Falcón to be the epitome of a *bête noire*.

As Haley, Thomas and Moss sat together in the cafeteria sipping coffee after lunch; Haley was fiddling with the salt shaker. She glanced up at the single camera mounted in the corner of the room. After thinking for a moment, she unscrewed the top of the salt shaker and poured a small mound of salt onto the table. As Thomas and Moss watched, Haley spread the salt in a flat layer in the center of the table. Using her index finger, she wrote WHAT NOW in the salt, and then, having made sure the men had seen it, she quickly rubbed out the letters.

Thomas and Moss sat motionless impressed with Haley's on-the-spot communications innovation. Thomas then reached out and wrote HELP FROM ALICIA, and quickly rubbed it out.

Moss reached out and wrote HOW?

Thomas just grinned and wrote AFFAIR—FLIRTED 4 LONG TIME—PAID OFF

Moss reached out and wrote HOW?

Thomas wrote ROOM WITH CAMERAS OFF. Moss pointed to his ear with a quizzical look. Thomas wrote NO MICROPHONES. Haley and Moss both grinned. Thomas then wrote IN LOVE WITH ME.

Haley wrote LOVE??

Thomas looked sheepish and wrote SHE ADDICTED. Both Haley and Moss gave Thomas a puzzled look. Thomas wrote TO MY LOVING. Haley and Moss laughed out loud. Then, to their utter amazement, these words were written as if by magic in the salt: THOMAS IS A MAJOR STUD—YOU ARE NOT ALONE. The three of them sat in stunned silence, hardly able to believe their eyes. Haley and Moss, thinking Thomas had executed a clever little parlor trick, began to laugh uproariously.

One of the guards noted their previous frivolity and came walking over. "What's so fucking funny?" He asked.

"Oh, silly me," Haley replied, "Someone played a practical joke and unscrewed the top of the salt shaker, and I spilled it all over the table."

"Stupid Yankees," he retorted, "you all behave like children." He then took his hand and brushed the salt into Haley's face. Thomas saw Moss instantly flinch in anger, and forcefully reacted by grabbing his arm before Moss could stand up. The guard had seen the anger in his response, and smirked as he taunted Moss, "What you going to do, cripple, kick my ass?"

Suddenly, the guard flew forward on to their table as though some one had kicked him quite forcibly in the posterior. As the furious guard got up to retaliate, no one was there.

CHAPTER 25

A s pre-arranged with Alicia, Thomas was fully dressed when he heard the door to Moss's and his room being unlocked. Moss was pretending to be asleep. Alicia opened the door as quietly as she could, and as the hall light spilled in, and smiled when she saw Thomas was dressed and ready for their "date" in the gymnasium, where Thomas believed the cameras and microphones were turned off at night because it was presumed all the patients were securely locked in their rooms for the night. As Thomas walked out into the hallway, Alicia winked at him and took his hand in hers. Together they wound their way through the halls in silence. When they reached the doors of the gymnasium, Alicia removed a key from her pocket and unlocked the door.

Once they were inside, Alicia stood in front of Thomas and began unbuttoning his shirt, saying "How is my big stud muffin doing tonight? Have you been thinking about me all day, sugar?"

Thomas responded by leaning down and kissing her passionately. As he unbuttoned her smock, he whispered in her ear, "You're practically all I can think about." He then teased the opening of her ear with the tip of his tongue as he simultaneously unhooked her bra.

Thomas then led Alicia over to one of the exercise mats, and pulled her down with him as he lay down. Discarding the rest of their clothes, Thomas marveled at Alicia's full breasts with their silver-dollar sized areolas. One at a time, he lavishly suckled her nipples as she moaned.

Thomas then knelt between Alicia's legs and trailed his tongue down her belly very slowly until he got to her mound. He was a patient and practiced lover, and Alicia groaned loudly as she came.

After she'd regained her breath and sat up, Alicia looked down at Thomas's erection, which was the largest she had seen on any man. "Roll over on your back, sweet pea—I got me some ridin' to do."

When they were both fully sated, and were lying in each others arms, Alicia said, "I have a present for you." She got up and reached into a pocket on her smock, and produced a key ring with two keys on it.

"What are those for?'

"One is for your room; the other is to the gymnasium. Now you'll be able to meet me here when we want to hook up without me having to come and fetch you."

"But won't the cameras see me?" Thomas asked.

Alicia laughed. "Silly boy, once you're locked in your rooms, no one monitors the cameras or microphones at night in either the hall ways or the patients' rooms! The security guards are in short supply…for this kind of operation they need people they can trust or control 100 percent, and they don't grow on trees. Besides that, Dr. Falcón figures that, after making you watch what they did to Richards, no one would dare to even think about escaping."

CHAPTER 26

At breakfast, Thomas, Haley and Moss were discussing the patient status report posted on the cafeteria bulletin board. Dr. Falcón had recently decided it would be good for patient morale to see that the experiments were resulting in a number of cures, particularly for diabetes and Parkinson's disease. Not listed was the handful of deaths due to experiments gone awry, nor the patients who had developed serious complications.

"Well," Moss said, "at least some patients are improved. But I didn't see anyone with a spinal cord injury listed. Thomas, if you put your doctor's hat back on, why is that the case?"

Thomas thought for a moment, and then speculated, "Even if they can re-grow neurons in the central nervous system, recovery from paralysis might not be possible because muscles atrophy beyond repair after a period of time."

"How long would be too long?" Haley asked.

"That answer would be purely theoretical, since normally the central nervous system—the brain and the spinal cord—can't repair themselves, and without enervation, muscles literally wither away in about a year. It is possible to stimulate the muscles with electrodes, but that would be pointless without a known cure."

"But if the paralysis is less than a year old, you think the muscles might recover if the paralyzing injury were corrected?"

"In theory, yes," Thomas answered. Both Haley's and Moss's faces lit up at this answer, since both of them had noticed increasing feeling and some movement in their lower bodies over the last few weeks. Neither of them had let on to the staff that these changes were happening, and they were hesitant to let themselves get their hopes up, although both of them were secretly delighted that feeling had returned to their genital areas. But, other than being able to wiggle their feet a little in private, neither of them had managed any movement of their legs.

Moss posited, "So, theoretically speaking, a person who had been paralyzed for less than a year could conceivably walk again if the damage to the spinal cord were corrected?"

"Maybe," Thomas answered, "but only with a rigorous rehab program."

"You mean the kind of rehab program a Walter Reed physiatrist could design?" Haley wondered.

Thomas smiled broadly, "Yes, the kind of rehab program a Walter Reed physiatrist could design."

CHAPTER 27

After "lights out" when all the patients were securely locked in their rooms, Moss was drifting off to sleep when he heard Thomas's voice, "HELP me." Moss sat up, rubbing his eyes.

"What's wrong, Thomas?"

He could see Thomas because the full moon was partially illuminating the room, and he showed no obvious signs of distress. None-the-less, Moss turned on the bedside lamp and made a "what-the-hell" gesture with his arms. Thomas was looking directly at him as he shook his head and made a "shhhh…" sound indicating nothing was really wrong. With a puzzled look on his face, Moss listened as Thomas spoke, not shouted, "Help me!" three more times over a 15 minute period. No one had come to investigate.

Thomas then stood up, walked over to Moss, where he pretended to try to strangle him for three minutes. Again, no one came to investigate.

"Huh, I guess Alicia was telling the truth about no one monitoring our rooms at night. Apparently, Security runs a skeleton crew at night with no one monitoring the cameras or microphones in our rooms."

"You mean we've been watching our 'p's and q's' needlessly all this time?"

"Well," Thomas reasoned. "Needlessly in hindsight, maybe, but instilling a 'big-brother-is- watching' mentality is a highly effective way to instill obedience."

"That and eviscerating a guy while we are forced to watch," Moss added.

"I believe we can talk freely, at least at night," Thomas said. "So, how are your legs doing?"

Moss grinned and replied, "I think all the feeling is back in my lower body, although I'm doing my best to conceal it from the staff. I can wiggle my feet, but my legs feel like lead weights."

"Wow!" Thomas exclaimed," That means, I think, that with intensive therapy you will likely walk again!"

"Therein lies the rub," Moss answered," How am I going to get intensive therapy? If we want to have any chance of escape, I have to walk again without Dr. Falcón knowing about it. How is that going to happen?"

Now it was Thomas's turn to grin. "You've seen how well equipped with equipment the gymnasium is? That's where Alicia takes me when she wants to fool around, and she has given me my own key as well as the key to our room. You and I could go there nights and work on your rehabilitation."

Moss beamed. "You really think I'll be able to walk again?"

"There is no reason to delay this. They've already asked me to assist with rehab, so if we get caught, the consequences should be manageable...I'll have to fabricate a plausible story so as to not get Alicia in trouble. Now let's get you in your chair and head down to the gym."

CHAPTER 28

The key to their room worked perfectly. As Thomas and Moss navigated their way to the gym, Moss asked Thomas, "I was wondering about the room key Alicia gave you. Have you noticed that every time she comes to our room she only has one key, not a ring of keys with her?"

Thomas thought for a moment, and then responded, "I believe you are correct. Why do you ask?"

"Because when Alicia comes to see us, she is making rounds, and sees other patients as well, all of whom are also locked in their rooms. Since it is unlikely that she goes back and forth to get a different key for each room, it is likely that she carries a master key that opens all the rooms."

Thomas was stunned. "I know Alicia likes me, and trusts me to a certain extent, but do you really think she'd be so stupid as to give me a master key?"

"No, I don't think she's stupid, but it may have been the only key she could copy. She only told you it was a key to your room, figuring you'd never guess it was a master key. It probably wasn't a risky move in her mind. But we're speculating. We don't know for certain that it is a master key to all the patients' rooms."

"There is one way to find out," Thomas said as he made a detour towards Haley's room.

When they arrived, Thomas nervously slipped the key into the lock and turned the handle. He grinned as he heard the click of the latch opening and said, "Bingo. Wait here."

Thomas entered the room as silently as he could, not wanting to wake Haley's room mate. He needn't have worried, as the woman took a sleeping pill every night that knocked her out for a solid eight hours. Haley, however, was a light sleeper and her eyes had opened when she heard the door unlock. There was no mistaking Thomas's huge silhouette in the moonlit room. He had his finger to his lips indicating Haley shouldn't talk. He pointed to the door and walked over to Haley's bedside, scooped her up in his strong arms and then deposited her in her wheelchair. He then quietly rolled her out into the hallway where Moss was waiting.

Thomas quickly explained to Haley how he had come into possession of the keys, and how Alicia had told him about the lack of monitoring in the patients' rooms, hallways and gym at night. At first, Haley was concerned for their safety, but the look of concern on her face slowly changed to one of relief. "You mean we can now talk freely?" Haley asked.

"We believe so, Haley," Moss answered.

"How are you doing, other than being scared to death like the rest of us?" Thomas asked with genuine concern, "And more specifically, how are your legs doing?"

"Other than living in sheer terror, I'm OK I guess. My legs definitely have feeling in them, and I can wiggle my toes and feet…although I've kept it a secret. So, how are you two doing?"

"I too have regained all feeling in my lower body, but, like you, I don't want anyone to know, which is hard. The other day in the cafeteria I found myself tapping my foot to the music they pipe in. My legs, however feel like they're filled with a mixture of acid and concrete—they feel extremely heavy, and it hurts like hell when I try to move them. On a positive note, Thomas appears to be totally cured of his Parkinson's disease."

Haley's eyebrows shot up at this news, as Thomas interjected "It's true. No more tremors." To prove his point, he held out his arm, which was steady as a rock. "And," Thomas added, "Given the return of feeling you've both had in your lower bodies, I am betting I can get you both walking again if you're up for some pretty intense and, to be totally frank, painful therapy."

"You're kidding, right?" Haley asked, trying not to sound too hopeful.

Thomas responded immediately, "No, I am not kidding, as you'll soon find out. Let's head over to the gym right now."

CHAPTER 29

As the trio entered the gym, Thomas said, "The first thing I want to do is give you each a quick checkup to evaluate the extent of your neurological recovery, and to make sure you're healthy enough to undergo a strenuous and maybe painful rehab program."

Because the gym was an extraordinarily well equipped rehabilitation facility, Thomas had all the things he needed to do a thorough evaluation of both Haley and Steve. A half hour after they'd entered the gym, Thomas pronounced them both fit enough to proceed. "You've both had significant muscle atrophy, but since your paralyzing injuries are relatively recent, we should be able to get you walking again. It will not, however, be a rapid process. Fortunately, we have both a LiteGait treadmill and the equipment for semi-automated loco-motor training. Why don't you both wheel over to the LiteGait and we'll get started."

Moss and Haley followed Thomas over to an odd looking contraption that looked like a parachute harness suspended over a treadmill. "Haley, you're first." Thomas gently lifted Haley out of her chair as though she were a feather and strapped her in to the LiteGait harness. "The idea is to suspend almost your entire weight while we work on getting your legs moving again," he explained. Thomas set the treadmill for 1.0 mph and turned it on, then knelt down by Haley's feet. He used his arms to move her feet, one foot in front of the other. After a few minutes, Thomas stood up but left the treadmill running. "Lordy, lordy, will you take a look at that!" Haley and Moss looked down at her legs, which were now moving on their own. Moss's jaw literally dropped, and tears ran down Haley's cheeks. After five minutes of Haley's legs moving on their own, Thomas stopped the treadmill, extracted Haley from the harness, and put

Moss in her place. His legs also moved a little on their own, but with results poorer than Haley's. Nonetheless, all three of them were euphoric with the proof that Haley and Moss had overcome paralysis of their lower bodies. Hugs and back slapping followed in abundance.

Thomas had clearly morphed back into his doctor persona as he explained: "You both have months of therapy ahead of you. Your muscles have to get built back up, and your spines need to gradually get used to bearing your weight. Fortunately, we have all the equipment we need to work at night. I will perform period re-examinations on both of you. During the days, I want you to be very careful not to let anyone else see you moving your legs or feet. If we ever want to get out of this place, your recoveries must remain secret."

CHAPTER 30

PraxMed's corporate headquarters sat in the midst of a ten-acre parcel that looked like a park. 18 months had passed since the en mass kidnappings of the experimental subjects now in Bogotá, and Ted Mallick had an appointment with the PraxMed CEO. He entered the main tower through an impressive two story lobby and walked up to the guard desk to check in. The guard was an ex-marine who had a no-nonsense air about him.

"May I help you?" The guard asked.

"Ted Mallick, vice-president, special marketing operations. I have an 8:00 appointment with Mike Pellizari." As he spoke, Mallick reached for his wallet to produce the required identification, and handed it to the guard before being asked.

"Please be seated. I'll call Eileen and let them know you're here." Eileen, a former marine, was the CEO's battle-axe assistant, an out-of the-closet bull dyke no one dared ridicule, and immune from sexual harassment. With a hormone-enhanced muscular physique and a Tae Kwon Do black belt, Eileen was also Pellizari's bodyguard. Mallick took a seat in the plush waiting area, knowing he would be kept waiting for at least 15 minutes because that was the CEO's way of saying 'I am the biggest dog on the block.'

It was nearly 8:30 when a tall attractive blonde stepped out of the elevator and strode over to where Mallick was seated. She smiled as she greeted him, nearly crushing his hand with her incredible grip. "Mr. Mallick, how nice to see you again," Eileen said frostily. "Please follow me—Mr. Pellizari is eager to meet with you."

Mallick followed like an obedient puppy as he rode up to Mike Pellizari's penthouse office suite in a private elevator. The elevator exited to Eileen's outer office, which was larger than most senior executives' offices. Pellizari's ample bottom was perched on the corner of Eileen's desk. As they entered, he sprang up and said, "Teddy Mallick, how the hell are you?" Pellizari always used the diminutive form of a subordinate's name. Mallick thought *I'm just fine, you overpaid fat fuck,* but "I'm just great, Mike, how are you and the family?" came out of his mouth. Before entering the building, Mallick had switched on the receiver and recorder in his car. His right cufflink was actually a microphone and miniature transmitter; he knew that of all the PraxMed meetings he'd recorded over the years, this meeting with the CEO would potentially be the most valuable. After exchanging a few more pleasantries, Pellizari invited him in to his office.

Mallick marveled at the office's size and opulence. Rather than sitting behind his desk, Pellizari sat down in a large arm chair, and signaled for Mallick to take the chair next to him. They were facing a large fireplace that looked like it belonged in an exclusive gentlemen's club. After Eileen had brought them coffee, Pellizari asked, "So, Teddy, how goes our advanced research projects?"

"Mike, I am delighted to tell you we have found real cures for both diabetes and Parkinson's disease, and great progress in other areas, using a combination of stem cell treatments along with newly developed pharmaceuticals. It's clearly time to start the legitimate human trials!"

After digesting this incredible news, Pellizari looked concerned. "What is our risk that the Bogotá experiments will be discovered?"

"Virtually none," Mallick replied. "We have a number of options for assuring no one ever finds out that we've been doing illegal human experimentation on subjects whose kidnapping we authorized." For the benefit of his recording, Mallick wasn't going to mince words. If he ever needed to negotiate his way out, he'd leave the biggest dog no wiggle room whatsoever.

"And those options are…?"

"The first option is that we never release any of the subjects after we are done with them. They can be housed quite comfortably for the rest of their lives. This option would be fairly expensive, and there is always the risk of someone escaping some day. The second option is the termination of the subjects at the conclusion of the experiments. The benefits would be low cost and minimal risk."

"But still some risk? I prefer no risk at all. I don't want to spend my hard-earned retirement years in some penitentiary!" Pellizari interjected.

Hard earned my ass, Mallick thought." There is a third option," he offered.

"Let's hear it."

"We could arrange an 'accident' at the Bogotá facility when it has outlived its use to us. Unfortunately, all staff and patients would perish along with all their records."

Pellizari reflected silently for nearly a minute. "I like that third option best."

Gotcha, thought Mallick. Had he known that Mike Pellizari was a first cousin of the Falcón brothers, he would have realized how truly cold-hearted the PraxMed CEO was.

CHAPTER 31

T wo months after Mallick's meeting with the PraxMed CEO, Jake Jackson sat in his Senate office reading the <u>Wall Street Journal</u>. A headline on the front page caught his attention:

PraxMed Receives FDA approvals to Begin Stem Cell Trials

Jake began reading the story:

During a press conference yesterday, PraxMed CEO Mike Pellizari announced the company has received FDA approvals to begin a number of human trials involving a proprietary set of treatments using embryonic stem cells in concert with new drugs the company has developed.

"We have made great strides in our animal research recently. PraxMed believes we are on the brink of developing cures for a number of human maladies, including diabetes, Parkinson's disease and other diseases.

"The FDA has granted approvals today for PraxMed to begin human trials involving embryonic stem cell therapies. These trials will involve both stem cells and a range of new pharmaceuticals, which, in combination, may provide total cures…"

The remainder of the story talked about the recent surge in PraxMed stock, and how far behind the competition was. Jake wondered how in the world this company had apparently made so many advances in comparison to other drug companies. Better scientists, perhaps? Or maybe they had simply thrown a lot of money in their research and development pot? Whatever the reason, Jake was heartened by the fact that this news would be an arrow in the heart of the pending legislation to block the use of embryonic stem cells by researchers. Maybe not a killing blow, but enough to give pause to the crucial swing voters in both chambers.

A knock at his office door interrupted Jake's pondering. It was Sally, who had become far more than his official spokes person over the past few months as their romance blossomed.

"Turn on CNN!" Sally shouted, clearly excited about some news story. "Take a look at this…" She walked over and flipped on the TV and tuned to CNN. A reporter's staccato voice was saying that Arizona's Senator Anthony Brown had just succeeded in getting a restraining order blocking PraxMed from proceeding with human trials involving embryonic stem cells. In addition, his Senate sub-committee has subpoenaed all of PraxMed's research records involving the use of embryonic stem cells. They were now going to show a clip of Senator Brown talking about why he had gotten the subpoena and a restraining order.

"We took this drastic measure to protect the unborn's rights from ruthless exploitation for profit. Until the court hears this case, there will be no human trials involving the use of embryonic stem cells, no matter how promising PraxMed claims are. I should also point out that, by the time this matter gets to court, the use of embryonic stem cells in medical research will likely be illegal, since legislation is currently pending to make it so…."

Brown went on to reiterate his arguments about the sanctity of life and that the use of adult stem cells should be explored more fully. Both Jake and Sally shook their heads in disgust.

"How did Brown get a judge to issue a restraining order based on those lame arguments?" Sally asked rhetorically.

"My guess would be that he did some homework and found a judge sympathetic with his views. There are a lot of people who share Brown's views, you know. Anyhow, PraxMed will surely appeal," Jake suggested.

Sally shrugged her shoulders in glum acceptance. "I can't believe that Brown would feel this way if he personally suffered from an affliction that would benefit from PraxMed's work."

CHAPTER 32

Ted Mallick sat fuming in his elegantly furnished study in his Tudor home. He had just watched the CNN report on the asshole Arizona senator's attempts to block PraxMed's trials from going forward. His funk was disturbed by the ringing of his phone.

"Mr. Mallick? Please hold—I have Mr. Pellizari wanting to speak with you." Mallick reached over and hit **record** on the digital recorder he had attached to the phone.

A minute later, Mike Pellizari was asking Mallick if he'd heard the news. Mallick said that yes, he'd just watched it on CNN.

"Not _that_ news, Teddy! We have offers from Canada and the UK to conduct our trials in their countries. Senator Brown can go fuck himself. The only thing we have to be concerned about is the subpoena of our research records. Is our ass sufficiently covered?"

"Do you mean are there any records of our human experiments in Bogotá?"

"Of course that's what I mean," Pellizari snapped. "Also, are we sure we have sufficient animal studies to back us up?"

Mallick thought for a moment before replying. "All of the Bogotá records are written as though the experiments had been done on animals rather than humans."

"No, I mean do we have any actual animal studies at all? I'm not sure if we want any references to Bogotá at all in the documents we have to submit."

Mallick suddenly had an idea which he excitedly explained to Pellizari—ignoring is question. "Say Mike, I've just had a brainstorm which may just get us out of this situation completely!"

"Well spit it out man!"

"Senator Brown's restraining order and subpoenas are predicated on the basis of the use of <u>embryonic</u> stem cells. What if we told them we had a way to harvest embryonic stem cells without using an embryo? I just read about a new technique where the stem cells they drew from amniotic fluid donated by pregnant women held much the same promise as embryonic stem cells."

"That would unhorse the assholes, wouldn't it?"

CHAPTER 33

J ake had just received a very good phone call. PraxMed had succeeded in a court challenge to Senator Brown's restraining order based on their argument that no embryos would be used at all in their human trials. Rather, they were planning on using a newly developed technique to extract stem cells they drew from amniotic fluid donated by pregnant women. The court, however, was unwilling to rescind the subpoena for PraxMed's research records since those were needed to substantiate the source of the stem cells.

Fabulous, Strike one up for Research and Development! Jake thought. The PraxMed human trials were going to go ahead as planned. In the back of his mind, Jake held out hope that Haley was still alive, and that someday stem cell research would yield a cure for her paralysis.

At lunch, Jake took Sally out to Murray's for one of their famous butter-knife steaks. Their relationship had blossomed, and both were comfortable sharing their thoughts with each other. Their conversation eventually led to the FBI investigation of the kidnappings.

"Jake, I know this is hard to discuss, but what do you honestly think are the chances Haley and the other kidnapping victims are still alive?"

Jake put down his silverware and reflected silently for a moment. "The FBI has hit a brick wall. There have been some less professional kidnappings, but with no discernible connections. I don't think they have collected one shred of physical evidence. There have also been no ransom demands for any of the victims. Personally, until proven otherwise, I will always believe Haley is alive and that one day we'll find her. However, pure blind luck will have to prevail, since there are no clues, or even any plausible theories as to what happened."

Tears were forming in Sally's eyes. She reached out and took Jake's hand in her own. "We'll never give up hope!"

Later that afternoon, Jake received an unexpected call from Senator Brown. "Senator Jackson, How are you?" Jake was less than happy to hear from this senator, whom he personally disliked intensely. After some brief obligatory pleasantries, he cut to the chase. "To what do I owe the honor of this call?"

"You've probably heard by now that PraxMed got our court order reversed?" Brown whined. Jake replied that he had indeed heard that. "However, the subpoena for their lab records was upheld. We received the first batch yesterday, and there is something fishy about them," Brown continued.

"What do you mean by 'fishy'?" Jake asked.

"The records are supposed to be the results of their studies on animals, and all the documents support that."

"So what's the problem?" Jake asked.

"There is no problem with the documents at all, but the prepared microscopy specimens do have a problem."

Jake speculated that Brown was nitpicking, but played along. "So, what is wrong with the specimens?"

"Well, we would have missed this if we only had our staff reviewing the PraxMed material, but fortunately we had a cellular biologist examine the specimens under a microscope."

Jake was beginning to lose his patience. So what did he find?"

"Well, it's really hard to tell for sure until more tests are done, but his preliminary opinion is that the specimens aren't from animals...they're from humans!"

It took a moment for Jake to comprehend the fact's significance. "Has anyone asked PraxMed about this?"

"Not yet, because it may point to the fact that they've been experimenting on people and the logical question is what people would voluntarily subject them to that kind of risk?"

"No one would volunteer if they had a brain in their head," Jake replied.

"Exactly," Brown said excitedly. "But what if they weren't volunteers at all?"

"What are you implying?" Jake asked.

"We have suspected for some time that PraxMed likes to take shortcuts with their research. What if they skipped animal testing completely and skipped straight to humans?"

"And where would they get these human subjects?" Jake asked.

"Jake, what if they're the ones behind the kidnappings?"

"That is a highly speculative inference from what is probably a laboratory screw up in responding to your subpoena. Unless you're up for getting sued by PraxMed, I'd suggest you not go public with this supposition. That said, I do think we need to talk to the FBI about this."

CHAPTER 34

Mike Pellizari was furious. He'd spent the last hour in a meeting with the FBI about the materials they had subpoenaed. The FBI wanted to know why human cells rather than animal cells were present in the accompanying specimens. Those wankers in Bogotá had screwed up in the rush to respond to the subpoena and included specimens from their human subjects thinking no one would actually examine them microscopically. He'd been forced to invent a story about a big mix-up at their research facility in Bogotá…something about laboratory samples being mislabeled, and now the FBI wanted to send someone down there to interview the lab personnel! Mallick had assured him that there would be no problems, but now they were knee-deep in alligators. Pellizari decided he was going to ream that boy a new asshole.

"Get me Mallick on the phone right now!" He bellowed to his assistant. Within a minute, she'd located Mallick and informed Pellizari he was holding. Once again, Mallick reached over and hit **record** on the digital recorder he had attached to the phone.

"Mallick, you are a son of a bitch!"

Mallick was taken aback, as he was unaware of the FBI's visit with Pellizari. "Mike, what on earth is wrong?" Pellizari filled him in on the problems with the material sent from Bogotá in response to the subpoena, and how they now wanted to go down there and interview the lab personnel.

"Listen, Mallick, our tits are in a wringer. We simply can't afford to have the FBI poking around in our knickers down in Bogotá. I'm thinking we need to do something."

"What exactly do you mean by 'do something'?" Mallick asked.

"I want you to arrange that 'accident' we discussed. Make it look like a gas explosion or something like that. I don't want any survivors or any evidence to be found," Pellizari commanded. "One more thing, Mallick, I want you to know I hold you personally responsible for this mess. Once this is over, your career at PraxMed is finished. You'll be given sufficient funds to disappear and live handsomely for the rest of your life. Do you have a problem with that?"

"No problem, Mike." Mallick realized two things. First, he was being unceremoniously sacked. Second, What Pellizari meant by "the rest of your life" referred to the short period of time until they could get him out of the country and arrange an "accident" for him. Pellizari didn't know that Mallick knew exactly how Pellizari dealt with problem employees, or that he now had tape recordings of Pellizari ordering murders.

CHAPTER 35

After months and months of late night therapy sessions, Haley and Moss had both regained full use of their legs. Not only could they walk again, but they were having late-night foot races in the gymnasium, and Moss began teaching Haley and Thomas the first few *hyungs,* or basic forms, of Soo Bahk Do. These are like martial arts "dance steps" which emphasize technique, balance and control; the *hyungs* were excellent therapy for all of them.

Thomas and Haley expressed curiosity about how Moss had come to be a Soo Bahk Do Master, so he told them the story about being reared by his aunt and uncle, and how Uncle Sumner began teaching him the philosophy and the art of Soo Bahk Do when he was six years old.

"I understand what martial arts are, but please explain what you mean by the philosophy of Soo Bahk Do, "said Haley.

"There are eight keys concepts of Soo Bahk Do, "Moss explained, "They are: *Young Gi* (courage*), Chung Shin Tong Il* (concentration), *In Ney* (endurance), *Chung Jik* (honesty), *Kyum Son* (humility), *Him Cho Chung* (control of power), *Shin Chook* (tension and relaxation), and *Wan Gup* (speed control). There are also the 'ten articles of faith' which are: Be loyal to one's country; Be obedient to one's parents and elders; Be loving to one's husband or wife; Be cooperative to your brothers; Be respectful to elders; Be faithful to your teacher; Be faithful to friends; Face combat only in justice and with honor; Never retreat in battle; Always finish what you start. I hope you got all that, because there will be a quiz tomorrow night." Thomas and Haley both laughed at that, and Haley gave him a good natured punch in the arm.

"Uncle Sumner had been an Army Major and spent many years in Korea, both during and following the Korean War. During that time, he became friends with an older Korean gentleman who was an accomplished martial artist in Soo Bahk Do; he convinced my uncle to become a student."

Thomas, who had been both a Golden Gloves and Marine Corps boxing champion, eventually began sparring with Moss. It was classic boxing versus Soo Bahk Do. Even though Moss was a seventh dan instructor, Thomas's size and impeccable technique enabled him to hold his own. Thomas's rehab program, on top of the stem cell treatments they had received, had worked miracles. Both of them had been successful in concealing their recoveries from Dr. Falcón and the hospital staff. This was made easier by the fact that none of the other paralyzed patients had made any kind of substantial recovery. Thomas had explained that the likely reason was that all the other cases had been paralyzed for years and their muscles had atrophied too much.

These days, their time was spent fighting boredom. Moss had organized a little chess club, but was having trouble finding any real competition among the patients who played. Haley was teaching an aerobics class, even though she did it in her wheelchair. A number of the patients, particularly those who had been afflicted with Parkinson's disease or diabetes, seemed to be totally cured, and welcomed the activities as a way to stave off boredom.

Moss was in the middle of a chess game (he was up by a rook and two pawns) when one of the security staff approached him. "Dr. Falcón would like to see you in his office," the man said.

"Can it wait, as I'm in the middle of a game?" Moss asked.

The guard paused, and then kicked the chess board, sending pieces flying. "Your game is over, gringo. You are not the guest at a fucking resort!" He grabbed the handles of his wheelchair and headed for the hall.

Once the security man had deposited Moss in Dr. Falcón's office, he was anxious that they had found out about Haley and him being able to walk again, and that they were about to suffer horrendous consequences. However, he quickly discovered that he was worrying needlessly.

After a moment of silence while Dr. Falcón continued reading some papers on his desk, He addressed Moss. "Colonel Moss, how are you? Enjoying our wonderful hospitality, I hope? I hear you are quite the chess player!"

Moss considered his words carefully before responding, since spewing the vitriol he felt could be dangerous. "How am I doing, aside from being here against my will? Well, all of the experimental procedures you've subjected me too seem to have been worthless, as I'm still in this damned chair. And yes, I do play a little chess now and then."

As Moss was speaking, Dr. Falcón brought out a chess set and began arranging the pieces. "Regrettably, we've had very little progress treating spinal cord injuries, but I'm not apologizing for trying. I've not had any real chess competition for years—I am here at the hospital most of the time and have little opportunity for leisurely pursuits. Shall we play?" When Moss appeared less than eager, Dr. Falcón made an offer, "Look, if you play me and win, I'll allow you to send a letter to whomever you want letting them know you are alive. Of course, it will be reviewed by me first, and mailed from another country. You will make no reference to our little experiments or the location and nature of this facility. Agreed?"

Moss was momentarily stunned by the offer. "What if I lose?"

"I expect you will lose, but there will be no repercussions if you do. I simply want some real competition, and I suspect without proper incentive, you wouldn't play to the best of your abilities. Shall we begin?"

"I'll play you to the very best of my abilities on one condition…that all of the patients being held against their will also be allowed to send a letter, subject to the same restrictions you described." Moss realized he was in no real position to negotiate, so he was surprised at Dr. Falcón's reply.

"I don't like it, but I'll agree to it anyway. I trust that you will now be sufficiently motivated. Now, let's begin, and I'll even give you white so you can move first."

Moss opened with a "King's Indian" attack. He was not surprised to see Dr. Falcón respond with a move that he recognized as the French defense, used by every world champion since Steinitz, except for Fisher. The game developed quickly, and the doctor proved to be a highly skilled adversary. As the end game approached, they were nearly even, so Moss took a risk and appeared to blunder when he moved a rook to an undefended position where Falcón's queen could capture it. The gambit paid off when the doctor smiled and said, "You play well colonel, but your knight no longer protects your rook." He then took the rook with his queen, giving him the apparent advantage of a major piece.

However, Moss's move had been a gambit for which the doctor had fallen, enabling Moss to move a knight to a position forking the doctor's king and queen. Now Falcón had no choice but to escape check and forfeit his queen, giving Moss a winning advantage. The smile evaporated, and the doctor glared into Moss's eyes as he grudgingly tipped over his king, a way of resigning the game. "That was very clever, Colonel. I clearly underestimated you. I won't embarrass myself further, so I'll resign. Since you've won, you may write your letter, and I'll inform the staff that all the other patients may write their letters as well."

"Will you actually send them? Or was your offer just a ploy to ensure I'd play competitively?"

"I would hope we could play many more games in the future, so I'd be a fool not to give you what you earned. Colonel Moss, you may think me an evil man, but I do honor my word, so yes, the letters will be sent, every last one."

While they'd been playing, Moss had been looking at the cozy fireplace in the corner of the office. It was made of a kind of stone he hadn't seen before. On the mantle was a framed picture of an ancient castle in ruins. Next to it was another picture of a castle; this one was massive and majestic. Moss decided he would ask about the fireplace and the pictures.

Dr. Falcón seemed pleased that he'd noticed. "The fireplace stone is from the castle in ruins you see on the mantle picture on the left. That castle is in Scotland, and was the ancestral home of our mother, who was a Scottish Lady. Even though she abandoned us in our childhood, we inherited it after she died from cancer, the same type your wife died from, Colonel Moss. Over the years, my brother Eduard and I have had the castle fully restored to its original magnificence; you see it pictured on the right. It is fully staffed all year round, and has over 300 rooms…even a dungeon equipped with medieval torture apparatus which my brother has lovingly restored. Eduard and I go there every year for a visit. It is the only place in the world I feel totally safe and secure."

Dr. Falcón seemed eager to share his family lore. He wheeled Moss over to the fireplace so he could feel the stones. "I like having my family history next to me. Now go write your letter."

CHAPTER 36

Bolstered by the recent "benevolence" of Dr. Falcón, Moss was eager to share the news with Thomas and Haley. After "lights out" Thomas and Moss made their way down to Haley's room. Thomas could tell that Moss was excited about something, but he wouldn't tell him until they'd gotten Haley and trekked down to the gym.

"I think I have some exciting news!" Moss exclaimed. He told them all about the impromptu chess game with Dr. Falcón, and the unexpected reward he'd negotiated. "If Falcón is a man of his word, and I believe he is, we'll be out of here fairly soon."

"This is great unexpected news, "Thomas responded, "but how does send-ing a bunch of letters of get us out of here? What am I missing?" The quizzical look on Thomas's face was matched by Haley's. Moss explained how, no matter to whom they sent their letters, some would likely get to the FBI. Once there, agents would likely try to lift finger prints to verify authenticity. He explained further that his letter to his cousin Jim would use a code he'd learned in the military for prisoner-of-war situations. He was sure Jim, who had also been in the military, would suspect that the letter should be given immediately to the FBI. The only problem, Moss explained, was his inability with this code to safely specify their location. He further explained that the code was fairly com-plex; teaching it to them would simply take too long. Thomas and Haley were thrilled with his plan and eager to write their own letters home.

"If you two don't mind, I'm going to go back to the room and think about the letter I'm going to write to my sister. Why don't the two of you get some exercise?" Thomas said. He knew that Haley and Moss, forced to conceal their recoveries during the day, relished the opportunity to be out of wheelchairs at night.

After wishing each other a good night and sharing a group hug, Thomas went back to their room.

"Before we exercise, could we just chat for a bit—there are some things I'd like to ask you," Haley said.

"No problem," Moss answered. "Ask whatever you want."

Haley looked a little embarrassed."

I am going to be frank with you. After my accident, I still had sexual feelings, even though I had zero feeling in the lower half of my body. But I would often have sexual dreams, and I think I even had orgasms. Now, though, all the feeling has returned to my lower body...to all the parts. I was wondering if it was the same for you."

Moss paused for a bit, wondering where Haley was going with it. "Once I recovered from my accident, I was very depressed for a lot of reasons. But eventually I too would have sexual dreams and have a sticky awakening. But now, all systems seem to be fully operational again.

Haley, why in the world are you asking me that question now?"

Haley smiled. "Steve, you may not know this. I've had a crush on you since the first time my brother introduced you to me."

"As I recall, that was when my wife was still alive and I was happily married. But, since we've been here, guess who my fantasies have been about?"

Moss took Haley's hand and looked into her deep blue eyes. As their lips were about to meet, Haley whispered, "Maybe we should go for another kind of exercise."

Their love making began tenderly as a gentle reawakening of sensations that had long lain dormant for both of them. Long passionate kisses and tentative explorations preceded a rapid flinging of garments aside followed by kisses and nibbles strategically placed to tantalize and maximize sensations. Both of them were trying to go slowly, but when Moss entered Haley, their hips took on minds of their own. The tempo moved to_allegro, and the volume of Haley's moaning went through a crescendo from *pianissimo* to *fortissimo*. When finally they had exhausted themselves, Moss lay with his head on Haley's chest. "I can hear a happy heart," he said.

Haley giggled, "Takes a licking but keeps on ticking."

CHAPTER 37

One of Jake's staffers, who was responsible for opening the mail each day, rushed into Jake's office excitedly. "I think you've received a letter from Haley!" The man handed Jake the letter. Jake's hands trembled with joy as he immediately recognized his sister's handwriting.

Dear Jake,

I've been allowed to write you this short letter to let you know I'm alive and well. Say hi to Sally, Katie, and everyone else for me. I am safe for now and being well fed. I'm sorry, but that's all I'm allowed to tell you.

Your loving sister,
Haley

After all his months of suffering, Jake wept with the apparent proof that Haley was alive. He then had the presence of mind to look at the postmark. The letter appeared to have been sent from Mexico. Jake immediately called Scott Wroblewski at the FBI to give him the news and read him Haley's letter.

"We've also received a similar letter from our old comrade in arms Steve Moss. His letter was sent to his cousin Jim Baker, who gave it to us; it is quite a bit longer than Haley's. But, like Haley's, it contains no details about where he is being held or why. Interestingly, though, he rambles on at length about our time together in the war. It's kind of weird, actually. And his letter appears to have been sent from Argentina."

Jake knew Steve Moss well, and had never known him to "ramble on" about anything. A light bulb went off in his head.

"Scott, Steve was a colonel in the Army. Do me a favor and have your cryptography people take a look at his letter. It just might be more than it appears!"

"I should have thought about that right off the bat," Scott replied contritely. "We also have his fingerprints on file, so we can check the stationery to see if we can lift some prints. Let me get right on this and I'll call you as soon as we know anything more."

Less than three hours later, Scott called back. "You were right! Steve's letter contained an encoded message in his "ramblings": Our cryptographers discovered he'd used an old code designed for officers taken prisoner. Steve says he doesn't know the exact location, but believes it is in Columbia where he's being held, and he makes reference to others, including 'the senator's sister'. He says there are a number of prisoners, and they are being used for medical experimentation."

Jake began to tremble with excitement as he put two and two together, "I think I know where they are! Remember the odd material received from PraxMed in response to a subpoena for their medical trials on animals? The documentation was all fine, but the microscopic samples they sent contained human cells. I believe Haley and Steve are being held by PraxMed goons in Bogotá, Columbia."

Wroblewski paused for a moment, thinking it through. "Jake, I think we need to get the CIA involved post haste.

CHAPTER 38

Ted Mallick had just arrived in Bogotá's El Dorado International Airport, traveling with a counterfeit passport and an assumed identity. He had a hospital full of patients he was expected to destroy, leaving no survivors. He couldn't just bomb the place—he had to make it look like a tragic accident. The details of how to pull this off were beyond the scope of Mallick's personal skills, so he had employed a 'specialist' in creating seemingly accidental gas explosions. Mallick knew the entire Falcón facility was heated with natural gas, so his associate assured him all they needed was a little unsupervised time in the medical center's basement. He had already scheduled a meeting with Dr. Falcón and his brother Eduard, so gaining access to the facility wouldn't be a problem. His associate would do the necessary work while he kept the meeting going. The plan was in install an acid-dripping device that would slowly eat through the gas main, and after the explosion look like natural deterioration of the pipe to investigators. An igniter triggered by a cell phone would enable him to initiate the facility's destruction via a phone call when they were safely out of the country.

In spite of the risks, Mallick was not at all squeamish about his assignment and he certainly wasn't going to miss those asshole Falcón brothers. There was only one person he cared about—a hot nurse he had had an affair with while they had met in a drug rehab program…maybe he could get something going with her again. He would make a point to arrange a lunch date with Alicia Jones and make sure she was absent when the place went up in a massive fireball. Even in the worst case, Mallick knew that if his plan failed or he was found out, his tapes of Pellizari ordering the murders would enable him to cut a deal and escape a long prison sentence.

Mallick and his associate took a taxi to their hotel and checked in under assumed names. After calling the Falcón hospital, he confirmed his appointments for the next day and managed to convince Alicia Jones to have lunch with him. He was perplexed by her initial hesitancy, but Alicia agreed when he assured her that his intentions were entirely platonic. He then spent a leisurely afternoon touring *Museo del Oro* and *Museo Nacional*, both of which were within easy walking distance of the hotel.

CHAPTER 39

Mallick and his associate arrived in separate cars at the Falcón medical facility an hour before his scheduled appointment, with the latter dressed as a repairman. The "repairman" entered the building first, and presented a bogus work order that would get him into the furnace room in the basement. It was only when he walked out and flashed Mallick a thumbs-up that Mallick got out of his car and strolled leisurely into the building.

He announced himself at the main reception desk and stated that he was here for a scheduled meeting with Dr. Nicolas Falcón and his brother Eduard. Mallick was determined to go on the offense in this meeting, laying full blame for the government's scrutiny on the doctor's head. He would then schedule another meeting for three days later (a day before the government's team of investigators was due to arrive), and insist that both Falcón brothers be present. However, there would actually be no meeting, since that would be the precise time that Mallick would by remote control initiate the acid drip on the gas main. One hour later, after enough gas had leaked out, he would turn the place into a fireball. The Falcón boys and all evidence of PraxMed's involvement would be reduced to ashes.

The meeting was brief but cordial. Dr. Falcón assumed full responsibility for not having personally reviewed the materials that had been sent in response to the subpoena and assured Mallick that the people who had sent the microscopy slides containing human rather than animal cells had been punished severely. He didn't mention that "punished severely" meant that Eduard had tortured them before their executions, or that their organs had been harvested for sale on the medical black market.

Alicia Jones was waiting for him in the lobby at noon, as they had pre-arranged for their lunch date. Mallick took her to a restaurant which he knew to be fairly quiet around noon. Over a sumptuous meal of prime rib and local vegetables, they discussed politics, the weather, and, after the small talk was over, how their personal lives were going. Mallick recalled why he had been attracted to Alicia in the first place. She was intelligent and witty, attractive, and great in the sack. He acknowledged to himself that he still had strong feelings for her, and couldn't tolerate her death in the disaster he was orchestrating.

After they had finished eating and were enjoying some fine Columbian coffee, Mallick took her hand in his and, against his better judgment, said, "Alicia, how long has it been since you've taken a real vacation?"

Alicia thought for a moment before answering. "Too long, I guess…five years ago when I went down to Rio. Why do you ask?"

Mallick smiled with a gleam in his eyes. "How does next week in Paris with me sound? It would be my treat, of course."

Alicia was momentarily taken aback by Mallick's out-of-the-blue vacation offer, and pointed out that her vacations had to be planned, with adequate notice given at work. "Why next week…and why are you so suddenly interested in my vacations?"

"Because next week something very bad is going to happen where you work, and you want to be miles and miles away when it happens."

"Do you mean people will be arrested?"

"No, it will be much worse than that." After obtaining a vow from Alicia that she would never reveal what he about to tell her, Mallick told her what PraxMed's CEO had ordered him to do. Alicia was horrified and tried hard to dissuade him but to no avail. Mallick went on to explain that United States government investigators were coming and why. "Look, dear, if the investigators come, there is a good chance they'll find out what really has been going on in Bogotá, and a lot of people, including you and me will be going to prison for a very long time. We can't take that risk, so when I take you back to work, just tell them you're taking next week off."

As soon as Alicia returned to work, she called Dr. Falcón to ask for the following week off, citing job stress and car problems as the reasons. He kindly told her he knew she had been doing an excellent job in a very difficult environment, but taking next week off was out of the question. Dr. Falcón sympathized, "God knows you haven't had a vacation in a very long time, but I need to tell you the confidential reason I can't grant your request. Next Tuesday we have a team of investigators from the United States government paying us a visit. I won't bore you with the reasons they're coming, but I need all of the staff available since we have no idea as to the nature and scope of this investigation. But, since you are having car problems, I will have my personal helicopter pick you up and take you home until your car is fixed. OK?"

Alicia panicked, but had no choice to agree. As her home was adjacent to a large empty field, there was no practical reason to decline. She would have to think of some way to prevent the patients at FHRI from all being burned alive.

CHAPTER 40

Sated after their regular Saturday night sexual rendezvous in the gym, Alicia lay in Dr. Thomas Jefferson Hunt's strong arms. In spite of trying hard not to fall in love with this studly hunk of man, she had failed. "Thomas," she began, there are some things I need to tell you. Bear with me, it's a long story." Alicia told Thomas of the relationship between the Falcón brothers and PraxMed, and explained the motivations for the unseemly relationship. PraxMed's were simple: huge profits earned by leapfrogging the competition in stem cell treatments and related pharmaceuticals. Their research in Bogotá would provide them with all the answers enabling them to avoid prolonged and costly legitimate trials that could take years The Falcón brother's motivations were far more complex. As Thomas listened patiently, she explained the early childhood of the Falcón boys and how Dr. Falcón literally owed his brother his life. Thomas was surprised to learn Eduard Falcón was a paraplegic—a gunshot victim. Alicia told him of Dr. Falcón's maniacal drive to restore his brother to health. When she stopped, Thomas said, "Alicia, why are you telling me all of this now?"

"Because people fucked up in responding to a subpoena sent by the United States government, a team of investigators is due to arrive here next Tuesday. Our contact at PraxMed told me today to go away for a week; their CEO has ordered him to blow the place up and make it look like an accident."

Thomas was stunned." When is this supposed to happen?"

"He didn't say for sure…just that I should take next week off. Big guy, we've got to get out of here before the shit totally hits the fan."

As soon as Thomas got back to their room, he woke Moss up and told him everything Alicia had related, emphasizing the need for escape before the entire place went up in smoke. Moss listened in stunned silence, only interrupting for clarification. When Thomas was finished with his narrative of impending doom, Moss asked, "Does Alicia have any ideas about how we'd get our collective asses out of the frying pan?"

"Actually, she does have an idea, albeit a highly risky one. It all depends on you, though." Responding to the puzzled look on his face, Thomas added, "You used to fly helicopters in the military, didn't you?" Moss nodded, and asked why that was relevant. "It just so happens that there is a helicopter parked on the roof. If you think you can fly it, Alicia says she can probably steal the keys."

"Did Alicia know what kind of helicopter it is?"

"I thought you might want to know that so I asked her. Fortunately, Alicia has flown in it a few times and chatted with the pilot. It's 206B3 Jet Ranger III. Are you familiar with it?"

Moss grinned. "I've flown the military version a few times, so yeah, I could fly it. However, I'm sure they don't leave their helicopter unguarded, and we'd have to get to the roof undetected—so this will be extremely difficult! Let's go see Haley…we've got some planning to do."

CHAPTER 41

The missions of the Federal Bureau of investigation and the Central Intelligence Agency are commonly confused. The mission of the FBI is to uphold the law through the investigation of violations of federal criminal law; to protect the United States from foreign intelligence and terrorist activities, and to provide leadership and law enforcement assistance to federal, state, local, and international agencies.

On the other hand, the CIA is the nation's first line of defense. They accomplish what others cannot accomplish and go where others cannot go. The agency carries out its mission by, among other things, conducting covert action at the direction of the President to preempt threats or achieve US policy objectives.

When the disappearances of Haley Jackson, Steve Moss, Dr. Thomas Hunt and the others occurred, they were at first believed to be kidnappings within the United States, hence under the purview of local and state law enforcement and the FBI. But when evidence came to light that caused suspicion the kidnapping victims had been transported out of the country, the CIA had to be brought in, especially because a covert foreign mission was likely the only way to rescue them.

The FBI director briefed the president, showing him the letter from Haley and the decrypted message from Steve Moss. These, along with the human rather than animal cell specimens received from PraxMed's Bogotá affiliate was all it took.

The president directed the FBI to give all its collected evidence to the CIA. He then ordered the CIA to compile intelligence on the Bogotá medical facility including satellite imagery in preparation for a possible covert rescue mission if the intelligence warranted it. He further ordered that every effort be taken to keep PraxMed from discovering they had been found out.

The next morning the head of the CIA began briefing the president on the intelligence collected over night. "We believe the kidnapping victims are most likely being held at to the Falcón Hospital and Research Institute, or FHRI." He then placed a satellite photo of the facility on the president's desk. "We believe we have a good chance of rescuing them with a lightening-like operation." Next he outlined the covert mission to the president. He pointed out in a photograph that, in one section of the medical facility, all the windows had bars in them. "We believe this is where they are being held. We'll go in strong and take out whatever guards there may be, locate the kidnapping victims and evacuate them as quickly as possible. We will take prisoner any medical staff that impedes us."

"If I give permission to proceed, when could the rescue mission be executed?"

"They are expecting a team of FDA investigators to arrive in a few days. That should happen as planned to give us an on-site intelligence report. Barring anything unusual, we would storm the facility once the investigative team has exited safely. Mr. President, do we have your authorization to proceed?"

The president was a decisive but cautious man, and he barely paused before speaking. "Be extremely cautious in selecting the investigative and assault teams...give them their mission details only after they are en route; and limit the people who know about this to those you trust implicitly. Permission granted and Godspeed."

CHAPTER 42

J ake had received an early morning briefing about the CIA's impending covert rescue mission in Bogotá. He had mixed feelings about it. Foremost in his mind was excitement and relief about a possible rescue of the kidnapping victims. But he was a realist, and knew there would likely be casualties—he just hoped Haley and his friend Steve Moss wouldn't be among them. As a seasoned combat veteran, Jake had succeeded in cajoling the CIA director into allowing him to go along with the rescue team. He hadn't told Sally yet, because he knew she would likely disapprove of his unnecessarily stepping into harm's way. But since Jake was planning to ask Sally to marry him, he figured he better go tell her what was going to be happening shortly.

As Jake walked into Sally's office, she immediately spotted the pensive look on his face. "What's wrong, honey?" she asked. Jake outlined the CIA briefing he'd just had and patiently answered Sally's questions. "So when is this covert mission going to happen?"

"It will happen next Tuesday, barring unforeseen developments," Jake said haltingly. "But there is one more thing I need to tell you about the mission. I'm going along."

Jake had expected an immediate negative reaction, which was not what he got. Instead, Sally just sat, looking at him thoughtfully. Knowing she was unlikely to be able to talk him out of it, she told him she understood, and just hoped he would be very careful.

Jake was surprised by her response, but then remembered that her calm demeanor in the face of adversity was one of the many reasons he loved Sally. Jake stood up to leave, then turned back to Sally and said, "This isn't when I planned to ask you this question, but given that this mission has come up, it can't be put off any longer."

Sally had no idea what he was talking about. "What is your question?"

"Sally Peters, if I come back from this mission alive, will you marry me after Haley is rescued?"

After an immediate albeit teary-eyed affirmation, they strolled down the hall to tell the staff their good news. Jake also told them he needed to go out of the country for a few days without providing any details, and the staff knew not to ask.

That evening, Jake took Sally and his daughter Katie out for a celebratory dinner. He had weeks before told Katie that he was intending to ask Sally to marry him after Haley was either rescued or her fate was known; he had worried needlessly about a possible negative reaction. His wife's suicide had hit them both very hard. He had doubted he would ever get married again because he had loved his wife so deeply, but that was before Haley's accident, when Sally had moved in with them. Sally provided Haley the care and attention she needed to adapt to life as a paraplegic, and simultaneously exerted a subtle maternal influence on Katie. Both the women had come to love Sally as a friend and surrogate mom to Katie. So when Jake had first intimated his marriage idea to Katie, she had given her immediate approval.

Over dinner, Jake swore Katie to secrecy and told her of the impending rescue mission. Katie was ecstatic until Jake informed her he was going along. Katie, breaking into tears, sobbed, "I know this is going to be dangerous! I want Haley and the others rescued, but why do you have to go along?"

Jake had thought about this long and hard. "Katie and Sally, I know you're both puzzled by my need to go on this mission, so I'll try to explain. After Haley's accident, I almost resigned my Senate seat, thinking I should be there full time for Haley. But, thanks to Sally, I felt you and Haley were in good hands. But Haley's abduction made me realize how vulnerable she was and how maybe, had I been there for her, it could have been prevented. If I don't go along on the rescue mission, and something goes wrong, I'd never forgive myself. I'd always be thinking that, had I been there, I could have helped Haley. So, in my mind, I don't have a choice…I have to go."

CHAPTER 43

Thomas, Haley and Moss believed they had developed an acceptable escape plan, although they had yet to discuss it with Alicia, who would have the first and pivotal role. She would need to obtain not only the keys for the helicopter, but ensure that it was fully fueled. In addition, she would have to obtain the security guards' schedule to determine when there would be a shift change, which was likely their best time to make a dash for the helicopter. Haley and Moss would accompany Thomas to his weekly scheduled tryst with Alicia tonight, where they would collectively try to hammer out the final details of the plan.

That night after lights out, Alicia had gone down to the gym to meet Thomas. The blueprints for the entire medical complex were tucked under her arm. When she walked in, she was surprised that Thomas was not alone. The senator's sister and Thomas's roommate Steve Moss were there also in their wheelchairs. Thomas explained that, if there were to be any escape, these two were coming along. "I know Steve Moss used to fly helicopters in the military, but don't you need to be able to use your feet for the pedals?" Alicia asked. She was not privy to Moss's and Haley's recoveries. Moss looked over at Thomas and saw him nod his head.

"For a variety of reasons," Moss began, "We haven't wanted the staff to know about this." He then stood up and walked over to Haley. Extending his hand, she took it and also stood up.

"Jesus, Mary and Joseph... when did these miracles happen?" Alicia exclaimed wide-eyed while crossing herself. Thomas explained that they weren't miracles at all, but cures effected by the stem cell treatments and months of covert nightly physical therapy. He also explained the rationale behind the need to conceal the recoveries, betting that an escape opportunity might present itself.

Over the next two hours, the group worked on the details of their planned escape. Alicia already knew where the keys for the helicopter were kept. She sat down on the floor and casually unrolled the facility's blueprints. "Are those what I think they are?" Moss asked. Alicia just grinned and nodded.

"How in the world did you get your hands on those?" Thomas interjected. Alicia just grinned some more. "I hope you didn't have to put out for some slime-ball guard to get those," Thomas continued with a touch of jealousy in his voice. He clearly had more than lust in his heart for Alicia.

"Actually, they were stored in the hospital archives. I just told the clerk Dr. Falcón was thinking about possibly adding a new wing, and the architect had requested them." Alicia then oriented them by showing them where their rooms were, the cafeteria, Dr. Falcón's office, and the guard stations. She then showed them the layout of the roof, where the two helicopters were kept.

"The helicopter keys are kept here," Alicia said pointing to a rooftop guard shack. "The guards are all armed with automatic weapons."

"Any ideas as to what magic trick you'll do to get the keys?" Moss wondered out loud. Alicia reached in a pocket of her nurse's smock and pulled out a block of wax. She explained how she'd tried to get next week off, pleading job stress and car problems. While Dr. Falcón had told her she couldn't have the week off because of the impending arrival of the FDA investigative team, he had offered to have his personal helicopter take her to work.

I've been practicing." She said. Holding up two car keys, she added, "One of these is my original car key and the other is one my friend made for me from a wax impression of the original. Both seem to work fine."

"May I ask what your friend does for a living?" Haley asked.

Alicia gave a sly grin. "Haley, I believe it would be fair to say he is in the 'car liberation' business." All four laughed out loud at this euphemism for car theft. "So here is my tentative plan. When the pilot picks me up on Monday at the parking lot of the market by my home, I'll look to see where the key is inserted. Once we land on the hospital roof, I'll tell the pilot that Dr. Falcón wanted him to immediately refuel the helicopter—I believe that they have fuel stored right there—because of a trip out to his brother's estate in the afternoon. While I'm exiting the helicopter, I'll 'accidentally' spill the contents of my purse on the floor. I'll suggest he start to refuel while I pick up. With any luck, he'll leave the key while he gets out for refueling…at which point I'll quickly make a wax impression of it. I'll meet my friend for lunch and give it to him to make a copy. He'll drop off the duplicate key later in the afternoon."

"I'm impressed, "Moss complimented, "You've obviously put some very creative thought into this. Only one thing remains to be done."

"What would that be?" Haley asked.

"Getting the guards' schedules so we'll know when there is a shift change." Every room in the hospital, including the gym, had a computer tied into the hospital's network. Alicia stood up and walked over to the gym's computer and logged in to the hospital's network as "Juanita Sanchez" and typed in a password.

"Fortunately for us, Juanita, who works nights, is very careless about her password and keeps it taped to her keyboard. All employees' schedules are stored online for convenience in scheduling." Alicia explained. After a few key-strokes, the weekly schedule for the rooftop guards popped up on the screen. After a brief look, Alicia grinned broadly. This couldn't be any better for us!" she exclaimed. "Next Tuesday the guards change at 7:00 PM, and the guard who is coming on at that time is Manuel."

"May I enquire why that is good for us?" Thomas asked.

"Manuel is notoriously late for work. Guards are supposed to wait for their replacements before leaving their posts, but everyone got tired of waiting for Manuel, so they just leave when their shifts are done. If Manuel is true to form, we'll have about a 15 minute window where the helicopters are unguarded. One more thing…since I'm not sure about when they plan to blow up FHRI, I'm going to try to find a way to delay it."

CHAPTER 44

The Lockheed C-130 Hercules is a four-engine turboprop cargo aircraft. Capable of short takeoffs and landings from unprepared runways, the C-130 was the aircraft of choice for the covert rescue mission to Bogotá. The versatile airframe had been fitted with beds for as many patients as the bird could hold. Armored personnel vehicles and two Boeing CH-47 Chinook helicopters were already in place for the evacuation of the kidnap victims. Jake and the CIA team were going to Bogotá ahead of the FDA investigative team, which had a scheduled appointment Tuesday morning at the Falcón Hospital. The plan was for one member of the investigative team to go in with a hidden video camera that would be transmitting back to the CIA's staging area. This would provide valuable reconnaissance regarding the amount of armed security at the facility as well as possible entries and exits.

All members of the CIA team had studied the mission plans in great detail, and each man knew his responsibilities well. To reduce stress, the conversation among the men was light and intentionally about any subject except the mission. Currently they were exchanging stories about the cleverest thing they'd ever heard anybody say. Most of the stories were about parents or teachers. Two of the stories were not.

Jerry Carter, who had been a middle manager for a Fortune 500 company prior to joining the CIA, told a funny story about an employee at his old company. "The cleverest guy I ever met was a former Marine Corps captain who was working for us as an engineer. Ben Miller, in spite of his military background as an officer, wanted nothing to do with going into management... he had had his fill of that in the military. Ben simply wanted to be an engineer responsible for nobody's work but his own. Shortly after one of several management reorganizations, he ended up with a new supervisor named Ron Langlot who was hell-bent on employee development classes.

"One day in a group meeting Langlot announced that all of his employees would be required to take a class called 'Leadership Effectiveness Training' taught by one of the company's industrial psychologists. Ben, who was already a proven leader with no management ambitions whatsoever, clearly did not need this class; however, as a good troop who knows how to take orders, he did as he was told and took the class. The industrial psychologist was an attractive young woman fresh out of graduate school; her favorite teaching technique for this class was role playing. 'Let's pretend—one person at a time—that you are a supervisor and I am your employee. I have just arrived in your office for an appointment I made to discuss some job concerns I have. Your job is to address these concerns with the techniques we have discussed this past week in class. Remember to use good listening skills, and please be courteous and considerate.'

"When it was Ben's turn at role-playing, he went up before the class and sat down in the chair facing her. 'OK, Ben, I have just arrived in your office for an appointment I made to discuss some job concerns I have, so here we go. Are you ready?' Ben nodded yes.

She began: 'I am not being challenged sufficiently by my current assignments. I also do not believe that I am being adequately compensated for my work. Furthermore, I believe my coworkers are talking about me behind my back.'

Ben had sat there patiently listening politely, nodding as he paid rapt attention to her every word. 'Now Ben, you are the supervisor, how do you respond?' He scooted his chair over it until he was almost nose-to-nose with her. 'You whining maggot… get your ass back to work.' The young woman at first had a mortified look on her face; she then smiled and said, 'Let me guess… you were in the military?' 'I was a Captain in the United States Marine Corps, Ma'am, and damn proud of it!' Ben's supervisor never asked him to take a leadership class again."

All of the men, most of whom were ex-military themselves, laughed uproariously. The other out-of-the-ordinary story was told by Jake Jackson.

"The cleverest person I have ever known is my older brother Luke who is now director of the National Security Agency. I know the rest of you have pointed to a teacher, a government figure, or even a co-worker. But none of them is as smart or clever as my brother Luke was at 12 years old." Jake paused for dramatic effect as the other men's curiosity picked up. "I was only 8 years old when this event transpired. We lived across the street from a kid named Lance Smith. Lance's main claim to fame was that his alcoholic dad was in charge of the July 4th municipal fireworks display, giving Lance access to some hellacious and powerful firecrackers. I'm not talking about little cherry bombs here—these suckers were designed to impress a grandstand full of people.

"Anyhow, Lance's family owned a big black lab named Bondo, who was kept in an open pen off to the side of the house. It was Lance's job to clean out Bondo's pen every week, which involved shoveling up the crap and then hosing off the concrete floor. So one day right before the 4th of July, my older brother and I were over at Lance's house playing Monopoly when his old man came in drunk and demanded that Lance stop playing RIGHT NOW and go clean out Bondo's pen. We were going to just go home, but Lance asked us to stay and talk to him outside while he cleaned out the pen.

"Lance clearly had skipped a couple of weeks on this particular chore, as there was a copious amount of dog crap he was shoveling into a pile in the middle of Bondo's pen. I asked Lance why he was shoveling it into a pile rather than into a garbage can. Reaching into the pocket of his jeans, Lance just smiled and pulled out the biggest firecracker I'd ever seen. 'Because I'm going to vaporize it,' he smirked. As Lance pondered the firecracker's ideal placement in the massive doo-doo pile, Luke took me by the hand and said we had to go home now. I argued strenuously that I wanted to witness the *vaporization*. My brother said fine…but we'll watch from the curb across the street. Grumbling, I followed him across the street where we turned around to face Lance's house. We sat down on the curb to watch. I thought Lance was a pyrotechnics genius for coming up with the *vaporization* concept. Luke just sat quietly with a Buddha-like smile. We watched as Lance carefully placed the mammoth firecracker under the pile, lit the fuse, and then ran like hell out of the pen. He turned to watch the *vaporization* when he was about ten feet out of the pen. When it blew, he turned to wave to us with a huge grin on his face, not realizing he had dog shit all over his shirt and face…even his teeth… and the entire side of the house. My brother and I, however, were clean as a whistle! Luke then leaned over and said to me, "Here is a little lesson about life: When you know shit is going to blow up, always try to watch from the other side of the street." At that particular moment, it occurred to me that Luke was the smartest guy in the world."

"Hey, a literal shit-eating grin!" one of the men exclaimed.

The men's laughter was interrupted by the plane's intercom, when the reality of the mission reasserted itself: "Gentlemen, please buckle your seat belts and hang on tight. We are beginning our descent and will be dipping below Columbian radar detection level, so be prepared to be tickled by some treetops. We should be on the ground in less than 15 minutes; Please make sure you have all your gear before exiting the plane." The pilot paused, and then added, "Once again, we thank you for flying CIA airlines . . . have a safe and successful mission."

CHAPTER 45

Alicia had received a disturbing phone call at her home from Ted Mallick. He had inquired whether she had succeeded in getting the week off, and she said no. After explaining her dilemma, Alicia asked if there were anyway Mallick could halt or at least delay the FDA visit. He reiterated that it was going to happen no matter how much she pleaded her case, but did allow as how a small delay might be possible.

"First, what difference will a delay make, and second, how much delay are you requesting?" Mallick asked.

"I'll be honest with you, Ted," Alicia lied, "I've still got feelings for you... I'd love to go to Paris with you, but I have to be alive to do that. I have a plan to get out of there Tuesday evening."

"How are you going to do that? They're not just going to let you waltz out of there."

"Of course they're not. I have a plan, but I can't share the details with you. I just need until 10:00 PM Tuesday. Can you at least do that for me?"

"I'd hoped to blow the place with the FDA investigators in it."

"Couldn't you delay it until Wednesday?" Alicia begged.

"I suppose I could do that, if I can think up a good enough reason."

Not wanting to leave it up in the air, Alicia offered, "What if I provide you with a real reason?"

"Like what?" Mallick asked with genuine curiosity.

"What if a car crashed into the hospital entrance Tuesday morning an hour before the FDA investigators are due to arrive? The place would be cordoned off by the local police with no chance for them to enter the hospital. There would be no choice but to delay their visit."

Alicia was thinking that she could call on her friend Diego who would be making the duplicate helicopter key for one more huge favor. After all, he literally owed Alicia his life. She had first met Diego late one night at her home with a bullet in his shoulder. His companions knew they couldn't take him to the hospital, since he had been wounded during a botched car theft. Alicia was known in the criminal community to be a last-ditch discrete provider of emergency medical care. After removing the bullet and giving the man a place to recuperate for three weeks, she had earned Diego's unending gratitude.

"I don't know how the fuck you plan to make that happen, but I trust you will. I'll wait until Wednesday until I turn the place into a literal hell," Mallick retorted.

CHAPTER 46

J ake had joined the preliminary reconnaissance team of five men who were parked discreetly in the FHRI parking lot...they were in a van that had an "Industrial Heating" sign in Spanish on the side. They had with them a television monitor which would be receiving a video transmission from one of the FDA investigators equipped with a concealed video camera. The FDA team was scheduled to enter the building within the hour. The CIA men were all highly trained professionals who were now intensely focused on the task ahead of them.

As they were testing the video camera's transmission, they were all startled by an old pickup truck speeding towards the main entrance. Close behind was a fast Suzuki motorcycle. Clearly the pickup's current trajectory would result in a serious crash into the building. About 100 feet before impact, the driver opened his door and rolled out on to the pavement. He was wearing a helmet and armored biker apparel to minimize his injuries. He appeared to be momentarily stunned by his fall, but quickly got on his feet and leapt on the passenger pillion of the waiting motorcycle, which immediately sped away. As Jake watched, he expected the truck to explode as it careened into the building. No strangers to the use of vehicles as mobile bomb platforms, the CIA men were surprised when the impact resulted in nothing more than the shattering of the entrance's glass facade. They looked over at Jake, who just shrugged and put up his hands, indicating he didn't have a clue as to what they had just witnessed.

A few minutes later, the small team's puzzlement was interrupted by a radio transmission from the FDA team leader. "I've just received a phone call from the chief of hospital security; the local police have instructed them to allow no one in or out of the building until they arrive. So, what do we do now?"

The CIA agent in command radioed back, "There obviously won't be an FDA inspection today. Call them and see if you can't set it up for the same time tomorrow."

He then radioed the temporary CIA command center a mile away and told them of the apparent botched terrorist attack, and that they should stand down pending further orders.

Later that day, the FDA team succeeded in rescheduling for the next day. Jake discussed the situation at hand with the CIA agent in command and agreed it was an amazing coincidence that an apparent terrorist attack would happen the same day as the planned rescue attempt. The men discussed at length whether or not it even was a botched terrorist attack. Some argued that it may have been a ploy to scare off the FDA investigative team, but Jake didn't buy that theory. Nonetheless, he didn't believe in coincidences of this magnitude. His gut told him something was fishy, but he couldn't figure out what it was.

CHAPTER 47

A licia's friend Diego had come through with flying colors; not only had he arranged the delaying crash in the morning, but he'd also made and delivered a duplicate of the helicopter key made from the wax impression she'd secretly made on Monday. Knowing the dangers Alicia and her friends faced on their escape attempt, he'd also brought her a 9 mm semi-automatic Luger. Alicia had feared needlessly that she wouldn't have an opportunity to make the wax impression, but her purse-spilling "accident" had gone exactly as planned.

Alicia lightly knocked, then opened the door to Steve's and Thomas's room. As she entered, Thomas beamed at her and said, "Are all the preparations complete for the party?"

Alicia grinned and replied, "Yes," as she walked over and handed Moss the helicopter key. She also reached in the briefcase she was carrying and produced the 9 mm semi-automatic Luger, which she also handed over with a somber look to Moss. "But I believe the most dangerous part of our plan is directly ahead of us. We need to go collect Haley and make our way to the roof without getting caught. The current roof guard's shift ends in ten minutes, so, assuming Manuel is late again, we have an unpredictable window of opportunity. I'll 'escort' you now down to Haley's room." After checking the Luger's magazine and safety, Moss slipped the weapon into the back of his waistband.

They were all anxious as they went down the hall, in spite of appearing to be doing nothing out of the ordinary. They passed a number of other patients heading back to their rooms after dinner who all greeted them casually. Thomas and Moss had prearranged with Haley to be ready to go any time between 6:00 and 7:00, but when they knocked on Haley's door, her roommate answered.

The matronly woman told them Haley had just been taken for another procedure and wouldn't be back for at least two hours. She added that Haley left explicit instructions that they should not wait for her. Both Thomas and Moss tried to keep the horror they felt off their faces.

Moss was still in his wheelchair as the three of them carefully approached the express elevator to the roof. The elevator required a key to operate, which Alicia had in her possession. One of the helicopter pilots was currently in the elevator holding the door open as he saw Alicia approaching. He nodded cordially to Alicia. "Going up to the roof?" he asked, knowing she was responsible for stocking the airborne medical supplies.

"Yes, I am, as I need to check the medical supplies on the air ambulance helicopter," Alicia said after noticing the man already had his elevator key in his hand. She turned to Thomas and Steve and said politely, "Thank you all for the pleasant chat, and Dr. Hunt, thank you again for your assistance with our patients' rehabilitation program!"

She extended her hand to shake Thomas's, with her elevator key secretly palmed.

As Thomas took her hand, he felt the key being pressed into his hand. "You are more than welcome, Nurse Jones. Now that Dr. Falcón has cured my Parkinson's disease, it's the least I can do to show my gratitude." Alicia then entered the elevator leaving the trio to watch the doors close in their faces.

"What is she doing leaving us here?" Moss wondered.

"I think she was trying to avoid any suspicion," Thomas answered showing Moss the elevator key Alicia had passed him.

They watched the floor indicator until it reached the top floor. After the indicator showed a red "R" they knew the elevator had reached the roof. Once the indicator had not changed for a full minute, Moss looked carefully to make sure no one was coming down the hall and said, "Now is as good a time as ever…let's go for it." He arose from his wheelchair as Thomas used the key to summon the elevator. Thomas then put the key back in his pocket. Once they were on the elevator, Moss removed the weapon from his waistband and cautioned Thomas to stay behind him when the elevator doors opened. In their planning, they had all memorized the roof's layout. They knew exactly where the guard and helicopter would be located, as well as all the large roof-mounted air conditioning units, which could provide concealment or cover if needed. They also knew where to hide Moss's wheelchair.

As the elevator door opened, Moss saw they were alone in a small room on the roof. Directly across from him was a door with a window in it overlooking the two helicopters parked on the roof. Through the window, Moss could see Alicia and the pilot; the latter had his back to the window. Moss caught Alicia's eye and she subtly shook her head signaling it wasn't safe to exit the room. He could see that the rotor on the air ambulance was already turning, and that paramedics were waiting in the helicopter for the pilot. After a moment the pilot waved goodbye to Alicia and strode over to the helicopter and climbed into the pilot's seat. After bringing the rotor RPMs up to takeoff speed, the pilot pulled up on the collective stick and the helicopter rose into a hover. After rising to 100 feet above the roof, the pilot pressed gently forward on the cyclic control and the helicopter slowly translated to forward flight. Moss looked over at Alicia and she again shook her head, but this time held up five fingers, which he interpreted as 'wait five minutes.' He glanced over at the guard house and could see through its front window a man dressed in a security uniform sitting at a desk. Alicia purposely strode over to the guard house and entered. As Moss continued to watch, he told Thomas it was safe to exit the elevator. They took turns surreptitiously peeking through the window on the door. After a few minutes, as Thomas was watching, he saw the guard, who was chatting with Alicia, look up at a clock, shake his head in disgust at the tardy Manuel and get up to leave.

"He's coming now...hide in the stairwell!" Thomas shouted. The stairway was provided as an emergency mode of getting off the roof; no one ever took it except when the power went out. As the guard approached the door, Thomas and Moss scrambled to conceal themselves in the narrow stairwell. They held their breath in unison as they heard the door open. Just as the guard was entering the elevator, Thomas sneezed mightily from the dust they'd stirred up in the little-used stairwell. The guard stepped out of the elevator and said in Spanish, "Who's there?" As the guard's footsteps approached the stairwell, Moss again pulled the weapon out of his waistband and signaled Thomas to go down the stairs. He hoped he wouldn't' have to fire it, as the sound of a gunshot would certainly bring guards running. But before he could even raise the weapon, the guard's AK47 was pointed at his forehead. The 6'4" muscle-bound guard, who looked like he'd been on steroids forever, eyed Moss curiously, and in broken English said, "What are you doing up here, gringo?" Before a word could come out of his mouth, Moss heard the elevator door open. The guard didn't take his eyes off Moss, probably assuming it was the always-late Manuel arriving, finally here to relieve him. "The gringo was trying to escape!" he shouted over his shoulder. But it wasn't Manuel behind him; Thomas had taken the stairs down to the next level, and then used the elevator key to come back up. "You are in so much trouble, gringo! They are going to cut all your organs out and sell them to the highest bidder!"

A deep bass voice from behind him boomed, I don't think so, amigo!" As the guard whirled around, he ran smack into a classic Golden Gloves right hook. The man was out cold before he even knew what hit him.

"Wow!" Moss exclaimed, "Move over Muhammad Ali!"

They were still dragging the unconscious guard's body to the stairwell when they heard the door open again. Alicia called to them saying it was safe to come out. "Good old Manuel, he's late again…what the hell happened here?" Alicia exclaimed when she saw what they were doing.

"We almost got caught," Moss explained, "but Thomas's quick thinking saved the day!"

Alicia responded, "OK, but we need to hurry, since the air ambulance was only going a short distance and could be back at any moment. They lamented on the unfortunate timing of Haley's latest procedure, which saddened them greatly.

"Our only hope for her is for us to escape, and then warn them by radio or phone to evacuate or find the bomb," Moss interjected. "We'll notify the CIA as soon as we can."

CHAPTER 48

Moss suggested they board the helicopter immediately. Once he was in the pilot's seat, he said, "We'll see how good your wax impression of the key was…not all keys made that way work properly." He held his breath as he inserted the key and attempted to turn it. "Oh shit, "he lamented, "It won't turn."

"That's not the only problem we have," Thomas added, pointing to their right. The air ambulance was returning, now just a speck on the horizon.

Moss jiggled the key furiously, hoping he could make it work. Just as he was about to believe all was lost, he gave an extra forceful turn of his wrist, and the key turned. Success! "Buckle your seat belts, we need to *vamoose pronto*!" he commanded as he started the helicopter's engine and engaged the rotor system. The air ambulance was less than a mile away and was already reducing speed in preparation for landing.

"You've got to go now!" Alicia screamed.

"I have to wait for the rotor to come up to flight speed!" Moss hollered back. The air ambulance was now hovering with the pilot eyeing them and looking perplexed. The rotor speed was approaching takeoff rpm, so Moss eased up the collective control and brought the helicopter to a hover. Alicia was in the seat next to him, and he asked her to turn on the com radio. "Do you know what frequency they use for air to air?" he hollered. Alicia nodded. "Then tune to that frequency now." Alicia did as she was told, and offered that the air ambulance pilot's name was Greg Alexander. Moss keyed the microphone and said, "Greg, this is Colonel Steve Moss aboard the helicopter that just took off—do you copy?"

After a long pause, the reply came back." What the hell are you doing in our helicopter? Land that thing right now!"

"Listen to me very carefully, Greg. You are probably unaware that a number of kidnapping victims, and I'm one of them, are being held against their will at this facility and being used for illegal medical experiments. We are in the process of escaping." His transmission was met by stunned silence. After a few moments a simple statement came back.

"I don't believe you."

"Well, you better believe this, then: A PraxMed executive is in town and there is going to be a US government inspection tomorrow. PraxMed can't afford for them to find out anything; an explosive device is in the building that will turn it into a raging fireball within the next 24 hours unless some one finds it and removes it. Look in the basement, and when it's found, tell Dr. Falcón that PraxMed has decided he's become a liability. Are you copying all this? If so, tell me back what I just said." The air ambulance was still hovering as the pilot haltingly regurgitated what he'd just been told. Moss eased the helicopter into forward flight and left the Falcón Hospital and Research Institute behind forever.

Alicia, who had been losing sleep over the impending doom of all the FHRI patients, breathed a sigh of relief when she heard Moss warn Greg Alexander about the explosive device.

Haley had known when they came for her late Tuesday afternoon for another "procedure" that she would miss out on their planned escape. She had debated with herself about what to do. As she was lying on the operating table waiting for the procedure to begin, Haley was fully conscious and not anaesthetized (since Dr. Falcón didn't know she'd regained all feeling and could even race Steve in the gym late at night). She glanced up at the clock and saw it was nearly 7:30; either the escape had succeeded or Steve, Thomas and Alicia had been caught, so any thing she did now would not jeopardize them further. Just as Dr. Falcón was about to make an incision in her lower back, Haley sat up and said, "Wait! You don't really need to do this."

Dr. Falcón smiled patronizingly and replied, "As you should know by now Ms. Jackson, these procedures are not voluntary. Now just be still, this will only take a few minutes."

Haley shocked every one in the room by standing up on the table. "No, you obviously don't need to do this since I'm perfectly fine, and have been for a long time. Furthermore, don't you think that you have become a liability to PraxMed? They have planted some kind of explosive device designed to send this whole place up, along with the FDA inspection team, in a fireball within the next 24 hours. I'd suggest you start looking for it now!" She then did a back flip off the table, a balance beam dismount maneuver she'd taught the girls in her gymnastic classes. Dr. Falcón and the surgical team were all speechless.

When Eduard found out about the escape and PraxMed's treachery, he was furious. He was also angry that Haley Jackson and Steve Moss had concealed their recoveries, thereby delaying his own recovery. He knew that Haley needed to stay alive for long term observation, and to perhaps assist in his own recovery, but it was not in his nature to forgive her…he would take his time and think of a way to make her pay for her behavior.

CHAPTER 49

Once again, Jake waited with the CIA rescue team outside the medical facility. The FDA investigative team had entered the building an hour ago, and had been transmitting recon video via their concealed camera. The team leader's radio came to life with a message from the FDA team saying that Dr. Falcón was nowhere to be found. A phone call to his private residence was answered by a maid, who said the doctor had left the country late last night to an undisclosed location. He hadn't said when he'd be back.

"That does it, "fumed the team leader, "we're going in right now!" He immediately issued the commands necessary for the rescue team to make a coordinated fully armed entry to the building; all the men were wearing body armor, expecting major defenses. But when they stormed through the entry, they met no resistance at all. One lone security man looked stunned when he saw heavily armed troops pouring through the door and asked in Spanish what was going on. All the men selected for this mission spoke fluent Spanish, and they asked him where the Americans were being held. As the man threw up his hands, a doctor walking by saw the soldiers and asked in perfect English, "Who's in charge here and what are you people doing with weapons inside our medical facility?"

The team leader said, in an unfriendly voice, "We are here to rescue the kidnapping victims being used for illegal medical experiments. Where are they being held?"

The doctor looked at the team leader as though he were crazy. "I have no idea what you're talking about, but go ahead and search the entire facility... you'll only find sick people and our staff."

"We'll soon see about that," the team leader said as he pulled out of his pocket a picture of barred windows on the buildings exterior and showed it to the doctor. "Can you tell me why these windows have bars on them?"

The doctor looked at the picture and began to laugh. "Is that what this armed intrusion is about? We have rooms that occasionally house sick inmates from prison, and we need a secure place to keep them. Come with me, I'll show you myself."

The doctor led the way, with the CIA men warily on guard for any eventuality. They finally arrived at a separate wing that had a combination lock on the door. As he doctor punched in the combination, he explained, "Sometimes, like during an influenza outbreak, this wing can be full. Currently, we only have two rooms occupied by two prisoners with suspected tuberculosis. But go ahead and see for yourselves."

The men broke into small groups and did a room by room sweep of the wing. All they found were two very sick Hispanic men. They spent the rest of the day searching the other 565 rooms of the hospital for the kidnap victims, but with no luck. A document search and an analysis of the computerized records showed no traces that the kidnap victims had ever been there.

CHAPTER 50

Mallick had planned to remotely trigger the firestorm by a cell phone triggered sequence once he was safely out of Bogotá, but his desire to see the grand explosion with his own eyes superseded his desire for safety. He was parked in the medical center's main lot, unaware that less than a hundred feet from him were parked the CIA team. Mallick had watched with glee as the FDA investigators entered the facility, relishing the thought of blowing them up along with the rest of PraxMed's research "gold mine" which had caved in. He carefully dialed the phone number of the cell phone mounted to the device which would begin the acid drip on the building's gas main and hit the send button.

Mallick knew the device had been configured to initiate the drip only after the twentieth ring to avoid an inadvertent early triggering by someone dialing a wrong number. Just after the third ring, he was surprised when someone answered the phone. "Hello, Mallick. This is Eduard Falcón. We have obviously found your little *present* to us, and I must say we're not very happy with you. What do you think would be a suitable *reward* we could give you?"

Mallick broke in to a sweat, as he was keenly aware of Eduard's reputation as a sadist. "Mike Pellizari is the one you want!" he blurted. "He ordered me to eliminate the problem you and your brother have created for PraxMed. I even have a recording of him giving the order that I secretly recorded. I'll give it to you!"

Eduard waited a long time before replying, knowing that Mallick was terrified at the possible repercussions. "I don't believe you. Pellizari is my cousin... he would never kill his own flesh and blood! I'll give you 72 hours to have the recording delivered to the following address. If I don't have it by then, I'll have your balls cut off and feed them to my dog while you watch. I'll then have you

161

slowly eviscerated before we kill you and sell your organs to the highest bidder. You can run and hide…but my cartel has eyes all over the world." To Mallick's great surprise, Eduard gave him an address in Scotland.

"Don't worry, I'll send it tonight if you promise never to kill me, or have anyone else kill me!" He knew that, in spite of being a criminal and sadist, Eduard Falcón always kept his word.

Eduard paused before answering. "You are in no position to negotiate, but I promise to never kill you myself, nor will I have anyone else kill you."

Mallick breathed a sigh of relief, believing he personally would get off the hook by giving up the PraxMed CEO. He then sped out of the parking lot and headed straight for the airport, shakily congratulating himself on his brilliance for having the foresight to record everything.

CHAPTER 51

A licia's "car liberation" friend Diego had agreed in advance to pick them up at a farmer's field in rural Bogotá. He had given Alicia the exact GPS coordinates when he had dropped off the copy of the helicopter's key. They had abandoned the helicopter after the short flight and, with Diego as their chauffer, were currently en route to Bogotá's only airport, *Aeropuerto Internacional El Dorado*, which handles all domestic and International flights. Thomas had suggested they immediately contact the Bogotá police, but Diego informed them that there were many policemen on the Falcón payroll. He had gotten them airline tickets and boarding passes—even luggage—for a flight to Toronto, Canada (knowing Falcón's people would be scrutinizing passengers traveling to the United States) and phony passports, as well as bogus but fully functional credit cards in the same names as the passports. Diego also gave each of them 20 $100 bills in US currency.

Diego had advised them that Eduard Falcón's drug cartel was incredibly powerful, with eyes and ears everywhere, including the Columbian government and reputedly even inside the United States FBI. As he handed them each a cell phone, Diego suggested that they not attempt any phone calls out of the country, as he knew many of the international phone operators were Falcón informers, and that the country's land lines and cellular network had been compromised. Diego had agreed to call Senator Jake Jackson with his satellite phone (thereby bypassing the cellular network entirely) once they were safely out of the country. Haley had given Steve and Thomas her father's unlisted private cell phone number, which Moss gave to Diego. As he knew the airport would be closely watched by Falcón drug cartel informers equipped with physical descriptions of the escapees, Diego had also provided them with elaborate disguises: Thomas and Alicia would be traveling as a priest and nun. Because Thomas's height was remarkable and difficult to conceal, a wheelchair had been provided for him. Alicia's stunning figure was concealed by a "fat suit" she was wearing. Moss's long hair had been cut short and dyed blond to match a fake moustache and goatee.

As they approached the airport, their level of anxiety grew tremendously. Their futures—their very lives depended on their success in getting out of Columbia undetected. Diego had provided each of them with a weapon that appeared to be a ballpoint pen, but was in fact a single-shot .22 caliber gun—effective only at point-blank range, but unrecognizable to airport security monitoring. When Moss expressed concern that the mass of even a single cartridge might be sufficient to set off a sensitive metal detector, Diego just grinned and told him that the cartridges were made from high strength ceramics and had no metal at all in them. He cautioned them that the weapon had only short-range effectiveness. After Diego pulled up to the airport entry to drop them off, he said "Stay in the car a moment, I have one more thing for you." He quickly hopped out of the car and popped the trunk open and extracted what appeared to be three bottles of drinking water. As he handed them out, he saw the puzzled looks on their faces and grinned once again." I'm not worried about your thirst. Hold the bottles up to the sunlight," he suggested. They complied, and Thomas said with amazement. "There is a clear blade attached to the lid!"

Diego explained, "Yes a razor-sharp polycarbonate blade with a clear handle attached. I pray you won't need them, but knife work is always quieter than a gunshot. You will not be permitted to take any liquids on the plane, so they are for your protection in the airport before you go through security. Even though I could have given you regular knives, you would not have them as close to hand as these." On that solemn pronouncement, they exited Diego's car after profusely thanking him for all his help. Diego got Thomas's wheelchair out of the trunk and he sat down in it.

Their entry to the airport was noted by two bulky men, who were surreptitiously comparing all those who entered the airport against photos and descriptions of Alicia, Thomas and Steve. One of the men had watched as Thomas got out of the car under his own power, and then sat down in a wheelchair.

"Do you think that is them?" the larger of the two men said.

"We'll soon find out," growled his companion. The two men followed them as they entered the airport.

With Alicia pushing Thomas in the wheelchair, Moss followed a few steps behind so as not to look like a group of three…exactly what the Falcón boys were looking for. With his military training in covert tailing techniques, Moss was hyper-alert to the probability they might be followed. He abruptly stopped, put down his suitcase, and knelt as though his shoe lace had become untied. "Go on without me…I'll meet you at the gate" Moss said to Thomas and Alicia. The two men behind him also stopped, making no attempt to go around Moss as busy travelers normally would have. He stood back up, glanced at his watch, and then began searching for a men's room. The two men did not immediately follow, but waited to see which way he would go. Seeing a sign with the international symbol for restrooms, Moss set off at a brisk pace in the direction the sign indicated. If the two men were indeed following him, they would be along shortly. As he neared the men's room, he slowed down, again looking at his watch. People passed by him on his right and his left; the two men, obviously not professionals, nearly bumped into Moss. Knowing now for sure that they were following him, he went in and noted there were only three other men there, two of whom were leaving. Moss directly went to the larger handicapped stall and closed the door and slid the latch into place. He stood on the stool so his feet would not be visible. He listened carefully, and soon heard a flush followed by the sound of running water. Moss then heard the restroom's door open and close. After several minutes, he heard the door open again.

"I'm sure I saw him go in here," a man's voice said. Moss silently took the water bottle Diego had provided out of his coat pocket and unscrewed the lid. He silently pulled out the polycarbonate knife, noticing that it had a stout little handle on it.

"Well, it doesn't look like he's here now," another voice complained. The men began opening all the stall doors, looking inside each one. When they came to the handicapped stall where Moss had hidden, one of the men pushed on the door to open it, but found the door latched. The men were now being quiet as one knelt, peeking under the door. He let out a blood-curdling scream when Moss drove the knife hard into his eye, piercing the socket and entering the brain. As the man fell dead, the other man withdrew a snub-nosed revolver from his jacket pocket and used his size 13 foot to cave in the stall's door. He was surprised to see Moss, backed into a corner of the over-sized stall, fiddling with a pen. A huge grin slowly evolved on his face and the last words of his life were, "Are you planning to write me a check?" The grin froze on his face as the small caliber ceramic bullet struck him between his eyes.

Moss now had two bodies to worry about. Once they were found, surely the airport would be locked down and departing flights would not be allowed to leave. He remembered seeing another door just as he had entered the restroom. Moss determined that the door had been left unlocked and led to a small janitor's supply room. He quickly dragged both bodies into the little supply room, grabbed a handful of rags, and cleaned up the men's blood on the restroom floor hurriedly. He hurriedly threw the rags into the supply room, hit the lock button on the door knob and, realizing some one surely must have heard the gun shot, exited the restroom as casually as his pounding heart would let him.

CHAPTER 52

J ake always carried two cell phones: one was for government business; the other a private one for family members and his personal staff only…he had instructed those he had entrusted with this private number never to give it to anyone else. He was about to get in his car when the private phone rang. Jake was surprised to hear a heavily accented voice he'd never heard before. "Senator Jackson?"

"Yes, and who might you be, and how did you get this number?"

"We have never met and we never will. My name is Diego. I am in Bogotá, Columbia. One hour ago I delivered your sister's three amigos to *Aeropuerto Internacional El Dorado* after they escaped from a hospital where they have been being held. Unfortunately, your sister Haley, who is not only well, but no longer a paraplegic, was unable to escape with them."

Jake was temporarily speechless. After the fruitless CIA trip, he had all but given up hope of ever seeing Haley again. "Where were these amigos of Haley's planning to go?" He added, "And what do you mean she is no longer a paraplegic?" Diego explained that they were heading to Toronto, Canada, and then summarized what he knew of the illegal stem cell experimentation being conducted by Dr. Falcón, and how that had led to Haley's full recovery. He also surprised Jake by telling him Jake's old military comrade Steve Moss—who was now disguised with his hair cut short and dyed blond to ma7tch a fake moustache and goatee—was one of the three escapees. Diego then gave Jake the names of the other two escapees and explained that they were disguised as a priest and a nun. Jake wanted to ask at least a dozen more questions, but the phone connection was abruptly severed. After a brief pause to digest what he'd just heard, Jake called Scott Wroblewski at the FBI.

When Scott answered, Jake simply said, "I just received a strange phone call from a man claiming Haley is alive but still being held captive. The caller also said our old friend Steve Moss, who is disguised with short hair dyed blond to match a fake moustache and goatee, and a couple other people, disguised as a priest and a nun have escaped and are en route to Toronto, Canada."

Wroblewski replied quickly, "Do you believe it?"

"I'm not positive, but how quickly can you get someone in your Detroit field office to Toronto to watch the in-coming arrivals from Columbia?"

CHAPTER 53

Thomas, Alicia and Moss did not begin to relax until their plane touched down at Toronto's Lester B. Pearson International Airport. Moss could hardly wait to deplane. He was anxious to initiate the rescue of Haley as well as the other kidnap victims, and bring the full force of the United States government down on Dr. Falcón's head. His first phone call would be to Haley's brother, his old friend Senator Jake Jackson.

Inside the airport, FBI agent Rodrigo Gomez, from the Detroit FBI field office, stood discreetly to the side of the arrival gate carefully watching the deplaning passengers. Gomez had gotten an order from the FBI deputy director personally to be on the lookout for three people who might be arriving from Bogotá, Columbia. He held a not-so-recent picture of Steve Moss in his hand, and had been advised of their disguises. He had been given no explanatory details; his orders were simply to take the three people into protective custody and await further orders. Gomez, who had relatives living in Columbia, didn't need any explanation—all he needed to know was that the Falcón cartel had a ten million dollar contract out to eliminate these three people before they could reach the United States. Gomez smiled…he was already planning how he would spend the money.

CHAPTER 54

Moss wanted to shout for joy at their escape, but he knew none of them would truly feel safe until they were back in the good old USA and had briefed the government about the situation in Columbia. He was about to call Jake Jackson when Moss noticed a Latino man in a dark blue suit looking directly at him. While he looked back at him, Alicia wheeled Thomas up beside Moss and exclaimed "We made it!" The man in the suit began striding quickly towards them.

As he approached, the man said, "Are you Colonel Steve Moss, Dr. Thomas Jefferson Hunt, and Alicia Janet Jones?" He began to relax as the man displayed his FBI credentials identifying him as special agent Rodrigo Gomez.

Moss replied, "Yes we are, sir!"

The FBI agent smiled. "Would the three of you come with me please? And, may I ask if any of you has made a phone call since getting off the plane?"

As they walked out of the airport and followed FBI agent Rodrigo Gomez far down the street, alarm bells started going off in his brain as Moss recalled Diego's admonition about the Falcón cartel having informers even inside the United States FBI. He glanced around and saw no other people near them.

Odd question, Moss thought. Why should agent Gomez care whether any of them had made a phone call since getting off the plane? He surprised Thomas and Alicia when Moss said, "Sir, we've come this far on our own, and we'll manage just fine from here."

The FBI agent drew his weapon. "You'll notice we are no longer in the view of any airport security cameras. You didn't really think you could escape unscathed from the Falcón brothers, did you? The Falcón cartel is now the largest criminal organization in the world," he bragged, "with eyes and ears in every major government and law enforcement agency. They have a ten million dollar contract out on you three!"

Moss realized their time to live would be limited if they did not escape this guy and find a safe haven. As a former bounty hunter, Moss knew that $10 million price on their heads would attract some seriously good talent.

None of them moved as they stood there with incredulous looks on their faces. As Gomez concealed his weapon from passing traffic, Moss made a snap decision and delivered a powerful spinning roundhouse kick to the corrupt FBI agent's jaw. He dropped to the ground like a rock. Gomez had gotten stunned, but had quickly retrieved his weapon and was now taking aim at Moss as he got back on his feet. Moss grabbed the hair on the back of Gomez's head, placed his other hand on his chin, and twisted fast and forcefully. The man's neck broke with an audible crack. Moss quickly bent down and took his weapon, FBI credentials and wallet. Moss didn't want to authorities to identify this body any time soon. A quick look in his mouth revealed no fillings at all, so there would likely be no dental records. A search of his pockets revealed a flask filled with whisky, a pack of cigarettes and a lighter. Moss opened the flask, sprinkled some on the man's coat, and then put it back in the dead agent's pocket. Making sure no one was near them, Moss used the lighter to quickly singe each of Gomez's finger tips; the burned tissue would not yield any identifiable finger prints.

Airport automobile traffic was zipping past them, although no one stopped or seemed to have seen what just happened. Moss dragged the body to the curb, and did his best to stand the dead FBI agent up. He waited for a car to come that would visibly be speeding. Luck was with him; in less than a minute he spotted a car roaring down the road towards them. Moss made as though to cross the street, assisting his "drunken buddy." The driver saw them too late to stop. Before hitting them was imminent, Moss let go of the body and leaped out of the way. There was a loud thud as the car hit the FBI agent's body, throwing it into the air.

"Follow me now!" Moss shouted to a stunned Thomas and Alicia as he began running back towards the main terminal.

CHAPTER 55

They headed back towards the airport where a short line of people were waiting for transportation. As a young couple were about to enter a taxi, Moss politely said as he stepped towards them with his extended hand holding five $100 bills, "Pardon me, but we're in a frightful hurry—may we have this taxi please?

The young man took a look at Moss's hand, grabbed the money and said with a look of glee, "It's all yours!"

They scrambled in, and Thomas, thinking quickly about a previous conference he'd attended, instructed the driver: "I'm a doctor, and I have an emergency surgery to perform at Toronto Mercy Hospital ...300 Elizabeth St. Please hurry!"

They rode to the hospital in silence, trying to calm down after the unexpected FBI "reception" at the airport. Moss marveled at Thomas's creative solution to their departure...he was clearly brilliant in many ways. Once they'd arrived at the hospital, Thomas explained to them that not only had he been here previously for a conference, but that he had an old friend from medical school, a Dr. Elizabeth Stanley, who was on the hospital staff. Not sure what or who we were up against, they agreed they needed a safe sanctuary until they could formulate a plan. The three entered the hospital and Thomas identified himself, asking for Dr. Stanley to be paged. They were escorted to a doctors' lounge, and told to wait there.

Several minutes later, a very tall majestic looking black woman strode in to the lounge, saw Thomas, and shrieked with joy. "Thomas," she sobbed, "when you went missing we imagined the worst!" She hadn't noticed Alicia and Moss yet. "You horny old dog...Where have you been? "Alicia grimaced. Clearly there was some history between doctors Hunt and Stanley. They held a long embrace and uttered some friendly pleasantries. Not having seen Thomas for several years, but knowing that he had been stricken with Parkinson's disease which often impairs the sufferer's motor skills and speech, Dr. Stanley exclaimed," Hey! What happened to your Parkinson's tremors, and your speech ...are you on some new drugs?"

"Liz," Thomas explained, "It's a long scary story, but I no longer have Parkinson's disease. I'll tell you the whole story later, but first I'd like you to meet some friends of mine." After the introductions, Thomas said "Liz, the three of us were kidnapped along with several people and subjected to medical experimentation in Columbia. We escaped, but our kidnappers are powerful people who are still after us." Thomas then explained what had happened with the FBI agent at the airport and told her they didn't know who they could trust in the government." Frankly, we need a place to 'lay low' until we can develop a plan. Can you help us?"

They stayed that night at Dr. Stanley's home. Moss called Jake Jackson and told him the whole story, from beginning to end, including the fact that The Falcón cartel is now the largest criminal organization in the world, with eyes and ears in every major government and law enforcement agency. Moss regretfully told Jake that Haley was not with them. He also told him they had a ten million dollar contract out on them. Jake told Moss about the CIA rescue attempt, and that all the kidnapping victims had mysteriously disappeared from the FHRI. Jake asked if he could put his fiancé and PR aid Sally Peters on the phone with them. They talked for two hours and hatched a plan that was largely Sally's idea. Basically, they wouldn't be able to trust anyone in their own government with whom they didn't have a long history.

The next morning they were flown to Minneapolis on Jake Jackson's personal jet. They used the bogus passports Diego had given them to get through customs. The pilot and co-pilot were both trusted guys Jake and Moss had served with in the military who had been briefed on their dire situation, and understood the need for secrecy. Later that week, Sally orchestrated carefully fabricated media stories which flowed throughout the country. The stories detailed how two missing kidnapping victims and an unknown woman had been found shot to death in an undisclosed location.

CHAPTER 56

E duard Falcón was sparring with an opponent in the gymnasium of his and Nicolas's magnificently restored family castle in Scotland. The castle featured a large central five-story keep. A 100 foot tower was located at each corner of the keep. A massive curtain wall surrounded the keep and multiple out buildings—essentially an enclosed village.

The Scottish government believed the castle estate was used as a very expensive and private drug rehabilitation facility (innocuously named "Oceanside Centre") for affluent seemingly incurable addicts who voluntarily chose to be "imprisoned" until cured. This reasonably explained the large security staff, daily deliveries and secrecy. Pictures of the castle had been on Dr. Falcón's fireplace mantle in his FHRI office; Dr. Falcón had completely forgotten about talking with Steve Moss about the castle the first time they'd played chess together.

Eduard and his brother had moved to the castle secretly two years ago, bringing along all of Dr. Falcón's 101 surviving human guinea pigs; the small number of patients who were not responding to treatments had been euthanized. Both he and Nicolas kept their residence at the castle secret from the outside world; only his closest lieutenants knew his exact physical location. However, given that he had a worldwide organization to run, they could easily contact him at a phone number that, if anyone were to try to track its exact location, would be found to move almost magically to different locations around the world daily. The covert evacuation of the patients from the hospital had been tricky, but the Falcón drug cartel's recently purchased Boeing 737 had made getting out of Columbia fairly easy.

Upon learning of the complete recoveries of Haley Jackson and Steve Moss, Eduard demanded and received the same stem cell treatments they had received, and now, after months of rehabilitation, had full use of his legs… which he was presently using to deliver an array of forceful martial arts kicks to his opponent's body and head.

As an added bonus, Eduard had received one other gift from his brother: a new flesh and blood hand to replace his prosthetic one. The hand had been taken from a living donor (an enemy who was about the same size and build as Eduard). Using a newly developed stem cell treatment combined with a nerve regeneration process, the hand's cells were seen by his body as his own; hence, no rejection. The hand worked as though he'd been born with it; his only regret, albeit a minor one, was that he no longer had the modified Ruger Super Redhawk Alaskan revolver concealed within his prosthesis.

He was currently demonstrating the hand's effectiveness by delivering a hammer fist blow to his opponent's clavicle. In his head, Eduard pictured striking the treacherous Mike Pellizari, PraxMed's CEO who had unsuccessfully attempted to blow up FHRI, as he continued the brutal attack on his opponent. He would deal with Pellizari and PraxMed when the time was right.

The gymnasium had been equipped with a wide range of gymnastic equipment, including uneven parallel bars, a horse, a springboard and a balance beam. This equipment was provided at Haley Jackson's request, to which Eduard at first refused, then diabolically agreed, upon the condition that she perform for him alone once a week totally naked. Eduard gave Haley two choices: she could comply, or if she refused, have all of her fingers amputated. Her humiliation was his retaliation for concealing her recovery, thereby delaying his own. How many people got to watch an Olympic medalist work out naked in their own private gymnasium? He knew that Haley's paralyzing injury had occurred on a balance beam; he had secretly marveled at the woman's dedication and courage as he watched her overcome her fear and once again master the apparatus.

CHAPTER 57

Oceanside Centre was a 1260 acre castle estate on Scotland's west coast, and was remote and heavily guarded by a small army of 185 highly trained mercenaries loyal to Eduard Falcón. Other estate protections included radar for detecting approaching aircraft, and a wide range of sophisticated weaponry. Anti-aircraft missiles and a heavily mined estate perimeter, along with a multitude of video cameras and sensors in the surrounding forest, made the castle itself fairly secure. There were also three more defensive weapons secretly developed for the Chinese government so highly advanced that no other government either had them or even knew of their existence; the prototypes had been built, but never delivered. The Falcón organization had paid a disgruntled Chinese scientist 5 million dollars for the EMP prototype weapons. The man had intended to give his unique designs to the highest bidders. The scientist died a month later from an "accidental" drug overdose before he could deliver his design documents to anyone else.

The first weapon was a powerful portable electromagnetic pulse (EMP) generator capable of producing a high-density electrical field in a focused beam that could be aimed. EMP acts like a strike of lightning but is stronger, faster and briefer. EMP can seriously damage electronic devices connected to power sources or antennas, but is relatively harmless to humans (unless they have an implanted pacemaker). This includes communication systems, computers, electrical appliances, and automobile or aircraft ignition systems. The damage spectrum ranges, depending on how powerful an EMP is, from a minor operational interruption to actual burnout of electronic components.

By using the portable EMP generator at its full power, any attacking force could practically be reduced to fighting as they did in medieval times. To protect the castle's own assets if the EMP weapon were ever used, "Faraday cages" were employed. This consisted of covering any vulnerable objects (like computers and communications equipment) with a grounded copper mesh which would stop virtually all electromagnetic radiation.

The second weapon was also an EMP device; however this one was not portable and was housed deep within the castle. This device, when activated, emitted continual EMP pulses that would mildly disrupt electrical activity in the human brain and peripheral nervous system, resulting in loss of coordination and massive cognitive disruptions...confusion so bad an effected person would not be able to function. This effect could be avoided by copper shielding; the Falcón brothers and all of the castle's defensive force had been fitted with a copper mesh version of a knight's armor that, in fact, was a personal Faraday cage. These Faraday cage suits of armor would be donned in the event the castle came under attack. This weapon's efficacy had been tested on the patients without their knowledge or consent; for two hours they had wandered the castle–aimless, uncoordinated, stumbling, falling down and confused–until the EMP weapon was turned off. An ecstatic Eduard Falcón had gleefully named the weapon "Discombobulator Supremo."

The third weapon was a variant of the second weapon, also housed deep within the castle. This device, when activated, emitted continual EMP pulses that would excite the molecules of gunpowder and other explosive material, including gasoline and other fuels, causing them to heat up and explode. This effectively negated the use of modern weapons and vehicles by potential attackers. The castle's defending force were all highly trained in horsemanship, hand-to-hand combat, the use of swords, bow and arrows, battle axes, and lances; they were literally modern day knights.

In the unlikely event that a takeover of the castle was imminent, Eduard would trigger a shielded massive explosive device located beneath the labyrinth of computers and communications equipment; the EMP weapons would be destroyed as well.

The tower on the northwest corner of the castle was topped by a massive copper-clad dome. Inside the dome, which could open up like a clamshell, was a Sikorsky X2 helicopter: At 288 mph it is the world's fastest. This helicopter was not for daily use; rather, it was a means of escape for Eduard and Nicolas Falcón, both of whom were reasonably proficient pilots. It had been fitted with four missiles: two air-to-air and two anti-ship missiles. The helicopter's passenger compartment had been extensively modified; it was water tight and it could be separated from the helicopter by exploding bolts. As the helicopter would necessarily fly over water, a life raft and Scuba gear were kept on board. A ballistic recovery system had been custom designed for a helicopter application. A solid-fuel rocket could be triggered to pull the parachute out from its housing and deploy the canopy fully within seconds.

The castle itself was situated atop a cliff 200 feet overlooking the ocean. The moat surrounding the castle had been stocked with Piranhas…a convenient dumping spot for the occasional enemy Eduard tortured and killed in one of his sadistic rages. Deep within the castle was a large crematorium suitable for incineration of multiple bodies at once. The estate included a long paved runway and a hangar (which was also a Faraday cage to protect the aircraft's avionics) for the Boeing 737.

A large courtyard with an Olympic sized swimming pool was for the patients' use. They were free to ride the many horses kept in the huge stable without supervision up to the estate's perimeter, which was double fenced. Even though the fences itself were no deterrent to escape, none of them dared cross them. They knew about the land mines between the fences—a few of them had a vivid accidental demonstration when a deer wandered out of the forest, hopped the outer fence, and was blown up before their eyes. They were puzzled by the daily horsemanship drills conducted by the castle's security force. Why did they need to be able to ride so well? They reasoned correctly that the approach road to the castle was mined, but those mines could be deactivated remotely for the daily deliveries of supplies.

Deep under the castle was a state-of-the-art communications and command center from which the global Falcón criminal operation was run. The computers and other communications equipment rivaled the best had by the CIA or NSA. All of the Falcón cartel outgoing operational directives used sophisticated techniques to conceal the originating location, and employed encryption that was theoretically nearly undecipherable.

There was also a massive vault containing (or so his security force believed) over 700 billion dollars in various currencies, and nearly 500 billion dollars worth of gold bullion; Eduard did not trust banks at all. While he wasn't a financial troglodyte–he relied on a variety of banks and financial institutions around the world—Eduard trusted only himself for the ultimate safety of his fortune. After his organization's international profits were consolidated and adequately laundered, he had them delivered by armored car to the castle, which his security force believed was more secure than Fort Knox.

Eduard believed that his global hegemony over the world's other drug lords was a continual state of war. As Sun Tzu had written centuries earlier, all warfare is based on deception. In fact, the bulk of his vast fortune was not stored in the castle at all; it was transported at regular intervals by submarine to six secret secure repositories distributed around the world. The four-man submarine crew would be totally replaced after each trip, and the preceding crew would mysteriously disappear or have accidental deaths within a month of their mission. These repositories were not banks; they were in unlikely and hidden locations, much like those used by pirates throughout history, with the difference that Eduard's treasure caches were all hidden in the midst of highly populated areas. No matter how safe and invulnerable he believed the castle to be, Eduard knew it was foolish to keep all of his eggs in one basket. The locations of these secret treasure caches were not encrypted or stored on computers or any other kind of electronic media; rather, there was an old-fashioned treasure map tattooed on his chest, along with the exact latitudes and longitudes of each location. The tattoo artist who had performed the work had gone missing years ago. Each treasure cache was defended by a small group of highly paid mercenaries who had no idea of what they were protecting.

Deliveries to the secret locations consisted of large sealed containers; in each container was, along with huge amounts of gold and cash, a pressurized cylinder holding enough bio-toxic gas to wipe out an entire city. Each cylinder was equipped with a timing device; they would count down for an entire year, and if not reset with the proper code within that time, then release their deadly contents. Eduard's rationale for these extreme measures was that the treasure caches could be used as bargaining chips if he were ever captured. The existence of the deadly canisters protected his life; he would die before giving up the code needed to reset the timing devices. The defending mercenaries were told to never attempt to open the large sealed containers, as they contained tamper-detecting sensors that would cause a massive explosion; they were monitored by a webcam at each location. The mercenaries were required to consistently have a minimum of six defenders; any attempts to disable the webcam monitoring them would result in immediate termination of their lucrative contracts. Every year Eduard would make a trip around the world to visit his treasure caches to pay the defenders in cash, and to reset the timers—he had just returned from his annual trip. Eduard's will was the only place where the existence of the deadly cylinders and their annual need to have their timers reset was written down; the will was stored in a special briefcase equipped with a transmitter that would notify Eduard if the briefcase were opened. The lawyer had been informed that opening the briefcase prior to Eduard's death would lead to his own execution. The locations of the deadly cylinders were not recorded in the will; it was written that the locations could be found on the large map tattooed in mirror reverse on Eduard's chest.

A cell phone jammer assured that none of the patients could make a call if they somehow got their hands on a phone. Ownership of the castle could not be linked to the Falcón brothers as they had "sold" the estate to a complex network of international investors shortly after they had inherited it.

CHAPTER 58

H aley and the other patients (all were now mostly cured of their prior afflictions) were captives deprived of their freedom, but were otherwise treated like royalty. Dr. Falcón and Eduard were, in spite of being criminals, grateful for the sacrifices the patients had made. They also realized that, in order for the long term efficacy of the patients' cures to be evaluated, they needed to be kept alive, healthy and happy...much like prized livestock. Dr. Falcón, thanks to his illegal experiments, now had cures established for diabetes, Parkinson's, Alzheimer's, a few forms of multiple sclerosis, and a cure for some cases of paraplegia and other injuries to the central nervous system. He had also discovered a technique for rejection-free transplantation of organs and limbs.

Now that their former partner PraxMed was an enemy, there was no clear way Dr. Falcón could profit from his work; therefore, he documented all his experiments and derived curative procedures in several journals and notebooks which were securely encrypted and stored on a set of DVDs kept in his personal vault. One day soon, he believed, the world would forgive his moral transgressions and see him for the medical genius he clearly was!

Unbeknownst to Dr. Falcón was the fact that the combination to his personal vault was known by one of the Falcón organization's senior security staff members. Dale Vandermeer, who (hoping for some leverage in dealing with the Falcón brothers) had secretly placed concealed miniature video cameras in the personal living quarters of both Eduard and Nicolas; Dale had one digital recording of Nicolas entering the combination to the vault, and another of a complex and curious tattoo on Eduard's chest.

Haley and the other patients had been told that the escapees from FHRI, Steve Moss, Dr. Thomas Hunt and their accomplice, Alicia Jones, had been killed before they got to the United States; they were reminded of the macabre penalties for attempting to escape. Haley had gone in to a deep depression at this news; she had come to love Steve Moss as she had loved no man before him. She still broke down in tears occasionally thinking about Steve and the life that could have been theirs together.

The patients were free to roam and explore the restored portions of the magnificent castle and surrounding estate unescorted during the days, and each evening gathered in the opulent dining hall where they enjoyed gourmet meals prepared to their individual preferences. They had unrestricted access to the castle library, and could request books, magazines, and music, which, if not already on the shelves, would be ordered for them. They could also order any items of clothing they desired from a wide variety of catalogs. Movies were shown every night in the castle's theatre, which was ornately decorated. So secure was the castle estate, their captors believed, that no attempt was made to monitor or supervise the patients at all. They each had a weekly medical checkup, but no other attention was paid to their activities. They were all required to attend a weekly meeting, where Dr. Falcón would address them. Only the Falcón organization's communications and command center, which, along with the castle's massive vault, were heavily guarded, and the Falcón brothers' personal suites were off limits to the patients.

Some parts of the castle, particularly in the lower levels, had never been restored. Dr. Falcón, believing curiosity, adventure and exploration was good for the patients, allowed them to wander freely...he had begun to think of the patients less as captives, and more like his permanent guests. To allow them to explore where there was no electricity, each patient had been issued a flashlight with a generous supply of rechargeable batteries. He even encouraged them to make maps, as neither he nor his brother had ever fully explored the bowels of the castle. He had looked into the history of the castle, and was surprised to learn that the current castle was actually the fourth castle built on this location. People had occupied this piece of land for nearly 2000 years. Three books had been written about the history on the castles. Dr. Falcón had them all, and encouraged the patients to read them. He pointed out to the patients that there were multiple references in the books to the castle being haunted; he jokingly advised them to be on the lookout for ghosts! While most of the patients chuckled at this, some were stone-faced; on more than one occasion strange sounds had been heard late at night, and odd unexplained sightings in the castle hallways of people not known to be either patients or employees had been experienced by several of the patients.

Their treatment was so good that some of the patients were exhibiting the Stockholm syndrome—a response sometimes seen in an abducted hostage, in which the hostage shows signs of loyalty to the hostage-taker, regardless of the danger in which they have been placed. They were all very pleased with their recoveries; but some seemed to have forgotten the previous atrocities committed by Dr. Falcón and his macabre minions.

What they all lacked, however, was structure and meaning to their everyday lives. Gone were jobs and careers, family, friends, community involvement, and the general sense of purpose and self-direction in their lives. No matter how well they were treated, there was an underlying sadness at the loss of precious freedom, and little hope of ever going home again.

CHAPTER 59

wo years had passed since their escape from FHRI. Thomas, Alicia and
Moss had been graciously invited to live in Jake Jackson's mansion. Jake
knew that the Falcón Cartel had placed a huge price on their heads, but now
likely believed they were dead; they needed to keep it that way. None of them
could let any of their families or friends know they were alive…they were now
living in a virtual witness protection type situation created for them by Jake.

Moss still thought about Haley every day, and realized he had come to love
her. Love had never come easily to him. The only other woman he had truly
loved was his wife Susan, with whom he had planned to grow old. When Susan
died from cancer, and especially after he became a paraplegic, Moss believed
he would never find love again. Haley, in spite of the horrific circumstances of
their kidnappings and the situation at FHRI, had changed that belief. He worried that she may have suffered terrible consequences after their escape, and he
held little hope of ever seeing her alive again.

The Jackson mansion, situated on Lake Minnetonka, was huge—over
10,000 square feet, and exquisitely furnished. During Jake's illustrious baseball
career, he had earned a multi-million dollar salary for several years as one of the
top pitchers in the American League, and he had invested wisely. The mansion's
rooms included a large ballroom, a library, a lounge, a billiard parlor, a theatre,
and a well equipped exercise facility. It even had a well provisioned "safe room"
with TV monitors for viewing all the other rooms in the home. Throughout
the mansion were valuable works of art. Attached to the mansion was an extra
large conservatory that housed tropical plants, a swimming pool and a large
whirlpool. Behind the conservatory, which overlooked Lake Minnetonka, were

a large boathouse and long dock. In the boathouse were a 36 foot long cruiser, a ski boat, two jet skis, a sail boat, and a pontoon boat for fishing.

As a cover for their residing at the mansion, they had been given actual "jobs" as household staff and paid quite generously by Jake. Thomas was the "tropical plant gardener" while Alicia was the second "cook." Moss was the "chauffer and mechanic" (they all had gotten new driver's licenses, checking accounts and savings accounts using their phony passports that Diego had provided them as identification). To allay suspicion from the existing household staff and visitors, they actually performed those jobs and even enjoyed them. Including them, there were now seven members of Jake's household staff: Chris Meyer, majordomo; Gabriel Sanchez, gardener; Gail Ford, maid; Jane Wang, cook.

Jake was an animal lover. Residing at the mansion with them were two dogs and two cats. The older dog, a Greyhound retired from racing was named Slim. Much younger was a German shepherd, a former police dog who had been retired after a gunshot wound, was named Mr. Judge (due to the quizzical look he would give to strangers while deciding whether they were friend or foe).

A black-and-white cat, one of the most intelligent felines Moss had never seen, was named Scheme due to the fact that he could pretty much figure out how to do anything he wanted to, including leaping onto a doorknob (all of which were the lever type in the mansion) and twisting with his paws until the door opened. Slim and Mr. Judge had figured out that Scheme had this capability to open doors. On a couple of occasions they had witnessed Slim and Mr. Judge run up the stairs from the lower level of the mansion when the doorbell rang only to find the door to the upstairs shut. They only had to bark a couple of times before Scheme would come running and open the door for them. The second cat was a regal angora named Camay. Even though she was the smallest of all the pets, the other three acquiesced to her dominion over the household. They enjoyed and had come to adore all four of Jake's pets; Slim and Mr. Judge would joyfully accompany Thomas and Moss on their morning runs, and ride in the boat with them when they went fishing.

Thomas, Alicia and Moss all used aliases. Diego had been wise in picking their bogus names; he reasoned correctly that they might slip up if he gave them first names different from their real ones. Therefore, Thomas Hunt was now Thomas Harvey; Alicia Jones was now Alicia Henderson; Steve Moss was now Steve Peterson.

Thomas, in addition to his medical training, had a significant background in botany. He began growing lovely orchids in the conservatory. Alicia actually was a gourmet cook; it had been her hobby for many years. Moss was thrilled to drive and maintain Jake's impressive multi- million dollar classic car collection, which included a 1961 Ferrari GT 250 SWB California Spyder, a 1931 Bugatti Royale Kellner Coupe, and a 1937 Mercedes-Benz 540K Special Roadster.

Only Chris Meyer, Jake's majordomo and a former Navy SEAL, knew their situation and real identities. Chris was the person who spoke, made arrangements, and took charge for Jake in his absence. Chris had quickly become their close and trusted friend. Chris, who looked as though nothing was physically wrong now, had himself been totally paralyzed temporarily a few years ago by multiple strokes following heart surgery.

Like Haley and Moss, Chris had had to learn to walk again. Although he didn't limp, if one looked closely, one could see that Chris's gait and coordination were a little abnormal. Moss knew that variants of Soo Bahk Do training had been taught successfully to students with a wide range of disabilities, helping them improve in numerous ways, including balance and coordination. Moss talked with Chris about this, and he immediately expressed interest.

Jake's large ballroom, with its hardwood floor, was a perfect spot for their martial arts training and workouts. Chris progressed rapidly, with marked improvements in his balance and coordination. The other members of the household staff, including Thomas and Alicia, asked if they could join them. They now had their own little *Do Jang*!

They established a routine: Mondays, Wednesdays and Fridays they would do martial arts training and cardiovascular exercises; Tuesdays, Thursdays and Saturdays they would do weight training. Thomas, in addition to being a specialist in rehabilitation, had been a bodybuilder prior to being afflicted with Parkinson's disease; he tailored a strength and flexibility regimen for each of them. They included elements of the incredibly strenuous Navy SEALS workout routine Chris shared with them. That routine greatly enhanced the Soo Bahk Do attribute of *In Ney* (endurance). After two years of this, Moss was in the best shape of his adult life, as were the others. He could hardly believe that his entire lower body had been paralyzed... not only did he have full use of his legs again; he could kick harder and higher than he ever had before! Chris also benefited tremendously... his gait and coordination now appeared to be absolutely normal.

As a United States senator, Jake spent most of his time in Washington, so they usually had the house to themselves. Two weekends a month, Jake and Sally would fly back to Minnesota. On those weekends, Jake would give the regular household staff, other than Chris, time off, and report to them the latest news about the secret on-going federal investigation regarding the vanished patients from FHRI.

As they were finishing a delicious meal of prime rib and Yorkshire pudding prepared by Alicia, Moss asked if there were any new developments in the investigation. Jake told them not much had been found, but they had determined that the multi-national Falcón drug cartel was indeed the largest criminal organization in the world—exerting hegemony over the drug business worldwide—with a huge number of police, judges and law enforcement personnel on their payroll.

They had learned that Eduard Falcón had been indicted only once; all of the evidence collected by the police had mysteriously disappeared. Of the six witnesses lined up to testify for the prosecution, four died in "accidents" and the other two went missing before the trial even began. The case was dismissed. The Falcón criminal organization's virtually unlimited financial resources allowed them to employ top-notch computer, communications, and paramilitary personnel. This included informants and operatives inside even Interpol and the FBI. "We really don't know who we can trust...the Falcón cartel seems to have eyes and ears everywhere...even inside the military," Jake bemoaned. "We know that Eduard Falcón continues to head the organization, but no one seems to know where his operation is headquartered since he vanished from Columbia. Highly encrypted messages have been detected on the Internet, but their originating source appears to be totally random. The Falcón brothers' family background is being thoroughly checked to see if there is some safe haven to which they could have fled."

A light bulb went off in Moss's head as he recalled the chess game in Dr. Falcón's office. He remembered the pictures on the fireplace mantle, and what the doctor had said: "It is the only place in the world I feel totally safe and secure."

Moss recounted the event to the others as best as he could recall it. "I think the investigators should focus on Scotland and see what's going on with that castle the Falcón brothers inherited and restored."

CHAPTER 60

S hortly after they had come to live in Jake's mansion, Moss discovered that both Thomas and Alicia were pool players; they spent many fun evenings competing in the billiard parlor. While Thomas was a good player, and Moss was a great player—Alicia was one of the best amateur players Moss had ever seen! She and Moss began playing in small local tournaments together.

One Thursday night, Alicia and Moss drove into downtown Wayzata to a nearly new billiard parlor in Jake's 1961 Ferrari GTO—even very expensive classic cars need to be driven once in a while—to practice on the tables they'd be playing on for the upcoming weekend nine ball tournament. They had been playing for about an hour when a tall handsome young guy in a leather jacket swaggered in the front door. At the moment, Moss was sitting at the bar taking a break and sipping on a Diet Coke. The young guy got himself a beer, and then casually surveyed the assortment of players at the tables. Moss noticed as his gaze locked on Alicia, who was bent over the table lining up a shot... she was apparently playing alone. Even though she was not wearing a low-cut blouse, her ample and attractive bosom was obvious. Conspicuous on her wrist was the diamond encrusted Rolex watch that Thomas had given Alicia on her last birthday.

The guy casually sauntered over to her table, and watched her make a couple of shots.

"Hello there, pretty lady ... I've been watching you practice and noticed that you are quite good ... I do not mean to disturb you, but I could sure use some tips and pointers; do you think we could maybe play a couple of games together?" he inquired politely. Alicia pleasantly agreed, saying as she extended her hand, "My name is Alicia. As long as it's only pool you want to play, that's fine. I already have a boyfriend who I would guess is roughly twice your size." The guy introduced himself as Jason Baxter, and assured her that his only interest was improving his billiard skills.

Moss immediately recognized this Jason Baxter as a probable pool hustler; he had previously regaled Thomas and Alicia with his own youthful exploits as a pool hustler, as well as explaining to them the plethora of hustling techniques used by him and others. Usually those hustling techniques involve misdirection, deception, or both. As the table next to Alicia was vacant, Moss secured that table for himself and began practicing, with no acknowledgment that he even knew Alicia, but Moss was close enough that he could hear and see everything going on at her table. Alicia surreptitiously glanced over at Moss and gave him a sly grin; she too had recognized the guy as a probable hustler.

Alicia was playing with her own professional quality pool cue, while Mr. Leather Jacket was planning to use one he had pulled off the rack. "Why don't we play a simple game of eight ball? I'd appreciate it if you gave me some pointers as we go along." He racked the balls and suggested that Alicia break. Jason played fairly well, but with some glaringly obvious faults in his technique, which Alicia identified and pointed out to him politely, making gentle suggestions for improvement. She easily won the first game. "Wow, you really are good. I'll be honest with you; I am actually a better player than I let on...I just wanted to meet you and maybe chat a little bit, "Jason said with a charmingly boyish grin on his face. "I hope you're not mad at me. Maybe we could play another game, this time for a beer?"

Jason Baxter is pretty smooth Moss thought to himself. He would intentionally lose the next game, but not by much. Jason would then suggest a third game; this time for a small amount of money. Losing that game by a very small margin, he would suggest a fourth game, this one for a significant amount of money—which he would plan to win. At least, that would be a standard pool hustler *modus operandi*.

The guy did not disappoint Moss. He proceeded pretty much as Moss thought he would, but he was fairly surprised by Alicia's strategy. She held back, occasionally missing a shot or two that he knew she could make... she was hustling the hustler! But in the fourth game—with a $500 bet riding on the outcome—Alicia sank her first ball on the break, and then ran the table except for the eight ball, which would win her the game if she could make the final shot, although it looked nearly impossible to make… her last difficult shot had resulted in very poor shape. Alicia had no clear shot; the cue ball was in the middle of a triangle defined by three of her opponent's balls. "Hey Jason, you want to up the stakes by another $500?" she asked. Believing the shot to be impossible, Jason agreed, thinking he could likely make all of his shots and win the game after she missed this shot. Alicia made an incredibly skillful, albeit extremely lucky, jump masse' shot that caused the cue ball to hop over the seven ball and then go backwards and sink the eight ball in the corner pocket. Jason Baxter had not even gotten a shot! A small group of other players had gathered to watch. Moss assumed they were fans of Jason who had wanted to see him fleece this newcomer, but they applauded Alicia's brilliant shot nonetheless. They, as well as Jason, were stunned as Jason had lost his big-money game without making a single shot. Jason was furious, and refused to pay Alicia the $1000 he owed to her. "You hustled me, you black bitch! I'm going to smack you silly," he said raising his pool cue over his head.

Moss was too far away to intervene in time. As it turned out, he didn't need to. As Jason ferociously began a skull-cracking swing with his pool cue, his feet were suddenly swept from beneath him by a diminutive Asian woman who had been standing right behind him—he crashed to the floor. Cursing mightily, Jason said, "Jesus Christ, Poppy, what the fuck did you do that for?" He got back to his feet and moved threateningly towards her.

"While I have been amused by your pool hustling the past, I draw the line at your attempting to club the shit out of someone who has turned the tables on you, Jason Baxter. Now pay the woman what you owe her and get your sorry ass out of here," Poppy demanded.

Jason made a mistake by attempting to throw a punch at Poppy; she skillfully blocked the punch, then stepped to the side in a cross-legged stance and delivered a spinning axe kick to his temple. He dropped to his knees, screaming in pain. "If you come at me again, I will cripple you for life. Now get your wallet out and pay the woman already," Poppy demanded of him. Jason grudgingly did as he was told. Alicia calmly put the money in her purse with a little smirk on her face. She had enjoyed seeing this small woman bring this hustling asshole (who was at least a foot taller and 100 pounds heavier) to his knees, both literally and figuratively. By this time, Moss had positioned himself between Alicia and this aggressive jerk. "Thanks for protecting my lady friend," he said to Poppy while extending his hand. "Are you a Tae Kwon Do student?" Moss inquired.

"No thanks are necessary. I am that, along with being a 'starving artist'," she replied with a confident grin and a firm handshake. Not bashful about her Sapphic inclinations, Poppy added, "I would have hated to see such a beautiful head bashed in." Poppy gave Alisha a coquettish wink, then turned and headed for the exit. Moss and Alicia followed Poppy out to the parking lot—Moss wanted to make sure she got to her car safely without Jason or his friends trying to retaliate. As they watched Poppy walk over to an old Chevy Nova spotted with rust, Alicia approached her just she was about to get in her car.

"Hey Poppy, hold your horses," Alicia said, "I'd like express my appreciation for what you did in there. What kind of artist are you?"

"I paint Minnesota landscapes; I have a couple in my trunk...wanna see them?"

Poppy pulled out two paintings. "They're a diptych—two pictures that together are of my favorite view of Lake Minnetonka. I did them for the Uptown Art Fair, but they didn't sell. I guess I should have taken the $300 offer...I was hoping for $500."

Alicia was impressed by Poppy's impressionist rendering of the beautiful landscape. "Would you sell them to me for $1000?" As Poppy nodded her stunned assent, Alicia waved Moss over. "Steve would you be a dear and load this lovely diptych in our trunk while I settle up with the artist?"

While Moss transferred the artwork to the Ferrari's trunk, Alicia handed Poppy the $1000 she'd won from Jason and gave her a short kiss on the lips.

CHAPTER 61

Haley and the rest of the patients attempted to establish a sense of community and stave off boredom amidst their "royal captivity." Eduard Falcón, with his brother's deference to his doctorate in behavioral psychology, reviewed and approved a variety of classes and activities for the patients. He understood well the duality of mind/body health.

Haley organized an aerobics and strength training class; she also taught a basic gymnastics class. Others, who had specialized skills or knowledge, organized their classes too. Laura Sandberg, a former English teacher, started a poetry writing class; Sherry Shenoy taught yoga; Patti Williams taught an art class; Dave Sanders taught a basic electronics class. All material, including art supplies and electronics kits were provided. The classes were not monitored by the security personnel, who viewed them as a harmless diversion.

Almost all of the class attendees were patients except for one: a tall lean athletic looking man in his late thirties named Andy who had befriended many of them and expressed great sympathy for their loss of freedom. He had earned their trust when he verbalized his hope that they could all one day return home to their family and friends, no matter what it took to accomplish that. He also expressed his sentiment that the Falcón brothers were the embodiment of pure evil. They all assumed Andy was part of the night cleaning crew, as several of them had seen him washing the castle hallway floors late at night. When asked directly why Andy, feeling as he did about their plight, continued to work at the castle, he'd responded with, "I am not here by choice; I can never leave." The patients were aware that many of the workers employed by the Falcón brothers were coerced to do so. They all felt sorry for Andy, who always looked sad; they made a point of being kind to him and encouraged him to attend their classes.

The class Haley liked best was a philosophy class taught by former Stanford professor Adam DuBois, who had been cured of his early-stage Alzheimer's disease. Their current situation, along with all the bad things that had happened to them, starting with their kidnappings, were difficult for a lot of the group— particularly the devoutly religious folks—to put in to perspective. One day Pete Hubbard, who had been cured of his type 1 diabetes but had been taken from a loving wife, three daughters and a great career as a geologist, asked a poignant question in a class on the existence and nature of God: "Why would a kind and loving God permit this to happen to us? Why aren't our prayers answered?"

Professor DuBois thought carefully before answering: "Pete, I personally am a freethinker, one who forms opinions on the basis of reason independently of authority or religious dogma, so that means I try to make sense of the world without reliance on an anthropomorphic omnipotent and omniscient god. I believe life is like a sailing ship; we are at the rudder and can set our sails in a multitude of ways, but we can control neither the tides nor the winds. While we can plan our journeys and destinations, we have to cope with the weather the best we can. Occasionally, our rudders may break and our sails may tear; perhaps we may hit a reef and get shipwrecked. Even a sea monster may arise and confront us on occasion. What can we do? We can pray, but we must remember God, whatever His true nature may be, is not a direct giver of gifts on request; if He were, don't you think God would have answered the prayers made by those poor souls in the Auschwitz concentration camp during World War II who were subjected to multiple horrors perpetrated by Dr. Mengele, the Falcón brothers' grandfather?

God may give us the strength to repair our rudders and mend our sails, but He won't do it for us. Events occur in all of our lives that we perceive as negative or even horrible relative to ourselves or our loved ones at the time they happen; however, we as mere mortal humans cannot fathom the ultimate good those events may have triggered, either for ourselves or, perhaps for people we don't even know.

We must craft our own destinies the best that we can, and play the best hand possible with the cards life deals us. If there is a way out of our captivity, we must figure it out for ourselves."

Pete became visibly agitated and literally bellowed: "You think there is a way out of here? Are you delusional? This place is more secure than San Quentin! I know you were out there the day that poor deer stepped on a mine and got blown to smithereens. Unless we can sprout wings and fly we are not ever getting out of here! We'll never be rescued either; everyone probably thinks we're dead!"

In stark contrast to Pete's outburst, Haley spoke in a calm even tone. "I'm not sure Pete is entirely correct about needing wings to get out of here. Last week a few of us went exploring and discovered an old passageway in the lowest level of the castle. It was partially blocked by rubble. Since we were curious about where it might lead, we cleared a small opening through which we crawled. We didn't go far, since we didn't have our flashlights with us and we were concerned about getting lost. But we went far enough to discover that the castle is built upon what appears to be a network of caverns."

Andy, who had been quietly listening, finally spoke up, "I recall reading a long time ago that some castles had secret routes to safety to escape from invading enemies. Maybe there is a way down to the beach."

Most of the other class members got excited; this was the only ray of sunshine they'd had in a very long time. Pete, however, clung to his dismal outlook. "OK, let's assume you found a way down to the beach. What are you going to do then…swim back to America?"

Professor DuBois was a fabulous logician and worded a series of hypothetical syllogisms: "If we take as a given that there is a way we could get down to the beach undetected by our captors, then we would need a means of contacting someone on the outside. If we could find a means of contacting someone on the outside, then we would have to convince them to help us. If we could convince them to help us, then they'd have to figure out how to get all of us rescued."

"That's an awful lot of ifs, Adam," Pete responded in a tone with a trace of hope in his voice, "but I think we ought to assemble a small exploratory team to see if Andy might be right about there being a route out of here unbeknownst to our captors. As a professional geologist and amateur spelunker, I'll volunteer to lead the team."

Professor DuBois responded with enthusiasm. "That would be great, Pete! Before we actually do that, a word of caution is warranted. As you know, there are a few of our fellow captives who seem to have formed an emotional bond with our captors. We don't know how they might react to the knowledge that we are actively searching for an escape route; we all need to watch what and to whom we say anything about this."

CHAPTER 62

The CIA's spy satellite was travelling at approximately 17,000 mph at an altitude of 150 miles. It was currently taking pictures of Scotland's west coast and transmitting them back to CIA headquarters at Langley. The pictures taken by this satellite had amazing resolution; individual people could be seen.

The request to take these pictures had alerted an informant of the Falcón organization; she covertly relayed this information to her designated contact. The terrorist group Brotherhood of Allah had also infiltrated the CIA; the satellite pictures would make their way surreptitiously to Fahim Al-Firaih, Eduard Falcón's arch enemy.

Jeff Florenzano, whose son Pete had played baseball with Jake Jackson for the Twins, was the CIA senior analyst who had asked for the pictures at Jake's request. Jeff had previously been a covert field operative doing "wet work" which was a euphemism for killing either in self-defense or to assassinate a bad guy as part of a covert operation. The CIA publicly denied that ever engaged in assassinations. He had, during his years as a field operative, acquired the dubious reputation of knowing 100 different ways to kill a man. Jeff was highly intuitive, perhaps even psychic; he could sense dangerous situations and adjust his actions accordingly. Jeff and Jake had shared an apartment with two other students during their college years at Yale. The four of them became lifelong friends.

When Jeff's son Pete became addicted to prescription pain pills following an injury, Jake had arranged and paid for Pete's rehabilitation, even letting Jeff's son live with him until he was well. Jake had effectively shielded Pete's addiction and rehabilitation from the media, preserving his career and reputation.

Jake had asked Jeff to hand pick a small team to investigate the goings on at a castle on the west coast of Scotland. His team had been told by the Scottish government that the castle was a clandestine alcohol and drug rehabilitation center for the rich and famous who did not want the public to find out about their problems. All of the patients had gone through failed rehabilitations previously, and voluntarily paid handsomely for their own incarceration. As Jeff looked at the satellite pictures of the castle estate in front of him, he saw the castle, the stable, an airstrip with a huge hangar, several small buildings, and what appeared to be a large barracks. He was puzzled by the number of uniformed men he saw—surely a rehab facility did not require that much security to keep their patients from leaving. Jeff decided a closer look was justified; he decided that assistance should be requested from Scottish law enforcement.

Jeff's and Jake's old college roommate, Ian McDonald, now headed the Scottish Crime and Drug Enforcement Agency (SCDEA), which is a police agency in Scotland responsible for disrupting and dismantling serious organized crime groups. Ian had been the best man at his wedding, and Jeff trusted Ian completely. He gave Ian a call on a secure line, explained the situation, and asked for Ian's help. Explaining the Falcón organization's deep penetration of law enforcement agencies worldwide, and further explaining that they were the probable kidnappers of Jake Jackson's sister Haley, he stressed that Ian needed to work alone in gathering intelligence about the private drug and alcohol rehabilitation facility called Oceanside Centre. Ian readily agreed.

Two days later, Ian called back. "Jeff, this is a curious situation. I have been monitoring all of the vehicular traffic leaving and entering Oceanside Centre; I've checked all of the license plates."

"Ian, how could you possibly have done that alone? I explained the need for secrecy!"

Ian patiently replied, "I did do it alone." Ian then explained their Automatic Number Plate Recognition (ANPR) system. ANPR is principally designed to be an alert system. ANPR is software which, when fitted to a camera system, can scan and read over three thousand number plates per hour.

Digital images are captured through the ANPR cameras located either in a mobile unit or a fixed site system. The digital image is then converted into data, which is then processed through the ANPR system. The system is able to cross reference the data against a variety of databases including the Police National

Computer and highlights vehicles of interest to police forces. "What is curious is that, while there are a variety of normal deliveries—like food and supplies—there were also three deliveries by armored cars with no company markings on them. The license plates are registered to a company with a fictitious address. I'm puzzled as to why a rehabilitation facility would need anything delivered by armored cars from an apparently phony company. I think closer surveillance might reveal more about what is going on there."

Jeff agreed and, knowing Ian had his own Beechcraft Bonanza, asked if he could do a multi-pass fly-over of the Oceanside Centre estate and shoot videotapes of it. Ian assured Jeff that he could, and would do it the next day.

CHAPTER 63

I an McDonald was unaware that his flight over the Oceanside Centre estate was being monitored from below. The castle's radar operator had first detected the aircraft approaching from the east at a speed of 125 knots and an altitude of 5,000 feet; it was obviously a small plane and he at first ignored it. But when the plane did a 180 degree turn and flew directly over the castle at 3,000 feet his interest was aroused. When the plane again turned and passed over at 2,500 feet, obviously doing some kind of surveillance, the radar operator alerted Eduard Falcón.

As Ian was calmly making a descending turn to the west to make his final videotaping pass over Oceanside Centre estate at 1,500 feet, the Bonanza's engine stopped running abruptly; he immediately tried to restart it, but the aircraft's starter motor would not work. His training kicked in and he quickly scanned his flight instruments. The GPS navigation screen was blank, as were all his other electronic instruments. Ian assessed his situation rapidly and realized he would shortly be over the ocean. He immediately tried his radio to make a mayday call, but the radio was completely dead. Ian had three choices: he could ditch in the ocean, circle back and try to glide to the paved airstrip he'd seen, or try to find a clear stretch on the rocky beach below. His altimeter and airspeed indicators, both non-electrical devices, were still working. As his airspeed dropped, Ian quickly realized he needed to trade altitude for airspeed before the aircraft stalled. This eliminated the option of turning around and making the paved airstrip. Ditching in the ocean would be perilous, and even if he survived the landing, he had not been able to make a distress call on the radio. He'd probably drown, as he'd never replaced the little emergency life raft after accidentally puncturing it a month ago. The only viable option was trying to find a clear stretch on the rocky beach below. As Ian eyed the rocky beach below, he couldn't see any clear stretch long enough for a landing; however, he did see a perfectly smooth stretch that was clear from the ocean up to the ascending cliff wall. The problem was the clear stretch was narrow and appeared to be less than a 100 feet long—too short for a conventional landing.

As Ian was coming to grips with the fact that a crash landing on the rocky beach was imminent, he suddenly recalled reading about an old former navy pilot who lived on a twisting river in North America. He routinely took off and landed on a short stretch of beach. Ian remembered the pilot's explanation: "If you are going fast enough, water is just like pavement."

Well, let's test that theory, Ian thought as he put the Bonanza into a gentle turn, descending and gliding towards the narrow stretch of clear beach. As he calculated his final glide path, Ian tried to picture a runway of normal length ahead of him. Fortunately the water was fairly calm and relatively smooth. At a faster speed than he'd normally land, Ian touched the wheels down on the water and immediately bounced up just as though the ocean were concrete. He quickly recovered control, then gently flared and again touched down. Rather than sinking, the wheels rolled on the water just as though on a runway. Just as the "pavement effect" was waning, the plane's wheels were on the beach. The Bonanza rolled 85 more feet onto the soft sand of the beach, then came to a stop completely intact. At this point, now that the emergency was over, Ian looked down at his shaking hands which had been rock steady during his handling of the dire situation. Ian wondered to himself aloud," What the hell just happened to my airplane?" He flipped open the hand-tooled copper cell phone case his son had made and given him as a birthday present. Ian had riveted it to the cockpit panel. As he called for help, he didn't realize that the only reason the phone worked was because the grounded copper case had shielded it from the electromagnetic pulse weapon aimed as his plane by Eduard Falcón. Ian requested and received a rapid evacuation—he didn't want to be here if an investigative sortie from the castle were launched.

Jeff Florenzano received a phone call on his secure line late in the evening from Ian McDonald. Ian told him about the mysterious engine failure and electronics malfunctions during his video surveillance flight over Oceanside Centre. "Jeff," Ian explained, "once we got my plane off the beach and investigated the engine, radio, video camera and avionics, we discovered everything electrical on the Bonanza was totally fried—as though I had flown through an electromagnetic pulse generated by a nuclear blast…the CAA inspector was flummoxed!" The Civil Aviation Authority (CAA) is the UK's independent specialist aviation regulator. Its activities include economic regulation, airspace policy, and safety regulation.

"Ian, exactly when did this happen? What specifically were you doing at the time everything went to hell in a hand basket?" Jeff asked.

"I was executing a series of descending turns with the video camera on. Everything quit working just as I passed over the castle heading west." Ian then explained the harrowing landing he'd made, including a description of how he'd used the water as a virtual runway. Jeff, Jake and Ian had all taken flying lessons during their college days at Yale. After much prodding, their fourth roommate Ross Ericson did too, but only after the others all agreed to take scuba diving lessons with him. Ross had gone on to earn a PhD in physics at MIT and eventually became a physics professor at Stanford. All four of the roommates were brilliant and logical men. They had been some of Yale's best debaters. The Yale Debate Association (YDA) is the most successful college debate team in the United States. Together, they led the YDA to win the American Parliamentary Debate Association's Team of the Year award. The approaches to thinking and analysis they mastered in debate carried over into many of their other life endeavors.

Ian was a natural born pilot, and had mastered flying much faster than Jeff, Ross and Jake. After Jeff, Ross and Jake had gotten their private pilot licenses, Ian had gone on to get many additional ratings. He had accumulated glider, instrument, multi-engine and helicopter ratings. Upon graduation, Ian went back to Scotland and enlisted in the Royal Air Force (RAF) where he eventually became an AV-8B pilot. The McDonnell Douglas AV-8B Harrier II is a family of second-generation vertical/short takeoff and landing or ground-attack aircraft. Ian was currently a pilot in the RAF Reserves.

"Christ almighty, Ian, I don't believe I could have pulled that landing off, and I don't know any other pilots who could either! The electrical damage to your Bonanza is totally weird. I've never heard of anything like it, especially since everything electrical failed simultaneously."

"I've never heard of anything like it either," Ian agreed. "I think I'd like to get Ross Ericson over here to look at all of the electronics that failed; as a physicist he might be able to come up with a reasonable theory. Would you like to join us?"

"Good idea...maybe I can get Jake to come too and we'll make it a reunion—maybe we can get some scuba diving in!"

The four college friends had all become proficient divers, and had explored many reefs and sunken ships together over the years during vacations, and were grateful to Ross for getting them to take scuba lessons. Jake's sister Haley and daughter Katie, had learned to scuba dive, and often joined the four friends on their diving adventure vacations.

"I'll call Jake and Ross tomorrow to set it up," Ian said.

CHAPTER 64

Pete Hubbard had cautiously solicited his fellow captives for volunteers to explore the caverns beneath the castle. He'd assembled a team of four, which included him, Adam DuBois, Sherry Shenoy and Haley Jackson. They would attempt to find a route through the caverns down to the beach below. Pete prayed that Haley was right about the ancient builders of the castle desiring an escape route. So far, the team had made three clandestine explorations only to discover the network of caverns was extensive and maze-like.

The team now possessed some dangerous knowledge about the castle's defenses. Laura Sandberg had struck up an ersatz romance with one of the senior security staff members named Dale Vandermeer. He had bragged to Laura about how the castle was virtually impenetrable. Dale's braggadocio extended to describing to her the EMP weapons, as well as the radio and cell phone jammers that made electronic communication in the castle environs impossible. Dale laughed hard when he told Laura about the patients' behavior when they unknowingly had been test subjects for "Discombobulator Supremo." She was surprised when Dale immediately apologized, and revealed a deep sympathy for all that the patients had been through.

Laura had verified Dale's claim about the jammer, as she had found a cell phone lost by one of the kitchen staff and kept it. When she tried it, all she got was a popping and humming noise. After sharing this knowledge with the others, a decision was made that the team should take the cell phone with them in case they found an escape route.

As a seasoned spelunker, Pete was careful to not get the team lost, and kept copious notes and maps. The corridor that led to the caverns split into five different routes; today the team was going to explore the fourth one. As soon as they began, with all of their flashlights on, Sherry Shenoy shouted excitedly, "Hey, look over there!" In the beam of her flashlight was what looked like an golden brick protruding slightly from the cavern floor; a few feet ahead of it was another golden brick, and then another. As the team advanced, Haley spoke up.

"I think this might be it!"

Pete, who was skeptical about finding an escape route, had a surge of hope. "Let's follow the yellow brick road!"

As the team proceeded, they found the golden bricks embedded in the floor every few feet; clearly they marked a descending path. They continued to follow it cautiously through a multitude of twists and turns, with Pete leading the way. He stopped abruptly as his flashlight shined upon a skeleton lying on the floor ahead of them; as they tentatively approached it, Sherry gasped, "Look at the skull!"

Atop the skull was a heavily jeweled crown. The cause of death was apparent, as an arrow protruded from between the skeleton's ribs. "Say hello to King Andrew, I believe," Haley said. "According to one of the books I read on the castle's history, a powerful clan chieftain, whose people proclaimed as their King, Andrew mysteriously disappeared early in the 13th century during an attack on the castle. It appears that he was wounded and trying to get to safety." The others were silent; the violent history of their environment was graphically on display in front of them, and the true antiquity of the place was sinking in.

"I think this further verifies that there is a route out of here," Pete added somberly. Let's continue following the golden bricks, but we should proceed slowly and cautiously, as there may be booby traps ahead."

"Pete, why would there be booby traps on an escape route?" Sherry Shenoy asked.

Adam DuBois, seeing the logic behind Pete's warning, answered for him. "Think about it, Sherry, if you were trying to escape from the castle, but attackers were in hot pursuit, how could you ensure the attackers' demise?"

Sherry grinned as she figured it out. "You'd have one or more fatal booby traps along your escape route that only you knew how to avoid." The others nodded in collective understanding. With Pete in the lead, the group cautiously moved ahead. His warning had been prophetic; Pete abruptly stopped just as the marked path took a sharp turn to the left, entering a huge cavern.

"What's wrong, Pete?" Haley asked.

"Look at the floor," Pete responded. "The spacing between the golden bricks has changed."

While the previous markers had been several feet apart, the golden bricks were now laid out in an end-to-end continuous row for the next 10 feet or so. Pete got down on his knees and struck the cavern floor hard with a hammer blow just to the left of where the end-to-end continuous row of golden bricks began; visible fractures in the floor appeared. Pete struck the same spot again, only harder. The floor in that spot shattered, revealing a hole that, when he shined his flashlight in it, appeared to be about 100 feet deep. Pete struck again on the right side of the bricks; visible fractures in the floor appeared again. With a second blow, the floor caved in, revealing the same dark chasm. Pete then struck the row of golden bricks, which remained intact. With a second blow, the only result was an aching hand.

"It is time for an experiment. Let's go find some heavy rocks to throw on the floor," Adam suggested, "I suspect the row of golden bricks denotes solid footing, and the sides of the path are thin rock that would cave in were someone to run or walk across it. We'll find out."

The experiment proved Adam's theory to be correct. After throwing a number of heavy stones, most of the cavern floor around the path had shattered, revealing a deep 10 foot wide chasm on both sides; the continuous row of golden bricks could now be seen to be resting atop an extremely narrow ridge. A step off that ridge would lead to a fatal fall. Stones thrown on the path past the ridge indicated that solid footing resumed once the chasm was crossed.

"I believe King Andrew must have practiced elsewhere extensively to develop the exceptional balance required to step across that chasm. Only one of us has the skill to proceed further," Pete declared while looking directly at Haley.

"Are you willing to go forward alone, Haley?" Adam asked.

Haley took only seconds to decide. She put out her hand and said "Give me the cell phone. If I get out, I'll try to call for help. Wait here for an hour—if I'm not back by then it means I got out or I'm dead."

"If you don't come back, they'll wonder where you are," Sherry noted. "What should we tell them?"

Pete grinned wryly, "We'll tell them we discovered the caverns and that Haley fell down that one seemingly bottomless chasm we nearly all fell in to yesterday."

Adam reflected on that idea for a moment and said, "We'd be taking a huge risk telling them that. First, they'd want to know when we discovered the caverns, and why we did not report our discovery…they may think we were trying to escape, and we all know the penalty for that. Second, we have no idea how far they'd go in trying to recover Haley's body. Third, once they see the caverns, they may launch their own explorations. Sooner or later, they'd find the golden brick path; our secret escape route would be blown."

Haley spoke up quickly. "Adam is correct, I believe. Even if I can find the way out without encountering a fatal booby trap, I'll have to come back. With luck, I can get out and far enough away from that jammer to make a call for help."

"Who could you possibly call?" Sherry asked. "We are in Scotland, not America—we don't know anyone here!"

"Actually, I know exactly who to call," Haley retorted. "Ian McDonald, my brother's old college roommate, heads the Scottish Crime and Drug Enforcement Agency. We used to go on scuba diving vacations with him. So wait for me." With that parting comment, Haley put the plastic bag containing the cell phone in her pocket, and stepped on to the golden "balance beam." In her best attempt at an Arnold Schwarzenegger impression, she said, "I'll be back."

Once Haley had crossed the chasm, she proceeded cautiously, following the golden brick path; the normal spacing between the bricks had resumed for a while, and once again changed to a continuous row of bricks, this time to the far left. As she stepped on to the first brick of the continuous row, Haley felt it shift downwards under her weight; she stood very still, waiting to see what would happen. More than a dozen sharp metal spikes sprang up forcefully from the center of the path, which would have impaled anyone in hot pursuit. Haley edged carefully past the spikes. She followed the path for another 500 yards, where it ended not at the beach, but at a glistening pool of water. Haley listened carefully, and thought she could hear the unmistakable sound of surf pounding on the beach. Maybe there was an underwater way to the beach. To test that hypothesis, she took out the plastic bag containing the cell phone and tied what she hoped was a waterproof knot. Haley took several deep breaths, and a final huge one; she the leapt into the pool. The water was extraordinarily clear, but she couldn't see any obvious exit as she looked from side to side. Just as she was losing hope of finding a way out, Haley looked straight down and saw a large opening about six feet beneath her. She surfaced and again took several deep breaths, and a final huge one. She did a surface dive and swam down to the large opening; she could see it transitioned immediately to a short horizontal tunnel. Haley swam through the short tunnel and saw the sunlit surface of the ocean above her. When she surfaced a small wave caught her and washed her gently onto the beach.

CHAPTER 65

Haley hoped that she was out of the range of the castle's jammer. She held her breath as she turned the cell phone on...a dial tone!

It was late in the afternoon when Ian McDonald's office phone rang. When he answered, it he nearly fell out of his chair when he heard Haley's voice. "Ian, This is Haley Jackson...I need to speak quickly because I don't know how long this cell phone's battery will last, so please just listen." Ian agreed to listen and immediately began recording the call.

Haley quickly explained that she and a large number of other kidnapping victims had been unwillingly subjected to experimental stem cell procedures, and 101 of them were now captives at Oceanside Centre. She explained her temporary escape through the caverns, and why she needed to return to the castle before her captors noted her disappearance. Haley asked Ian to contact her brother and tell him that not only was she well, but that she was no longer a paraplegic. She outlined the little she knew about the castle's defenses and three EMP weapons, especially the effects of the "Discombobulator Supremo" she had personally experienced. She cautioned him that ammunition and combustible fuel would explode if the third weapon were activated.

Just as she was going to ask Ian if he knew anything about the murders of Steve, Thomas and Alicia, the cell phone's battery gave out.

Ian was stunned as he played back the recording of the call; he now knew why his Bonanza's electronics had failed—it had been the target of an EMP weapon the military only dreamed about! He quickly arranged a secure conference call to Jeff Florenzano, Jake Jackson, and Ross Ericson...presently the only people he positively knew he could trust. Given the extraordinary weapons at Oceanside Centre and the fact that there were potential hostages, unconventional means would be required to conduct a rescue mission.

Once the four men were on the phone, Ian began: "I have incredible news! I spoke less than an hour ago with Haley Jackson, who is alive and well, although still a captive of the Falcón organization. She gave me a brief encapsulation of the situation."

Luke and Jake were nearly overcome with emotion. Luke said, "Ian, how was she able to call you if she is still a captive?"

Ian replied, "Hear it for yourselves; I recorded the call."

After the short recording finished playing, Ross Ericson spoke first. "Luke and Jake, I am thrilled that Haley is alive and well. My wife Noreen and I had feared for the worst for your sister. That said, as a physicist, I am amazed at the science behind the EMP weapons Haley described."

"My Bonanza was the target of a powerful EMP burst that took out my engine and electronics," Ian said. "I'm pretty sure it came from the castle." He quickly retold the story of his harrowing, albeit successful, landing. Ian paused for a bit in deep thought, and then continued. "I don't believe we can launch a conventional rescue assault on the castle for four reasons: First, they apparently have sophisticated weaponry unlike anything we've encountered before. Second, the minute they know we're coming, the patients would be used as hostages. Third, since we now know the Falcón organization has eyes and ears everywhere—even in the military—we would hardly be able to secretly plan and organize a rescue mission. Fourth, firearms and assault vehicles can't be used because they'd explode! We can only execute a rescue operation with people we trust completely!"

Jake was still trying to absorb the fact that his and Luke's sister was alive and well. "Why don't the four of us meet in my home as soon as possible? There are five other men besides us I trust to bring in on this, all with military experience, who we can include in the planning and execution of a rescue operation." Jake went on to explain that Steve Moss, who they all knew, and a Dr. Thomas Jefferson Hunt, a former United States Marine officer, had been captives of the Falcón organization. He further explained that, after their escape, a huge bounty had been put on their heads. They were now living in his home under new identities, and the Falcón organization believed them to be dead.

"So we four, Steve and Dr. Hunt, but who are the other three men?" Ian asked.

"Reliable men you all know: Chris Meyer, my majordomo, who is a former Navy SEAL, Scott Wroblewski, director of the FBI, and my brother Luke Jackson, director of the NSA." Jake answered. "Do you all think you could come to Minnesota this coming weekend?"

CHAPTER 66

I t was a beautiful April evening on Lake Minnetonka. Moss was as thrilled as Jake to learn that Haley was alive and well. Moss had previously revealed to Jake his love for his sister, so Moss was the first person he told after the conference call with Ian McDonald. Luke Jackson, Jeff Florenzano, Ross Ericson, Ian and Scott Wroblewski had all flown in to the Twin Cities for a rescue strategy meeting with Jake, Sally Peters, Chris Meyer, Thomas and Moss.

Thomas and Moss asked Scott Wroblewski if they could speak with him briefly. They told him the story of their encounter with FBI agent Rodrigo Gomez at the Toronto airport and how his death had not been an accident. Scott admitted he knew the FBI had been infiltrated by the Falcón organization, but there was little he could do about it.

After cocktails and an hour of all of them getting reacquainted, they sat down for dinner. They were at the moment all seated at the massive dining room table. Alicia had prepared for them a wonderful meal of grilled walleye (which Thomas and Moss had caught) and a delicious casserole made with Minnesota wild rice, which they had just finished.

Jake, who was the host, began their serious discussion about planning and executing a rescue operation. "This situation, as you all know, is extraordinarily complex. The Falcón organization is possibly the most sophisticated and insidious criminal hegemony in modern history. It used to be said that the sun never sets on the British Empire—that can now be said of the Falcón global operations. They have successfully infiltrated governments, law enforcement agencies, courts, and even militaries around the world. Now we know that they are in possession of weaponry seemingly out of a science fiction novel. That means

Oceanside Centre is virtually unassailable by conventional means without jeopardizing the people we need to rescue. Our small group here needs unique 'outside of the box' plans if we want to have any chance of rescuing the captives."

Luke Jackson added, "Because the Falcón organization uses perhaps the most sophisticated encryption, computers and communications techniques in the world, our government knows less about them than we know about any country in the world...meaning we have very little to go on. Let's discuss our options and do some brainstorming."

Sally, who had worked with him for a long time, interjected, "Luke is right about how little we actually know about the far-reaching operations of the Falcón organization. When I was working for NSA, some of our top cryptographers were lured away to the private sector by a company we later learned was controlled by the Falcón organization. Even I interviewed with them. I was offered nearly triple my NSA salary, incredible benefits and five weeks of vacation. I nearly accepted their offer."

Jake asked, "Why didn't you take their offer, Judy?"

Luke was flattered by her answer. "Because, Jake, your brother was the greatest boss in the world—next to you of course; my loyalty to him and my country were not for sale."

Luke's career had begun in the Army Security Agency where he'd been a Korean linguist. He had risen to the rank of general. Luke and Moss shared a strong interest and background in Soo Bahk Do. Luke had studied under some of the Korean Masters, and was a seventh dan.

During the brief time Moss had been stationed on the east coast, Luke and he were occasional sparring partners...practicing both Soo Bahk Do and Kendo. Kendo, is a modern Japanese martial art of sword-fighting based on traditional Japanese swordsmanship, which both of them had studied for many years. As with many serious martial artists, they both had experience in a variety of other self defense forms and styles.

"Before we begin our brainstorming, I'd like to ask Alicia, who worked with Dr. Falcón for a long time, to tell us what she knows about the Falcón brothers," Moss said. "Alicia, I know this will be a repeat of your debriefing by Sally, but kindly indulge us."

Alicia had not talked (other than her earlier debriefing) about the Falcón brothers, FHRI, or their escape for the past two years. But for the next hour,

Alicia told them everything she could recall. She explained that each of the brothers was a genius. However, while Dr. Nicolas Falcón, with a PhD in genetics in addition to his MD, was merely a sociopath and megalomaniac, his brother Eduard was a bona fide psychopathic manipulator and sadist made more dangerous by his PhD in behavioral psychology. "If there is a way to motivate, frighten or intimidate someone, Eduard knows how to do it!" She further explained PraxMed's relationship with the Falcón Hospital and Research Institute, and how going directly to the human trials would have allowed them to leapfrog the competition in stem cell research, treatments, and pharmaceuticals. Alicia stunned all of them when she revealed that, in preceding years, 187 patients (from an earlier round of kidnappings in western Europe) had died as a result of the PraxMed's and the Falcón Hospital and Research Institute's illegal experimentation.

Alicia's narrative concluded with the fact that Eduard Falcón was a sadistic torturer skilled in multiple martial arts. Prior to being paralyzed by a bullet, he had slowly beaten several enemies to death with his bare hands. At this revelation, Luke and Moss exchanged somber glances.

Three hours later they had a rough plan in place. Jake, Scott and Luke would brief the president on the situation. Ian would brief the prime minister. Ross would research possible counter measures to the unique electro-magnetic pulse weapons at Oceanside Centre. Thomas would consult with Ross on a neurological defense against the "Discombobulator Supremo" device. And, last but not least, Moss would plan the actual rescue operation.

CHAPTER 67

Fahim Al-Firaih had decided the time was right for the Brotherhood of Allah to strike a death blow to the Falcón organization. He had learned that global operations for the Falcón organization were being orchestrated out of Ocean Centre on the west coast of Scotland. He had an informant who believed that not only was Eduard Falcón residing in the castle, but that his entire fortune was stored there as well. The highly paid informant, who worked as a grounds keeper, had advised Al-Firaih about the mine field surrounding the entire estate. The informant had further advised him that the mines on the approach road could be switched off by special remote control devices to enable authorized traffic to and from the estate; the informant could gain possession of one of those remote controls. Of great convenience was the fact that the hangar that Al-Firaih had seen on the spy satellite photo contained a Boeing 737—perfect for transporting his men and the Falcón fortune out of the country! Two of his men were pilots; he'd made sure they had gotten 737 training prior to the mission. One thing the informant told him puzzled Al-Firaih: the Falcón security forces regularly conducted military drills on horseback wearing armor and carrying swords, lances and crossbows! He assumed these exercises were benign, and for the amusement of the eccentric Eduard Falcón. As a mere grounds keeper, the informant was unaware of the three EMP devices.

Al-Firaih meticulously planned a strike that he would personally lead; he desperately wanted to kill Eduard Falcón himself. 200 of his finest men—highly trained ex-military soldiers who sold their services to the highest bidder—would parachute onto the estate. Each man would be heavily armed, and each would have enough explosives to blast open any kind of vault securing the

Falcón billions. The two aircraft delivering them would never come within 20 miles of Ocean Centre; they would be flying over international waters.

The assault forces would be using black HiGlide parachutes and would bail out just before dawn using oxygen systems at an altitude of 32,000 feet—over six miles high. The HiGlide free-fall ram-air parachute system is designed for use in mission-specific applications. With a 6:1 glide ratio, the HiGlide canopy has the highest glide ratio of any military parachute in the world.

Each man's descent would be guided automatically by a GPS system to coordinates precisely inside the outer wall of the castle. Timed to coincide with the landing of the parachutists—five armored Al Fahd vehicles would arrive at the entry road to Ocean Centre. These vehicles were equipped with a turret on which 105 mm low recoil weapons were installed. The driver's stations were equipped with a suite of day and night vision periscopes. Al-Firaih himself would be in the lead vehicle; he would blast open the gates to the castle himself. The grounds keeper would signal with a flashlight indicating that he'd switched off the mines under the road. The outer massive gate to the castle would be blown down; Al-Firaih planned to make short work of the defending forces, find Eduard Falcón, and personally behead him in front of his own men. Eduard Falcón had insulted Al-Firaih years ago by stealing many of his organization's most profitable drug dealers by selling to them at less than his own cost...it was time to get even!

CHAPTER 68

E duard Falcón awoke to the furious pounding on his door. As he arose, he glanced at his clock—it was only 4:15 AM! The guard (wearing a full suit of copper armor) at the door excitedly explained that paratroopers were seen descending towards the castle; they had apparently come from high flying aircraft detected by the castle's radar. Eduard gave the order to immediately sound the alarm indicating that the "Discombobulator Supremo" device was about to be switched on; the patients had all been warned to immediately lie down if they ever heard this alarm. He quickly donned his own copper armor and made his way to the massive courtyard as the alarm began blaring. One of his men handed him a pair of night-vision binoculars and pointed to dots on the horizon. As Eduard gazed skywards with the binoculars, he saw dozens of parachutes unmistakably gliding towards the castle; he issued orders for all the castle's weapons containing gunpowder to be stored in their copper clad cases; all the estate's vehicles were kept in garages with copper shielding. When the head of his security forces assured him that the weapons were now all protected, Eduard ordered the EMP device which caused fuel and explosive materials to detonate to be turned on; it required several minutes to charge up. If necessary, Eduard could by a remote control discharge the device—instantaneously unleashing the destructive pulse. He further ordered that the horses be garbed in their protective armor and that the men mount up with their weapons.

"I don't believe these are military or law enforcement people...I think this invasion is from one of our rival organizations," the head of security forces surmised to Eduard.

As the first of the parachutists landed, their feet went out from under them as they hit the ground; they were now within range of the "Discombobulator Supremo" device and would suffer from confusion and lack of coordination. Even though Eduard saw the men were all armed and had packs strapped to their chests, he did not yet trigger the EMP device which caused fuel and explosive materials to detonate—the invaders would be too confused and uncoordinated to use their weapons. Eduard speculated correctly that there would be another component to this invasion. Dawn was breaking; his mounted men were laughing and pointing in amusement at the floundering "invasion force" on the ground before them, the main gate to the castle was suddenly blown inwards.

Five armored Al Fahd vehicles came roaring into the courtyard. As Al-Firaih looked through the lead vehicle's periscope, he was stunned at what he saw. His highly paid mercenaries were wandering and stumbling aimlessly about; a mounted force of men in armor was before him. Al-Firaih was suddenly confused—he could not remember why he was even here and why he was confined in the tight quarters of this uncomfortable vehicle. He clumsily got out and tripped immediately, falling on his face to the ground.

Eduard gave a command. His mounted men advanced on the defenseless paratroopers and systematically cut them to pieces before Al-Faraih's eyes. Eduard then ordered his men to pick Al-Firaih up off the ground and bring him over. Eduard then ordered the "Discombobulator Supremo" device to be turned off. The look of confusion on Al-Faraih's face was replaced by one of horror as he realized the carnage before his was the remnants of his own men.

Before the men in the five armored Al Fahd vehicles could fully regain their mental faculties, Eduard looked into Al-Faraih's eyes and spoke harshly: "Al-Firaih, you were an idiot to think you could attack me successfully. Before you die, behold what your foolishness has wrought!"

Eduard held up his hand in a silent command to his men; they quickly trotted their horses to the far side of the courtyard. Eduard easily shoved Al-Firaih over to where his men were. "Now watch this, you fucking camel jockey!" Eduard triggered the EMP device which caused fuel and explosive materials to detonate. The paratroopers, all of whom carried explosives in their packs, were blown to bits. He then drew his enemy's own sword and with a mighty stroke beheaded Fahim Al-Firaih. It took an entire week to clean the magnificent courtyard of the human gore.

CHAPTER 69

Mike Pellizari, CEO of PraxMed, was not a happy man. First came his failed plot to blow up FHRI, and for the past two years, PraxMed's stock price had been falling steadily. This was largely due to his announcement to the press that, contrary to their earlier position, PraxMed was withdrawing from stem cell research completely for "ethical reasons"; he had offered no further explanations. Next, his wife divorced him; he was now making exorbitant alimony payments. Pellizari was also greatly concerned for his life.

Ted Mallick had left PraxMed immediately following the botched attempt to blow up FHRI. As a "life insurance policy" he had told Pellizari he had been recording their conversations for years; a third party was now in possession of those recordings with instructions to take them public should Mallick die for any reason. He also told Pellizari he had sent Eduard Falcón the recording of Pellizari's orders to destroy FHRI. Mallick had demanded and received a huge severance package—large enough that he would never have to work again. He then purchased the best new identity money could buy and left the country.

Pellizari was now living alone in his penthouse overlooking Central Park. The only access to the penthouse was by his private elevator, which had a battery backup power supply. All of the windows had been replaced with bulletproof glass, and his security system was state-of-the art. Eileen, his assistant and bodyguard, lived next to him in her own elegant suite paid for by Pellizari. He could beckon her at a moment's notice via silent alarm, and she would enter his penthouse by a secret passageway, which contained a wide assortment of firepower from which Eileen could choose.

Late in the evening Pellizari's phone rang shortly after the building's fire alarm went off. The man identified himself as the building's security officer calling from the lobby. "Sir, there is a gas leak in the building; we need everyone to evacuate the premises immediately." Pellizari did not recognize the voice, and he knew the building's security officer Gene Williams well.

"You are not Gene Williams…who is this?" Pellizari demanded. The phone went dead. When he tried to call the lobby, he could not get a dial tone. He immediately pulled out his cell phone and called 9-1-1. All he heard were the sounds generated by a jammer. A panicking Pellizari, who could now smell the gas, activated the silent alarm to Eileen next door. It was a fruitless move, as Eileen lay dead on her kitchen floor with a high caliber armor-piercing sniper's bullet in her brain. When she did not respond, Pellizari decided he better get out now. He got in to his elevator and hit the button for the lobby…the elevator did not respond! The smell of natural gas was now unmistakable. The cell phone in his pocket rang—maybe it was working now! When he answered, he heard the unique sound of Eduard Falcón's voice: "Goodbye cocksucker, you traitorous asshole. You never should have gone against me. I promise you the same means of death you attempted to inflict on my brother and me." Less than 30 seconds later, Pellizari would have been incinerated as the otherwise evacuated building erupted in a gigantic fireball. However, Pellizari was no idiot when it came to self preservation; he opened the elevator door with its manual latch and ran down the hall to his fireproof safe room and sealed himself in with only seconds to spare. Pellizari knew that Eduard Falcón always tried to keep his promises, and Eduard always tried to get even…if he survived this, he would take extraordinary steps to protect himself; surely Eduard would try to kill him again.

CHAPTER 70

The French Riviera is a beautiful place, and was the current residence of Ted Mallick. He was relaxing in a lounge chair on the beach overlooking the Bay of Cannes. He was currently living in the most expensive luxury hotel in Cannes. He was watching teenage girls parasailing, and gleefully reading the newspaper's headline: "PraxMed CEO Pellizari Narrowly Escapes Death in Building Explosion." After leaving PraxMed, he made a rule to move every 60 days. Mallick had "negotiated" a $10,000,000 "severance package" and left the country. He was nervous at first, but two years of living high on the hog, with no signs of retribution from PraxMed or the Falcón brothers, had lulled him into a feeling of relative safety. With Pellizari's near death—surely orchestrated by Eduard Falcón, he wrongly believed the retribution for the failed attempt to blow up FHRI was complete. Mallick knew Eduard would eventually get Pellizari.

A super attractive busty blonde plopped down in the lounge chair next to Mallick. "This chair's not taken?" she asked with what he guessed was a German accent.

"*Nein, Fraulein*…it's all yours," he answered with a big smile. "Are you here on holiday like me?"

She smiled back and replied, "No, unfortunately, I am here on a work assignment for just one day, and then I have to fly back to Berlin." She was quiet after that, and began reading a magazine. Mallick gazed surreptitiously at her gorgeous long legs, and, breaking one of his own self-imposed survival rules— beware of beautiful women who approach him—tried to engage the woman in conversation. Being a vagabond meant that he was never in one locale long enough to form relationships, and, as he detested the idea of paying for sex, Mallick hadn't gotten laid in a long time.

She told him she was a journalist covering the upcoming Cannes film festival. The woman, who introduced herself as Anna Lupke, explained it is one of the world's oldest, most influential and prestigious international film festivals alongside Venice and Berlin. Her story's spin was to be how Berlin's is actually the best festival of the three.

Mallick was a huge film fan, and they spent the next hour discussing the best films of all time. He had introduced himself as Tony Emerson, a hedge fund manager from New York. With the dinner hour approaching, Anna thanked him for the interesting conversation, and then she got up to leave. Mallick threw caution to the wind and said, "Anna, wait! I haven't enjoyed a conversation this much in a very long time. Would you consider continuing it over dinner? It would be my treat, of course!"

She paused, as though she wasn't sure she should go to dinner with a man she'd just met. Then Anna smiled brightly and answered, "I'd like that a lot, Tony! Let me go shower and change. Could I meet you at the hotel's main restaurant on the ground floor in an hour? Perhaps afterwards we could go to my room for 'dessert'?" She winked at him, then turned and walked away.

CHAPTER 71

Mallick could barely contain his excitement. He was definitely going to get lucky tonight! He'd put three condoms in his wallet after showering and shaving. He dressed in an elegant cream colored silk suit and went down to the restaurant. He waited 15 minutes for Anna, worrying that she may have had second thoughts and might not show up for dinner with him after all.

Just as he stood up, disappointed and intending to leave, Anna walked in. She was elegantly dressed in what must have been a horrendously expensive designer gown in a pale yellow. Her hair was worn up—she looked like an actress arriving at the Academy Awards. Heads turned as she walked elegantly over to Mallick, and he swallowed hard. She pecked him quickly on the cheek and said, "You certainly clean up well, Tony... I'm starving—let's eat!"

They enjoyed a lovely dinner of grilled beef tenderloin and a medley of in-season vegetables; when the sommelier came to their table, Mallick, wanting desperately to impress this gorgeous woman, inquired if they had a bottle of Chateau Mouton Rothschild Pauillac 1986 in their wine cellar. Anna smiled radiantly, recognizing Mallick's request was for a very fine, albeit extremely expensive, wine. The sommelier, knowing that this particular wine cost nearly $600 a bottle, said that he would go check. If he were out to dinner with a woman as beautiful as this man's date, he would want to impress her too.

Their table had a glorious view of the sea. Towards the end of dinner, Anna excused herself to go to the restroom, taking her purse with her. On her return, she handed her purse to Mallick and said simply, "Look inside, Tony." Puzzled, he opened her purse to look. There were her panties, which she had apparently removed in the restroom." Now, drop your napkin under the table and go down to pick it up," she commanded. He did as he was told; while he was under the table, Anna spread her legs wide giving Mallick an unfettered view of her recent Brazilian wax job. He was blushing as he sat back up. "Now finish your wine and let's hurry back to my room for our 'dessert'!" Mallick finished his wine in a single gulp, registering an odd taste. They got the check and he paid in cash, leaving a generous tip.

***

Eduard Falcón hated Ted Mallick for two reasons: First, he had, at Mike Pellizari's direction, orchestrated the failed attempt to blow up FHRI; Second, Mallick had once, while drunk, raped and sodomized a woman who was Eduard's second cousin. He had escaped prosecution by threatening to have her husband, who was an illegal alien, deported.

It had taken the Falcón organization a long time to find the elusive Mallick, but finally he had been spotted checking into a French luxury hotel. He regretted that he'd promised Mallick his life, but he had something special in mind for him that the sadistic Eduard would enjoy more than killing him.

Mallick awoke sometime later with a pounding headache. When he tried to rub his head, he discovered his hands wouldn't move; panicking, he tried to sit up, but could not. He realized he was tied spread-eagle on a bed, with a plastic sheet beneath him. "Anna" was standing next to the bed, pointing a video camera at him. There was a grotesque looking burly man in the room who, upon seeing Mallick waking up held a tablet computer in front of Mallick's face. Eduard Falcón filled the screen. In spite of his fear, Mallick was surprised to see Eduard not in a wheelchair, but standing up and radiating pure hate. "Hello there Ted; I'm sure you thought this evening would turn out differently—I hope you enjoyed your dinner with 'Anna'! Unfortunately, it is the last food you will ever enjoy. As you recall, I promised not to kill you, but there are many ways of living worse than death," Eduard said diabolically. "Human beings have many parts not essential to life…like your eyes and tongue. Did you know a man can live without a stomach? Your digestion will be a little dicey, but nothing that can't be overcome in a nursing home."

Eduard continued, "Your lovely date this evening is actually a former surgeon with an insatiable heroin addiction, and my friend Emil, who is holding the computer, was a surgical nurse who loved to rape invalid men and boys. He also liked to euthanize old women patients. Both of them will be making sure you don't die tonight as they relieve you of your unnecessary parts which include, sadly, your penis and your testicles. You may recall, Ted, that you never paid for raping and sodomizing a woman who happens to be my second cousin.

Before the main event begins though, Emil would like to partake in the joys of your lily white ass. Oh, and a guy doesn't really need arms and legs to survive. You will live, if you want to call it that, a long time, Mallick—but not very happily. While I did promise not to kill you, I will give you the option of swallowing a little pill which will end your life with only fleeting discomfort. The choice is entirely yours to make."

Emil held a capsule out for Mallick to see: "Your decision please?" With tears in his eyes, Mallick nodded his head. Emil put the capsule in Mallick's mouth, and "Anna" gave him a sip of water. In less than a minute, he began convulsing and foaming at the mouth. Then Ted Mallick simply died. Eduard always tried to keep his promises, and Eduard always tried to get even.

***

PraxMed CEO Mike Pellizari, having narrowly escaped death, mistakenly believed his only current fears could be assuaged by beefed up personal security; he did not know Ted Mallick was mailing his attorney a postcard every week. The attorney had copies of all the incriminating documents and recordings Mallick had accumulated. His instructions were explicit: should he ever not receive a postcard for two weeks in a row, all the incriminating documents and recordings involving PraxMed and Mike Pellizari should be turned over to the FBI.

Attorney Jason Miller had been paid by Ted Mallick a huge retainer to basically do nothing. He had been given Mallick's will and a signed confession to his crimes committed while employed by PraxMed and the Falcón brothers along with a large sealed box with a detailed list of its contents. Mallick's instructions to Miller had been simple: should he ever not receive a postcard from Mallick for two weeks in a row, Miller should arrange to have his confession and all the incriminating documents and recordings involving PraxMed and Mike Pellizari should be turned over to the FBI.

Consistently for the past two years Miller had received a postcard from Mallick every week; it had now been three weeks since the last postcard. As he was instructed to do, Miller contacted the FBI and arranged to have the stuff delivered. As Mallick had not required it, Miller did not tell the FBI that the material was sufficient to sink PraxMed and put Mike Pellizari away for life; he just said he was fulfilling the instructions of a client's will. As there didn't appear to be any urgency, no one at the FBI bothered to look at any of the material Miller sent for several weeks.

CHAPTER 72

Haley overjoyed her escape-minded compatriots when she returned from the beach with news of her successful call to Ian McDonald. She told them about how the cell phone's battery had died, but only after she had told Ian about where they were being held and warning him about the castle's defenses. She stressed the need to somehow get their hands on a cell phone charger so she could go back to the beach and call Ian again to consult on whatever rescue mission might get launched.

One day shortly after the call to Ian, Haley, Pete, Sherry and Adam packed a picnic lunch and rode horses to a beautiful spot overlooking the ocean. As Haley was lamenting the fact that a cell phone charger was going to be nearly impossible to get, Sherry's face lit up. "We don't actually need a factory made cell phone charger...I bet Rob Sanders, our resident electrical engineer, could fabricate one for us! They get him any kind of components he wants for his electronics class."

Pete chimed in, "That's a great idea, Sherry! Maybe Rob could fabricate a cell phone charger powered by a small solar panel so it wouldn't have to be plugged in—I saw one of those once." Adam, who had taken Rob Sanders's class, agreed to make the request.

Haley nodded her assent. "We also should ask Laura Sandberg to get more information about the castle's defenses from her 'boyfriend' Dale."

"Any information on possible counter measures against the EMP weapons would be good to have too," Sherry added.

CHAPTER 73

Rob Sanders readily agreed to fabricate a solar powered cell phone charger; he already had all the components he needed. Over the next two weeks, Laura Sandberg elicited voluminous information about the caste's defenses and the workings of the EMP weapons.

Her "boyfriend" Dale Vandermeer, an MIT engineering graduate, loved to show off the depth of his scientific knowledge to Laura. He wasn't quite the jerk she had at first imagined him to be... he was, in fact, a decent and moral man who had early in his career, after serving as an officer for four years in the U.S. Army Criminal Investigation Command (USACIDC), found himself working for the Falcón organization. While Dale was indeed a stereotypical engineer, he was also a kind and gentle soul, and his affection for Laura seemed genuine... and Laura was actually beginning to fall in love with him. Dale was physically very attractive. He had sandy hair, blue eyes, and was about 6'2" tall with the trim and muscular physique of a former athlete who still worked out on a regular basis. Dale was always was well groomed and well dressed.

Dale had begun working for the Falcón organization not for the money or because he was evil, but simply because they possessed the most sophisticated computer and communications technology that he had ever seen. Dale had been recruited by a company named "Next Century Computing" shortly after he had finished his master's degree at MIT; he had no idea that the company that had recruited him was a wholly owned subsidiary of the world's largest criminal organization. They had agreed to postpone his employment until he finished his four year stint in the army.

When he eventually discovered he was working for a criminal organization, Dale had attempted to resign, but was informed in no uncertain terms that his appointment was permanent. Not so subtle threats regarding his personal safety and that of his family were made. As a personal insurance policy, he had over several months secretly copied all of the encrypted files regarding the Falcón organization's global infrastructure and operations. Dale had also located and copied the encrypted files in Dr. Falcón's personal vault containing all of the knowledge and stem cell procedures resulting from the Bogotá experiments. Lastly, Dale had secretly copied encrypted files containing details of the Falcón organization's command, control and communications. Dale kept the DVDs containing all the copied files not in his personal living quarters, but beneath a pile of rubble in an unrestored area of the castle. He told Laura that he one day hoped to escape the clutches of the Falcón organization and bring them down.

Laura decided to trust Dale; he was a potentially invaluable resource. She told him of their planned escape (omitting names and details), and Dale asked if he could go with them. As proof of his sincerity, he told Laura everything he knew about the castle's defenses.

Laura learned from Dale that the castle's security force was composed of men highly skilled in hand-to-hand combat, archery and swordsmanship. They drilled extensively on horseback to hone their riding skills. For immunity to the "Discombobulator Supremo" EMP device, each man was issued fine chain mail and armor made of copper…a personal Faraday cage. The horses had similar protection they could wear.

Laura also learned there was no defense against the EMP weapon that caused fuel and ammunition to explode. This meant any attacking force would be reduced to fighting as the knights of antiquity had. In addition, she learned that the handheld EMP weapon used against vehicles and aircraft had a range of nearly two miles.

***

Once Rob Sanders had fabricated and tested the solar powered cell phone charger, he delivered it to Adam. As the connector plug was unique to the cell phone, Rob dared not request one. His design worked by removing the battery from the phone to charge it. He delivered the device and the cell phone's fully charged battery to Adam, and gave him use instructions. Once Adam gave the battery and charger to Haley, who still had the cell phone, she installed the battery and turned the phone on. It powered up, even though it was not usable until she was outside the range of the castle's jammer. She requested a box lunch for the next day, determined to go back to the beach again for another call to Ian McDonald.

CHAPTER 74

The next morning, Haley rapidly followed the gold path through the caverns; she had the fully charged cell phone and solar charger sealed in plastic bags in her pockets. When she was on the beach, she immediately called Ian to give him the intelligence they'd gathered, including the countermeasure of copper armor to negate the effects of the EMP "Discombobulator Supremo." Haley cried for several minutes after learning that Steve, Alicia and Thomas had not been murdered; they were alive and well, living under new identities with her father! After regaining her composure, Haley explained that one of the patients, an electrical engineer, had fabricated a solar powered cell phone charger, meaning she would be able to call again. She told Ian of the unsuccessful attack on the castle by the Brotherhood of Allah forces. None of the patients had been awake at the time, but they had learned that all three EMP weapons had been used with devastating effectiveness; the patients had witnessed over 200 bodies in the courtyard—these had been disposed of in the castle's crematorium.

Ian, who had not expected Haley to be able to call again, asked her if she could call him back in an hour so he could set up a conference call with her brother Jake, Steve, Tom and whoever else on the rescue team he could round up quickly. "I'm not going anywhere; of course I will call you back—I can hardly wait!"

Ian scrambled and got Steve Moss, Thomas Hunt, Jake and Luke Jackson, Jeff Florenzano, Ross Ericson and Scott Wroblewski on a conference call, telling them only that it was an emergency. When Haley's call came in, Ian said, "Gentlemen, we have one more person joining this call." Ian then patched

Haley in to the conference call. After stating the names of the people on the conference call, Ian smiled broadly and said, "Go ahead, Haley."

They were all incredulous when they realized Haley Jackson was on the phone with them; Luke, Jake and Moss wept with joy; Haley and Moss exchanged endearments, explaining to the others that they were in love.

Haley was excited, albeit nervous, to hear that a rescue operation was in the planning stages...she repeated the story about the thwarted Brotherhood of Allah attack on the castle, and its grisly outcome. She admonished them to use extraordinary care in light of the proven effectiveness of the EMP weapons. Jake inquired about the patients' treatment and living conditions in captivity. They were surprised to hear how well the patients were treated. They were especially pleased to hear that the patients were relatively unguarded and unsupervised; they were pretty much treated as guests at an exclusive resort, although permanent ones. They were even encouraged to explore the lower levels of the castle which had not been restored—which serendipitously led to the discovery of an escape route!

For the next hour Haley told them everything she knew about the castle's layout and defenses. She also explained the countermeasures to the EMP weapons. Haley told them that the castle's defenders were highly trained in archery, swordsmanship and hand-to-hand combat. She reinforced the fact that Eduard Falcón was a psychopath and sadistic killer. Haley expressed little doubt that he would threaten to kill all the patients if the castle were openly attacked.

"There is only one way I can think of to get all of the patients out safely, but it would require a lot of luck and perfect timing." Haley went on to suggest that a small scuba equipped rescue force coming from the ocean could enter the castle by the same route through the caverns from which she had come. Haley said, "I've sometimes woken up just before dawn and gone for a walk. Nearly everyone else is still asleep...there are only a few security people around. That would be the time to get all the patients out." She described the escape route in great detail, including the short "balance beam" stretch over the deep chasms, which she believed would be difficult, if not impossible, for nearly all the patients to traverse safely. "There are over a hundred patients, so you'd have to have a ship right off the coast."

240

"We could stretch and secure a net over that short expanse of the path… not a major problem," Moss interjected. "I am more concerned about getting everyone out without detection. If they discover us before we can get everyone down to the beach, all hell will break loose…especially if they power up their 'Discombobulator Supremo' and the ammunition/fuel exploding EMP device before we are clear of the castle; any firearms we have would be worse than useless…we can't even risk having firearms with us!"

"I've got an idea about that," Ross Ericson said. "We could get fabricated wetsuits interlaced with copper and Kevlar—that would protect us against their 'Discombobulator Supremo' and give us limited protection from swords and arrows; if they employ the ammunition/fuel exploding EMP device, they can't use firearms either."

"We clearly have a lot of planning and logistics to figure out before we can proceed; Haley, sweetheart, can you call us back at this time one week from today?" Moss asked. They all agreed to convene another conference call with Haley next week.

CHAPTER 75

The small team had a lot of work to do before they could launch a rescue operation. Both the president and the prime minister had been briefed on the entire situation. Given the acknowledged deep penetration by the Falcón organization of law enforcement agencies worldwide, they were given authorization to plan and execute a covert mission outside of normal channels.

Getting the military involved was deemed too risky due to the fact that the Falcón organization was known to have highly paid informants in all branches of the service. The president, who had a huge family fortune, offered his 430 foot personal yacht named *Almirante Cochrane*. The yacht was named in honor of the president's ancestor, who had died in combat during the War of the Pacific in the late nineteenth century. The armored frigate *Almirante Cochrane* was a ship of the Chilean Navy on which he had served.

The president's *Almirante Cochrane* would transport them to Scotland and, should the rescue be successful, return the patients to safety. The prime minister would order an aircraft carrier to be cruising 50 miles off the coast of Ocean Centre. A specially shielded AV-8B Harrier was being prepared that would be immune to the EMP weapons. Ian McDonald would be on board the carrier ready to fly an emergency flight should all hell break loose at the castle. The only people going on the mission would be Jake Jackson, his brother Luke, Scott Wroblewski, Ross Ericson, Chris Meyer, Jeff Florenzano, Thomas Hunt and Steve Moss.

Even though they hoped to get all the patients out of Ocean Centre in the dead of night with little or no resistance, Moss had planned for multiple contingencies. As they would be entering the castle through the caverns Haley used

243

to escape, they would approach from the ocean using scuba gear. Anything they brought along would have to be light and small. The little team knew they needed high powered flashlights, a net and pitons to secure it for spanning the chasm crossing in the caverns. They would be carrying shielded radios proven to be immune to cell phone jammers. Each of them would have a tranquilizer dart gun; the darts would be propelled by compressed carbon dioxide cartridges rather than gunpowder. Just in case, they would also carry short swords.

Scott Wroblewski would be carrying a search warrant for Ocean Centre signed by the Prime Minister; he hoped he would not actually have to serve it, but it would effectively block accusations of trespassing in case they were caught during the rescue mission. And though they were betting that they could pull this operation off covertly with little or no opposition, their ace in the hole was Ian McDonald. If they met with serious resistance that they could not overcome by themselves, Scott would present the search warrant, point out that they had the legal right to search Ocean Centre, and collect evidence of the crime of kidnapping; obstructing the director of the FBI would result in an air strike that would totally destroy Ocean Centre.

***

Ross succeeded in getting wetsuits interlaced with copper and Kevlar fabricated for them. In case the "Discombobulator Supremo" got switched on before they made good on the patients' extraction from the castle, Ross and Thomas came up with the idea of bringing a big role of copper foil to make impromptu hat shields for the patients to wear. They would still suffer loss of coordination from the effects on their peripheral nervous systems, but they would be able to think clearly.

Moss began planning the mission logistics for execution at the end of the month. He asked all the other men to arrange their schedules to accommodate an entire two weeks. He also requested the president to immediately order the provisioning and preparation of the *Almirante Cochrane* for their voyage to the west coast of Scotland, as they needed to take into consideration the vagaries and uncertainties of the weather. With luck, they could safely extract all of the patients with no loss of life.

Luke and Moss provided basic hand-to-hand combat techniques to the rest of the rescue party, except for Jeff Florenzano, who probably knew killing and defense techniques not taught in any legitimate martial arts school. There was little time for thorough traditional martial arts training; therefore they decided it would quicker and more effective to teach a refresher course in something else which Luke and Moss had both studied extensively … Krav Maga.

Based on simple principles and instinctive movements, this system is designed to teach self-defense in the shortest possible time. Chris Meyer, Scott Wroblewski and Ian McDonald had already received some training in Krav Maga years ago, as law enforcement agencies and militaries around the world provided some training in this basic and utilitarian system of self-defense. Even Ross Ericson had received some minimal training in Krav Maga during his years as a naval intelligence officer.

Krav Maga is an eclectic hand-to-hand combat system developed in Israel. It was derived from street-fighting skills developed by Imi Lichtenfeld, making use of his training as a boxer and wrestler, as a means of defending the Jewish quarter during a period of anti-Semitic activity in Bratislava in the mid- to late 1930s. It has since been refined for both civilian and military applications. Unlike most martial arts, Krav Maga is essentially a tactical defense skill. Its philosophy emphasizes threat neutralization, simultaneous defensive and offensive maneuvers, and aggressive endurance in a 'him-or-me' context.

CHAPTER 76

B y the time Haley called again, planning for the rescue mission was nearly complete. Haley informed them that almost all the patients were excited, albeit nervous, about the possibility of being rescued. She informed them in a concerned voice about a small number of patients who she thought were suffering from Stockholm syndrome. Communication about the upcoming rescue mission was being withheld from that group until the last possible moment. Haley was worried that one of them, out of misguided allegiance to their captors, might spill the beans and blow everything.

The night of the rescue, which they agree to be the last day of the month, Haley agreed to meet them on the beach at 3 AM to guide them through the caverns into the castle. With her finely honed sense of balance, Haley would cross the chasm first and drive the pitons for securing the net into the stone floor. They would then stretch the net back across the chasm securing it to another set of pitons that they would have first driven in to the cavern floor. She would have with her copies of a map of the castle, including the patients' room assignments. They would attempt to evacuate the patients in very small groups, maximizing the chance that at least a few would escape even if things subsequently went to hell in a hand basket. They would shoot any security personnel they encountered with a fast acting tranquilizer dart.

They told Haley about their special wetsuits interlaced with copper and Kevlar mesh; Moss told her that they'd bring her one of her own. They also told her about the role of copper foil they would be bringing along to provide basic protection for the patients from the "Discombobulator Supremo" EMP device should it be activated.

"I want all of you to know that we patients had pretty much given up hope of ever getting out of here. No matter what the outcome, you have our deepest appreciation for even contemplating this dangerous mission. Luke, Jake and Steve, I love you all so much…I cannot wait to see you," Haley said. "I know this mission is very dangerous, I want you promise me to be as careful as you can possibly be!"

"We love you too sweetie and I promise we will be very careful "Moss replied.

"Steve is the best mission planner I have ever seen, "Jake said. "He is literally planning for every conceivable contingency, and even some contingencies the rest of us had not imagined."

CHAPTER 77

Gabriel Sanchez, the gardener at Jake's mansion, had really gotten into the Soo Bahk Do training sessions in the ballroom. He was fascinated by its history and underlying philosophy; he wanted to learn more about it. On his own initiative he began searching for anything having to do with Soo Bahk Do on the Internet. Gabriel was very surprised one day to see a picture of Steve Peterson on a website being awarded a trophy at a tournament; however, the name under the picture was Steve Moss, not Steve Peterson. An accompanying article gave a brief biography of the man, including the fact that he was a decorated war veteran. The biography did not agree at all with the background the Steve "Peterson" that Senator Jackson had given the rest of the household staff when he added positions for Thomas, Alicia and Steve. Gabriel, even though a gardener, was a very intelligent man. He reasoned correctly that if Steve's background was phony, it was likely that the backgrounds provided for Thomas and Alicia were probably phony too. He figured the Senator probably had his reasons, so Gabriel decided to regard his discovery as merely an interesting curiosity.

It wasn't until Gabriel mentioned in passing his interesting discovery to his older sister Juanita (who happened to be the same Juanita Sanchez whose computer network account Anita had accessed to check the guard schedule) on the phone that he discovered the likely truth. Juanita worked for a large medical facility in Bogotá Colombia. He wasn't quite sure what she did there, but Gabriel knew that Juanita was highly paid.

Juanita asked Gabriel to describe the other two new members of the household staff to her.

"Gabriel, "she said, "Listen to me very carefully. I think these are the same people who escaped from FHRI, where I work. We thought they had all been killed, but obviously not. There was a ten million dollar contract out to eliminate these three people … I am sure Eduard Falcón would still be willing to pay that amount to you if he found out they were still alive. You think you could take pictures of them and e-mail them to me?"

Gabriel had heard of Eduard Falcón, but did not know what his connection was with his sister's place of employment. "I can certainly try, but now that I think about it, all three of them seem to be shy around cameras."

"Take them with your cell phone camera, but don't let them see you doing it," Juanita replied. "Get them to me as soon as you can."

While Gabriel was basically a good man and loyal to his employer, the idea of a $10 million bounty overcame any scruples he may have had; he did as his sister requested and surreptitiously took pictures of the three and sent them to her.

It took less than a day to verify that Steve Moss, Dr. Thomas Hunt and Alicia Jones were very much alive and living under assumed identities in the mansion of United States Senator Jake Jackson. Eduard Falcón was promptly notified; he agreed to pay $10 million dollars to Juanita and Gabriel Sanchez on the confirmed deaths of Steve Moss, Dr. Thomas Hunt and Alicia Jones. He further said that Gabriel would not have to do the killing himself; Eduard would arrange for a professional team of assassins to travel to Minneapolis. All that Gabriel needed to do was specify a time when the targets would be in the house and then get out of the way.

CHAPTER 78

Moss had stayed up much later than normal on Saturday night chatting with Thomas and Alicia on the dock. Usually they retired by midnight; it was now 2 AM. As they dangled their feet in the water, sipping their wine, Moss talked about all the intricacies of mission planning that were weighing on his mind. As Thomas and Alicia were trying to assuage his fears and concerns, Moss spotted three heavily armed men dressed all in black arrive far down the beach in a small boat. After they beached it, they began moving stealthily from the beach towards the mansion.

All the lights were out because the rest of the household staff was off for the weekend, and Chris had already gone to bed. Cautious man that he was, and since Thomas, Alicia and Moss still had prices on their heads, Jake Jackson had the foresight install a small armory adjacent to the boathouse concealed by a large panel on hinges. As quietly as he could, Moss swung the panel out and removed two semi-automatic Benelli Super Black Eagle shot guns, handed them to Thomas and Alicia, and took a Beretta 92S 9 mm handgun for himself.

They had no idea who the men were or why they had come to the mansion. The fact that they were heavily armed led Moss to think that this was not a simple robbery; more likely it was a home invasion. It also occurred to him that someone may have found out that Thomas, Alicia and Moss had not been murdered after all.

So far the men did not seem to have seen them. Alicia had her cell phone with her; in whispered voices they briefly discussed calling 911, but rejected that idea for a variety of reasons. Most important of them was protecting their identities from too much police scrutiny.

The men were clearly professionals; they found the phone line to the house and cut it. As they entered through the front door, Thomas, Alicia and Moss waited for the security system to set off an alarm. It never did, which could only mean one thing: the men had typed in the correct security code to disarm the system. They waited for Slim and Mr. Judge to start barking, but realized they were likely asleep in their doggie beds located in the lower level. With the door to the downstairs closed, the dogs were unlikely to be awakened. It was beginning to look like an inside job. It was probably someone on the household staff, all of whom knew the security code.

They reentered the house from the conservatory door, which they had left unlocked when they went out to the dock. They took off their shoes and silently padded into the kitchen. Adjacent to the kitchen was the mansion's safe room, which was equipped with TV monitors from which they would be able to see every room. They tiptoed down the short hallway to the safe room, and eased the door open. Given that the safe room walls were reinforced and extremely thick, they could talk without fear of being overheard. Thomas switched on the bank of TV monitors and they could instantly see inside every room of the house. The intruders had likely figured out already that they were not in the house. The men were in Chris's bedroom showing him pictures of Thomas, Alicia and Moss. When Chris threw up his hands, implying that he did not know they were talking about, the largest of the men punched him in the face. When Chris said nothing, he then put a gun to his head. Beretta in hand, Moss dashed out of the safe room and yelled, "Thomas, come with me. Alicia, you stay here and don't let anyone in!"

Thomas and Moss bounded up the stairs and ran down the hall to Chris's bedroom. They startled the men as they crashed through the door. As one of the men was raising an automatic weapon, Moss delivered a spinning tornado kick, which has tremendous force, to the man's head... his neck snapped and he dropped like a rock. One of the other two men reflexively fired a short burst nearly hitting Moss, but before he could fire again, Thomas knocked him off his feet tremendous uppercut. As the man struggled to get up, Thomas blew a giant hole in his chest with his 12gauge shotgun. They could hear Slim and Mr. Judge barking now.

The third man was holding Chris close with an arm around his neck with what Moss recognized as a Steyr Tactical Machine Pistol pointed at his temple. The Steyr TMP is a 9 mm blowback-operated, rotating-barrel weapon that can fire 800 rounds per minute. He commanded, "No one escapes from Eduard Falcón and lives. Put down your guns or your friend dies."

Chris said in a stone cold voice, "I don't think so, asshole." He surprised all of them with a blazingly fast back fist (*Cap Kwon*) to his captor's nose followed by an elbow strike (*Pal Koop*) to the solar plexus; the man, clearly in pain, released Chris but quickly spun around to try to fire off a burst killing all of them. Before he could squeeze the trigger, Slim and Mr. Judge came rushing into the room; Scheme must've heard them barking and performed his door opening trick. Mr. Judge unbalanced the man by lunging at him and latching onto his arm with powerful jaws. The assassin attempted to redirect his weapon at Mr. Judge. All those hours at the shooting range in Phoenix finally paid off; Moss simply shot the man between the eyes before he could fire his weapon.

All three of the assassins lay dead on the floor before them. They searched them, but found nothing to identify them. They did, however, find a small block of plastic explosives and a timer to detonate them on one of the men. They surmised the intruders knew about the mansion's safe room and came prepared to blow the door off should they believe them to be inside. Chris, Thomas and Moss lavished calming praise on their two canine saviors. Their adrenaline levels were likely off the chart.

After calming down a bit, they called both Jake Jackson and Scott Wroblewski on a secure cell phone Jake had provided them for emergencies. They advised Scott and Jake that they had thwarted an assassination attempt by three men who had arrived by boat. Thomas, Alicia and Moss were clearly intended for execution; failing miserably in their attempt, three bodies were currently up in Chris's bedroom. After giving them the details of the attack, they needed to know what to do next. Scott Wroblewski, knowing that calling the police, with the possibility of Falcón informants, was not wise, came up with a well crafted solution. "Put all their bodies back in their boat. One of you drives the boat at least 100 yards out in the lake and sets the timer on the explosives; all that will be found by the authorities will be boat fragments and parts of three unidentifiably mutilated bodies. With luck, Eduard Falcón will hear about it and think his assassins put a bomb in your boat and that the remains are yours."

When Gabriel Sanchez never returned to work it was obvious who had set them up.

***

Their ruse worked. Two days later, Eduard Falcón, who had ordered the assassins to do the killings and then immediately leave the country, smiled as he read the online article in the Minneapolis paper; obviously, the professionals he had hired, had come up with a creative solution to eliminating the lives of Steve Moss, Dr. Thomas Jefferson Hunt and Alicia Jones.

CHAPTER 79

They were all shaken by the attempt on their lives, but they were getting over it successfully. There was no way of knowing how Eduard Falcón had interpreted the news stories about the boat explosion and fatalities on Lake Minnetonka. If the men were told to report back on the success of their mission, clearly Thomas, Alicia and Moss were out of luck. However, it was not inconceivable that the men were simply paid to do their job; resulting news stories would have been accepted as proof of their success. At this point, Moss couldn't worry about it, as the upcoming rescue mission demanded his full attention.

Thomas, Chris and Moss prepared for a trip to the east coast where they would meet up with Jake, Jeff Florenzano Scott Wroblewski and Ross Ericson. Their small rescue team had a final pre-mission teleconference with the president and prime minister. The president, acting in his role as commander in chief, surprised Moss by secretly and temporarily recalling him back into the army with the rank of brigadier general; effectively changing his status from an independent private citizen to a military officer under his command. President Paxton justified this action by asserting that the Falcón organization's penetration of militaries and law enforcement agencies around the world was tantamount to a global war. As Moss was trying to mentally process the unexpected action of the president's, the president also surprised Ross Ericson, who had been a naval intelligence officer with the rank of Commander, by recalling him temporarily back into the navy with the rank of Captain. The president wasn't done; he recalled Chris Meyer, who had been a Lieutenant Commander in the SEALS, temporarily back into the navy with the rank of Commander.

Two medical doctors would be traveling with them; they would be examining the patients once retrieved, as there was no way of knowing their physical condition. When cleared medically for travel, the patients would be flown by a military aircraft back to the United States, where, after a debriefing, they would be reunited with their families.

It would've been faster to fly to Scotland, but the sea voyage would enable them to plan and talk freely about the mission details at length. They had already prearranged mission details with Captain Jim Dexter of the *Almirante Cochrane*. Jim was an old and trusted friend of the president; they had served together as officers in the Navy. The media was keenly interested in the voyages of the president's personal yacht; a short press release had been prepared stating that the yacht was going to have multiple renovations at a shipyard in Scotland, and that neither the president nor any members of his family would be on board.

In spite of their anxiety about the mission, their transatlantic crossing was very comfortable and pleasant. With all of their major planning out of the way, they spent a lot of time talking about various contingencies and how they would react to them. They practiced Krav Maga skills every day; Luke and Moss ran the others through drills on basic sword fighting. They did this wearing their custom-made wetsuits interlaced with Kevlar and copper mesh in order to get used to them.

The *Almirante Cochrane*'s chef, Arnold "Arnie" Dixon, had also served in the Navy with the president. In addition to feeding them extraordinarily well, he was a great storyteller. Arnie regaled them with stories of famous Navy battles throughout history; they enjoyed most the ones about British Admiral Thomas Cochrane (after whom the *Almirante Cochrane* was named), 10th Earl of Dundonald, who was one of the inspirations for Horatio Hornblower, a fictional protagonist of a series of novels by C. S. Forester.

Days passed remarkably fast; as they approached the coast of Scotland their trepidation grew. All of them were keenly aware of the risks in their rescue endeavor: in spite of their plans for a stealthy retrieval of the patients, they might encounter resistance that would result in their capture or the loss of life. Two storms delayed their progress, but on the 11th day of their voyage the west coast of Scotland came into view.

CHAPTER 80

The day of the rescue mission had arrived. They anchored 10 miles off the west coast of Scotland. They contacted Ian McDonald, who was aboard the British aircraft carrier anchored even further off the coast. He would be monitoring all of their radio transmissions when the rescue mission began. Ian's Harrier aircraft not only had special shielding protecting it from EMP weapons, but missiles capable of flattening the castle; Ian would be called to action only as a last resort.

At 2 AM they donned their custom-made wetsuits, strapped on their short swords, made sure their shielded radios were working (Moss was bringing an extra one for Haley, along with an extra wetsuit), checked their tranquilizer guns, and packed the small number of items that they would take into the yacht's tender boat along with their scuba gear.

The yacht's large tender boat, capable of carrying all of the patients if tightly packed in, took them to within 500 feet of the shore, where they donned their tanks and strapped on the small amount of gear they'd be taking with them. Each of them had a holster containing a tranquilizer gun around their waists. With the fate of the patients at stake, they dropped into the ocean for their underwater swim ashore. Five minutes later they were on the beach, where Haley was waiting for them. Having removed his scuba gear as quickly as he could, Haley and Moss shared a long embrace and multiple kisses. It'd been over two years since they had last seen each other; mid-kiss, Jake tapped Moss on the shoulder and said "Hey buddy, that's my sister you are kissing!" Older brother and sister shared a long and tearful embrace. Luke interrupted. He hadn't seen his little sister in five years. Oldest Brother and sister also shared a long and tearful embrace. It'd been years since Haley had seen Ross Ericson, Jeff Florenzano, or Scott Wroblewski, and a long time since she had seen Chris Meyer. They all hugged her warmly and commented on her amazing recovery. Moss gave Haley the shielded wetsuit he had brought for her; the men all politely turned their backs to her while Haley quickly changed into it.

They were about to proceed when Jeff quietly said, "Don't panic, but I sense that we are being watched. Wait here…I'll be back shortly." Jeff's intuition was legendary; no one questioned what he was sensing. Jeff walked quickly but quietly towards a large boulder about 50 yards away that was more than seven feet tall. As he approached it, two men with sniper rifles stepped out from behind the boulder and pointed their weapons at Jeff and shouted, "This is the private property of Ocean Centre, and you people are trespassing. Put your hands up now or we'll shoot you where you stand." After observing that neither man appeared to be carrying a radio, Jeff's eyes rolled back and he collapsed on the sand as though he had fainted. The men approached him cautiously without lowering their weapons. As one bent over to check his condition, Jeff's hand shot towards his throat; the tiny scalpel-sharp knife he'd concealed in the palm of his hand severed a major artery in the man's neck; he fell to his knees clutching his throat. Before the other man could react, Jeff expertly stabbed the man in the thigh, severing his femoral artery. Both men would bleed to death shortly…they had already lost consciousness. Not leaving anything to chance, Jeff snapped both of their necks. The rest of the rescue party, who had seen these events unfold, came running over to Jeff.

"That was utterly fantastic! The stories about your psychic abilities are apparently true!" Chris exclaimed.

"Two men died doing their jobs, so 'sucktastic' is more like it," Jeff replied fatalistically. They dragged the two bodies down to the ocean and set then adrift.

Haley led them back into the water and showed them the submerged portal leading to the caverns. After a very short swim, they resurfaced in the cavern pool. She showed them the path marked by the golden bricks; soon they came to the sharp metal spikes in the middle of the path… a dangerous booby-trap Haley had triggered earlier. They carefully skirted the spikes. After walking further along the path, they came to the chasm Haley had described; it was spanned by an extraordinarily narrow ridge of rock. As they walked up to the edge of the chasm, all of them marveled at how deep it was; Haley simply smiled at them and said, "I hope you remembered to bring that net we talked about!"

Ross grinned and unzipped a small pack strapped to his side. He removed half the pitons and a net made of Kevlar fabric and handed them to Haley. "You think you can carry these and still keep your balance? I'll toss you a mallet for pounding the pitons in once you're on the other side." Securing the net on their side with the remaining pitons was easy.

They all stood with their mouths agape as they watched Haley rapidly traverse the chasm as though she'd never been paralyzed. Fishing lines for pulling the net back across the chasm trailed out behind her. Her incredible bravery and fully restored balance brought tears of joy to her brother's eyes. Now on the other side, Haley put down the net and pitons. "Toss me the mallet," she said.

As securing the net was a critical step, Moss had fortuitously anticipated that tossing the heavy mallet successfully on the first attempt would be difficult; he had tied a 20 foot length of fishing line to the mallet. The first time Ross tossed the mallet it fell short; as he had tied the other end of the fishing line to his wrist, he was able to retrieve it. His second toss was successful.

Haley drove in the pitons, securing the net on her side. Using the fishing lines, Ross retrieved the mallet, and they hauled the net back across the chasm. They then stretched the net tight as the surface of a trampoline; they tested it by throwing rocks into little piles on both sides of the net. It held nicely, Moss tentatively stepped onto the net slowly transferring his entire weight on to its surface—it held perfectly!

Once they all crossed the chasm, they continued to follow the path marked by the golden bricks. After a while they came upon a skeleton… they stopped in stunned silence.

"Oh my, I forgot to tell you about him! Say hi to King Andrew, I believe," Haley said. "According to one of the books I read on the castle's history, a clan chieftain, proclaimed King by his people, Andrew mysteriously disappeared early in the 13th century during an attack on the castle. It appears that he was wounded and trying to get to safety. Obviously, he did not make it."

After Haley indicated that they were approaching the entry to the lower level of the castle, Moss brought the group to a halt. "Let's quickly review the plan," he said. Haley had provided each of them a copy of the castle's basic lay-out, including a list of the patients' names and their room assignments. Each of the patients judged trustworthy had surreptitiously been told of the impending rescue mission; they would be ready to go and waiting in their rooms for them to come.

Moss laid out the immediate logistics: "We will first do a brief scouting patrol, shooting any security personnel we find with tranquilizer darts; we need to try to move each to a spot where they won't be easily seen. We will collect the patients in groups of 10; once the first group is collected, Haley will escort and guide them through the caverns and down to the beach. She will then come back for the second group, and so on. Once everyone is safely out, they will be ferried out to the president's yacht. If all goes smoothly, we will all be out of here before dawn. If anyone encounters a problem or resistance, hol-ler 'mayday' on your radio and give your location." Ross Ericson quickly dem-onstrated fashioning a hat from the copper foil they had brought along. "This will protect human brains from the effects of the 'Discombobulator Supremo' should it get turned on. We will fashion one of these for each of the patients."

CHAPTER 81

They advanced silently up to the main level of the castle's central keep; while no one was in sight, they did hear footsteps coming towards them echoing in one of the adjacent hallways. Luke Jackson held a finger up to his lips, signaling no one to talk. He unstrapped his tranquilizer gun and slowly moved towards the hallway. Before the guard could see any of them, Luke shot him with one of the fast acting tranquilizer darts; within seconds the man collapsed...he would be unconscious for at least 18 hours. They dragged over to an art alcove and Scott Wroblewski stuffed him behind a statue of a knight while the others proceeded on.

A second guard further down the hall saw Scott just as he stepped out of the alcove; he immediately drew his weapon from his holster and aimed it at Scott's face and ordered him to put his hands up. Scott reacted with a very fast Krav Maga move; he grabbed and deflected the weapon with his left hand and simultaneously delivered a crushing punch to the guard's face. As the guard's knees buckled, Scott retained his grip on the weapon and moved forward quickly, pinning the weapon to the guard's midsection. As he fell unconscious to the floor, Scott disarmed him and then shot him with a tranquilizer dart; he hid the man in the same alcove as the first guard. He ran quickly to rejoin the rest of the group.

They proceeded cautiously to a grand staircase leading to the second level, where half the patients' rooms were located; the rest were located on the third floor. Haley had told them that the patient accommodations were large and opulent mini two-bedroom suites, each with a shared sitting room and two private baths. The suites were distributed on either side of a massive hallway.

Unlike their accommodations in Bogotá, there was no video surveillance here and the patients were not locked in their rooms.

Previously, Haley had told them how the patients had come to be regarded not as prisoners, but permanent guests of the Falcón brothers. As their current treatment and living conditions, in spite of the fact that they could never leave, were superior to some of the patients pre-kidnapping life situations, Moss was mildly concerned about the Stockholm syndrome… Haley had warned them that a couple of the patients, two women who shared a suite, were afflicted the worst. Their suite was located on the third floor, and the team decided to collect them last. What if one or more of the other patients had become so enamored of their current lives at Ocean Centre that they didn't want to be rescued? What if they had blown the whistle and we were walking into a trap?

Haley also told them that Dale Vandermeer, an involuntary Falcón employee who had supplied many of the details about the EMP weapons, wanted to escape along with the patients; he would be waiting for them in Laura Berg's room,

Moss couldn't afford to dwell on these concerns as they needed to move forward quickly and efficiently.

They rapidly collected the first group of 10, all of whom were delighted to see them. Laura Berg and Dale Vandermeer were in this group. In hushed tones Moss told them Haley would lead them through an escape route in the caverns deep below the castle to the beach. They outfitted each of them with a quickly folded copper hat, warning them about the EMP weapon that could severely mess with their nervous systems. Moss explained that they would need to swim for a short distance twice: once for a few seconds through an underwater tunnel leading to an exit near the beach and again swim about 500 feet out to a large boat that would be waiting for them. Fortunately, everyone in this first group said they could swim. Haley would then return to the castle to escort the second group out.

As they went from suite to suite on the rest of the second floor, patients were universally glad to see them, and they only encountered one other guard, who they again shot with a tranquilizer dart; they stuffed him in a closet in one of the suites. They also came upon an extremely fit man who was diligently washing the floor. As Moss pointed his tranquilizer gun at him, Haley grasped his arm and said, "No need…this is our friend Andy—he doesn't work here by choice, and he wants us to escape!" Andy nodded and smiled, giving them thumbs up.

Half the patients had now escaped the castle; Haley, a strong swimmer herself, only had to lend slight assistance to a few of the patients. Moss made radio contact with the yacht's tender boat. They assured Moss that all 50 patients had successfully made the swim from the beach, and were now safely on board. They proceeded stealthily up to the third-floor. The first four groups of 10 patients were collected uneventfully and led by Haley for their journey through the caverns.

The rescue seemed to be going perfectly so far...it was almost too good to be true. With eight patients waiting in the hall for the final trek to freedom, their good luck went to hell in the last suite they had left (the one Haley had warned them about). The two women patients simply did not want to be rescued.

The older of the two, a woman named Harriet Beecher, said "Dr. Falcón saved me by giving me a new liver for which I don't even need anti-rejection drugs! My failing health had robbed me of a wonderful career in hotel management, but I now live the life of royalty. I have no family left back home, and my husband died 10 years ago. Jane Alexander here, who used to own and run a fabulous restaurant that her numbskull husband lost in a poker game, was cured of her severe diabetes, a disease whose complications killed her sister Jennifer when she was only 35 years old. Jane's adulterous husband beat her regularly, and her only child died seven years ago in a car accident, so she has nothing good to go back to either. We know that neither of us will be permitted to leave here ever, but we don't care, we're not leaving with you!"

This was a conundrum. Moss tried to reason with Harriet, pointing out that neither she nor Jane would ever be truly free if they chose to stay. Thomas joined in with the argument that someday the Falcón brothers may tire of their perpetual guests and simply eliminate them.

"I guess we'll just take our chances with that," Jane retorted. "No matter what you say, I'm not going with you!"

"We are sorry to hear that," Jake Jackson said with genuine remorse in his voice, "but we can't chance having you ruin other patients' chance for freedom." He then shot her with a tranquilizer dart; Jane collapsed within seconds. Upon seeing this, Harriet screamed and immediately began clicking a button on a small device hanging from what looked like a necklace. Jake then shot her too. They now had two tranquilized women lying on the floor in front of them.

Thomas walked over and knelt on the floor next to Harriet. He closely examined the device around her neck, and then began searching the room. "I think we may be in trouble... Harriet may have transmitted a distress signal. There is a button she pressed on that thing hanging around her neck. It looks a lot like the transmitters given to invalids and at-risk patients when they go home from the hospital. I am looking for the receiver, which would be hard-wired to a monitoring station somewhere in the castle. Oh shit, here it is! They will probably think she is having a medical emergency and will come quickly to investigate."

Moss walked over and retrieved the tranquilizer darts from the two women. "We can safely leave Harriet where she lies... it will take them a while to figure out why she is unconscious. Jane is another matter; we need to put her in her bed and hope they don't find her for a while." They moved quickly, hoping to escape through the caverns with the last of the patients before anyone came to investigate. They were not in luck.

CHAPTER 82

A s they cautiously peered out into the hallway, they could hear footsteps coming from the stairway. "Get in here!" Moss whispered to the patients waiting outside...there was no time to go to another room. They all had alarmed looks on their faces as they rushed into the suite; Haley, having returned from escorting the previous batch of patients, was with them. Fortunately, the people approaching had not seen them.

Scott Wroblewski looked at Haley as she was frantically tapping him on the arm. "The door has a dead bolt lock," she whispered. Scott managed to slide the lock shut just seconds before the people arrived at the door. When they couldn't open it, they began pounding on the door and a woman's voice shouted, "Harriet and Jane are you all right?" There was more pounding on the door, and again "Harriet and Jane are you all right? We're coming in!" When they heard the sound of keys jangling, Scott signaled frantically for them to retreat from the sitting room to the bedroom on their left. They just made it as they heard the sound of the door unlocking and opening. They again heard a woman's voice say, "Check for a pulse." A few seconds later she asked, "Do you think she had a heart attack?"

A male voice responded, "I don't know, but I think we better get her down to the infirmary." Raising his voice, he hollered, "Jane, are you here?" When there was no answer, the team heard the door to the second bedroom open. The man saw Jane lying in her bed sleeping. "It is still early, let her sleep and we will just leave a note that Harriet has been taken to the infirmary," the man said.

Just as Moss was breathing a sigh of relief, Ross bumped a floor lamp; it crashed noisily to the floor. "Who is in there?" asked the woman.

Moss had his tranquilizer gun ready as the door flew open; before the startled man and woman could utter a word, he shot them both with tranquilizer darts. They quickly dragged them into one of the bathrooms. "Someone else will come looking for them when they don't return … we need to get the hell out of here right now!" Haley exclaimed.

As quickly and quietly as they could, they left the suite and headed for the stairway down to the second floor. They made it down the hall way of the second floor headed towards the stairway leading to the main floor. They almost ran into two men coming up the stairs—when they saw them, the two men did an about-face and ran back down the stairs. Just before Ross shot them both with tranquilizer darts, he saw one of the men key the microphone on a walkietalkie and scream, "Intruders on the second floor… intruders on the second floor!" Their hopes of getting all the patients out undetected were now trashed.

CHAPTER 83

They all raced down the stairs and dashed for the exit leading to the lower level and their escape. Moss thought they were going to make it out with all of the patients, when suddenly they began stumbling and falling (except for Haley, who was protected by her wetsuit) with an abrupt loss of coordination, indicating that one or more of the EMP weapons had been activated. One of the men screamed as his pants pocket exploded; it dawned on Moss that he was probably a smoker, and that he likely had butane lighter in his pocket. Within minutes they were surrounded by men wearing copper armor; all were armed with swords or cross-bows, several of the latter were being aimed at them. "Don't move, or you are all dead," he shouted at them. Those of them who were still standing froze in their tracks. The man keyed the microphone on his walkie-talkie and said, "Intruders apprehended and detained on the main floor."

A few minutes later Dr. Nicolas Falcón and his brother Eduard strode towards them. Moss noted that Eduard was no longer in a wheelchair, as Haley had previously informed them. The brothers were looking very pissed indeed. They were not wearing copper armor, indicating that the "Discombobulator Supremo" had been turned off. This was verified by the patients who had stumbled and fallen, but were now standing back up with their coordination apparently restored. With their hooded wetsuits on, the Falcón brothers did not immediately recognize Thomas and Moss. As they got closer, a look of genuine surprise registered on both their faces when they recognized the pair of escapees. The Falcón brothers had no idea who the other men in the party of invaders were. Before they could utter a word, Scott spoke, keying the microphone on his radio: "We are currently being detained by a group of armed men. I will speak to them now, while I continue to transmit. My name is Scott Wroblewski; I am the director of United States Federal Bureau of Investigation. I have in my possession a search warrant, signed by the Prime Minister, giving us the legal right to search Ocean Centre, and collect evidence of the crimes of kidnapping and false imprisonment; obstructing or impeding us will result in an air strike that will totally destroy Ocean Centre." Scott slowly unzipped his wetsuit and pulled out the warrant which had been laminated in plastic; in spite of the crossbows aimed at him, he bravely walked over to the Falcón brothers and officially served the warrant. "You are all under arrest for the crimes of kidnapping and false imprisonment."

Before anyone could react, Moss spoke into his radio: "All parties monitoring this radio transmission, this is Brigadier General Steve Moss acting on orders of President Paxton. If our party is not safely on the beach in two hours, you are hereby authorized to commence an air strike on Ocean Center. The tender boat is ordered to immediately transport all passengers to the *Almirante Cochrane* then return to the beach and wait for the rest of us. All parties acknowledge now."

"This is Ian McDonald aboard the aircraft carrier Churchill; I copy you loud and clear General Moss. If I do not receive confirmation your party is safely on the beach within two hours, an air strike on Ocean Center will be initiated."

Next came: "This is Captain Jim Dexter aboard the *Almirante Cochrane*. I too copy you loud and clear General Moss. We have a clear view of the beach, and will be waiting for your party's safe arrival."

There was dead silence for several seconds; Eduard Falcón finally spoke. "I see you are now back in the military, Steve Moss, and, oh my goodness, you are now a general! And hello to you Dr. Thomas Jefferson Hunt; you are both clearly hard men to kill. I am predisposed to ordering my men kill all of you right now; however, I will offer you a proposition. First, will you have these five other gentlemen introduce themselves?" He pointed to Jeff Florenzano, Ross Ericson, Chris Meyer, Luke and Jake Jackson.

Jake went first: "I am United States Senator Jake Jackson. You made a big mistake when you had my sister kidnapped, you malevolent sons of a bitch."

Ross went next: "I am Captain Ross Ericson, United States Navy. You made a big mistake when you had all these people kidnapped, you sociopathic assholes."

Luke went next: "I am Luke Jackson, Jake's brother and director of United States National Security Agency. You made a big mistake when you had our sister kidnapped, you despicable wankers."

Chris went next: "I am Commander Chris Meyer, United States Navy SEALS. You made a big mistake when you had my friend's sister kidnapped, you abhorrent scum bags."

Jeff went last: "I am Jeff Florenzano, with the United States Central intelligence Agency. You made a big mistake when you had United States citizens kidnapped, you disgusting pieces of shit."

Eduard paused for a bit before replying. "It is a pleasure to make your acquaintance; I am pleased to see that you all hold my brother and me in such high regard. You seem to be forgetting that the reason Haley Jackson and Steve Moss are walking again is because of the brilliance of my brother."

Moss interrupted, "Let me tell you what I have not forgotten: you and your brother forced all of the kidnapped patients at your facility in Bogotá to watch as a certain Mr. Richards was tortured, skinned alive, and eviscerated for attempting to escape; I still have nightmares about that! The facts that Haley and I are walking again, and that the patients here appear to be cured of their maladies, while we are all extremely appreciative, in no way exonerates you or your miserable brother, nor does it forgive your diabolical and egregious acts."

Eduard Falcón continued, ignoring everything Moss just said. "It appears that we have an impasse here; clearly, you have won the war; it may turn out to be a Pyrrhic victory, as it doesn't mean that you gentlemen will survive this last battle. I am familiar with the martial arts expertise of Steve Moss and Luke Jackson. I'm also aware that Dr. Hunt has an impressive boxing background. Having just met Director Wroblewski, Mr. Florenzano, Captain Ericson, and Commander Meyer, I have no idea of their knowledge or experience in the arts of combat and self-defense; I am guessing that it is not insignificant. Here is my proposition: the seven of you will engage in hand-to-hand combat, one match at a time—no weapons—with me and six of my men. If you win, you all live and are free to leave with your entire party; if we win, my brother and I will be permitted to leave in our own helicopter with your personal pledge that we will not be shot down or pursued. The winner will be determined when one side or the other has won four out of the seven matches. Your only choices are to accept or be executed where you stand."

This was no choice at all. Moss quickly said, "We accept, with one condition: after you have selected your combatants, all your other men will leave, taking all of the weapons with them."

"You are in no position to dictate conditions; will you all kindly follow me to the castle gymnasium where our contest will commence?"

CHAPTER 84

They all followed Eduard Falcón to the gymnasium in silence with his armed men right behind them. Moss figured that, no matter what the outcome, they had succeeded in the rescue of most of the patients.

"Before we proceed, I believe you gentlemen would be more comfortable if you removed the hoods to your wetsuits," Eduard said in an icily calm tone.

Observing that none of the armed men had removed their copper armor, and knowing that EMP devices could be turned back on at any time Moss replied, "We are deeply touched by your concern for our comfort, but we will leave them on unless your men remove their copper armor and helmets." When Eduard gave the order, all of his men removed their armor and helmets; Moss and the rest of the recue party then removed the hoods of their wetsuits.

Eduard selected his six combatants; he ordered his other men to gather the captives' short swords, hand-held radios, and tranquilizer guns. Obediently, the men did as ordered. He was unaware that Haley also had a radio, which she had tucked into the waistband of her slacks; the bulky sweatshirt she was wearing completely concealed it.

"Here is how we will proceed," Eduard dictated: "spectators will form a ring in which the combatants will fight, one pair at a time; spectators may not provide any assistance at all to any fighter at any time. I will select the order of the fights, with General Moss and me going last. At the beginning of each match, I will have my selected fighter step to the center of the ring; General Moss will then select one of his men as the opponent. At the beginning of each match, Haley Jackson shall raise her right hand in the air; when she drops it, the fighting will commence. Each match will end when a fighter either gives up or is unable to continue. Please note that none of my men are permitted to give up; they will fight until they are either unconscious or dead. The fighters have no rules. The winner of the overall contest will be the side that wins four matches out of the seven fights. With these formalities out of the way, let us commence."

Everyone spread out in a large circle forming the ring in which their future depended. Eduard Falcón pointed to one of his men and commanded him to go to the center of the ring. The man did not appear formidable at first glance; he was an Asian and a few inches short of 6 feet tall. He was also quite thin. Moss looked closely and realized that he recognized the man. He was an internationally known martial artist named Mok Lee. He was wiry, surprisingly strong for his size, and quite a showman. Mok Lee could appear to defy gravity with his leaping and spinning kicks, but Moss recalled that he was not overly fast. He decided that Chris Meyer, with his amazing quickness, strength and conditioning, might have a chance. Moss asked him to step into the ring.

Mok Lee, with all his comrades watching, immediately began to show off. He traversed the inner circumference of the ring, demonstrating a wide variety of spins, mid-air twists and flying kicks amid the cheers of the Falcón forces. Moss had to admit that the man's skills were impressive. When Moss glanced at Chris, he was surprised at how calmly Chris was observing this demonstration. Mok Lee was apparently reveling amid the cheers and adulation; still showing off, he completely missed Haley raising her arm and lowering it when Eduard Falcón nodded at her to signify the beginning of the match. Chris and everyone else had clearly seen Haley drop her arm. Chris, knowing that the match had technically begun stood perfectly still and let his opponent continue to show off. Mok Lee was still demonstrating his impressive martial arts repertoire when his face spun into Chris's blazingly fast *Jang Kwon* (palm heel) to the chin; Mok Lee dropped unconscious to the floor. Stunned silence replaced the raucous cheering of a few moments ago. After a whole minute of immobility, it was clear that the fight was over... Chris had won with a single blow!

As Chris was exiting the ring, he was blocked by one of the Falcón men who was brandishing his sword. The man was very large and muscular. "Now that wasn't exactly a real fight, mate; I think it would be fitting if I lopped off that arm with which you struck our man when he clearly wasn't ready." As he raised his sword with two hands, intending to amputate with a mighty swing of his blade, a thunderous voice came from the back of the gymnasium.

"Halt! That man is unarmed—your fighter got what he deserved for his obvious grandstanding and lack of humility. If you want to see an armed battle, you with the sword and whoever your best swordsman is can together fight me alone—I guarantee you all an entertaining sword fight, the likes of which you've never seen before!"

Everyone turned to look at this unknown bold speaker. His head was covered by an ornate helmet, but his lean athletic body was unarmored. In his hands were two magnificent short swords with heavily jeweled hilts. Moss, whose uncle Sumner had been an avid sword collector, recognized the stranger's swords as Oakeshott Type XII—a type used during the High Middle Ages.

Eduard Falcón spoke: "Who the hell are you, and what are you doing here?"

"I am simply a humble bystander who is tired of watching idly as you and your ilk engage unchecked in truly evil acts."

"I think you are insane and suicidal," Eduard replied, "but we will happily accommodate you in your death wish. Please come forward into the ring. Unfortunately for you, you will be facing two of the very best swordsman in all of Europe." Eduard pointed to one of his men. "Andre, please join Jacque and our soon-to-be-dead guest in the ring." All the Falcón men cheered, whistled and applauded as the three men entered the ring.

The sword fight lasted less than a minute. The attacking blades of Andre and Jacques were skillfully parried by the helmeted stranger, who at first seemed to be simply defending himself.

"Come on lads, is that the best you've got?" he taunted. Angered, Andre and Jacque lunged at him together. Suddenly and quite unexpectedly, the stranger crossed his arms and executed a perfect back flip. Just before he landed, his crossed arms lashed outwards. The sword in his right hand decapitated Andre; the sword in his left hand simultaneously decapitated Jacques. There was stunned silence in the gymnasium.

"Clean up this mess, and then let your contests continue," said the stranger. No one attempted to block his exit from the gymnasium.

CHAPTER 85

The incredible appearance of the stranger—and the rapid dispatching of two of Falcón's best swordsman gave everyone pause; Eduard commanded his men to not comment about the peculiar gory scene they had just witnessed. The two men he had ordered to follow and capture the stranger departed.

The first match had been a fluke... a clear example of the risks of overconfidence. Moss surmised that they would likely not be that lucky again. He and the others were puzzled by the appearance of the helmeted stranger and his astounding rapid dispatching of two great sword fighters.

Eduard Falcón tapped a huge ruddy-faced man with a red beard on the shoulder and pointed to the ring. As he strode to the center of the ring, Moss estimated that he was nearly 7 feet tall and well over 400 pounds with no apparent fat on his body. While skill and technique can often overcome a substantial size difference in an opponent, a large advantage in reach and brute strength are difficult to overcome. While Thomas was not nearly as large, his own size and strength were formidable; he was clearly the best choice.

Moss announced that Thomas Hunt was his choice for the second match. Thomas stoically entered the ring. In stark contrast to his predecessor, this adversary wasted no time showing off as his foolish predecessor had. He began by walking around the ring, stretching his muscles; his eyes were glued to Haley, waiting for the signal to begin. When she dropped her arm after receiving the nod from Eduard Falcón, the huge man began cautiously approaching Thomas in a classic boxer's style. For several moments, Thomas feigned as though he were going to box the man. His stance appeared to be a standard boxer's defense. As his opponent was winding up for an uppercut, Thomas first crouched low, then leapt into the air delivering an *E Dan Ahp Cha Nut Gi* (jump front snap kick) to the other man's face. Infuriated, with blood streaming from his broken nose, the man abandoned his boxing attempts... he immediately retaliated with an effective leg sweep knocking Thomas to the floor. While down on his back, Thomas responded by hooking his instep behind his opponent's Achilles tendon and delivering a hard kick to his kneecap... they all heard an audible snap as the huge man's knee broke. Thomas quickly got to his feet as the man hopped backward in tremendous pain, cursing Thomas profanely. Knowing he was not permitted to give up while still conscious, the man valiantly raised both fists signaling his willingness to continue. Thomas, hesitant to attack a man who was clearly disabled, simply adopted a defensive pose. He bobbed and weaved, avoiding several gamely thrown punches and jabs. Very unhappy, Eduard Falcón screamed, "Finish it, or I'll have you both killed!"

Thomas moved into a *Sa Ko Rip Jaseh* (side stance position) and lowered his body by bending both knees. He jumped up with both feet at the same time, bringing his knees up high. At the maximum height of his jump, Thomas executed an *E Dan Yup Hu Ri Gi* (jumping side hook kick) with his head up and his non-kicking leg tucked in; the heel of his foot connected forcefully with his opponent's temple. The huge man literally crashed unconscious to the floor. The match was over. They had won two matches and witnessed a bizarre unplanned sword fight; five fights remained unless Falcón and his men got frustrated and killed all of them first.

As his men carried the unconscious warrior out of the ring, Edward Falcón said frostily, "Your side has had extraordinary luck so far...don't expect it to continue. By now I expect my men have captured your mysterious ally."

CHAPTER 86

The next combatant designated by Eduard Falcón was an average sized man. There was absolutely nothing remarkable about his appearance at all except for his totally shaved head. Moss noticed he moved with cat-like grace and superb posture as he moved confidently towards the center of the ring; Moss surmised that this man was a highly accomplished martial artist. Luke Jackson was his immediate choice to face him. Moss knew Luke had observed the same things he had, and had probably reached the same conclusion about his opponent's likely prowess.

Luke Jackson had the strongest *Moo Do Shim Gong* (martial arts spirit) of any Soo Bahk Do practitioner Moss had ever known. In realistic self defense, when one is threatened, the "fight or flight" response is activated, altering one's biochemistry, blood flow and energies in preparing for survival in a dangerous encounter. This is the point where their *Moo Do Shim Gong* can be activated and help keep them centered. *Moo Do Shim Gong* does not come naturally; it takes many years to develop. Moss could almost see Luke activating his *Moo Do Shim Gong* as he entered the ring, preparing to get this distasteful task done efficiently and effectively.

Both men kept a sharp eye on Haley, waiting for her signal to begin. Neither man engaged in any posturing or theatrics. At Eduard Falcón's nod, Haley dropped her arm. Both men began moving about the ring, neither sure of the other's training, skills and repertoire of techniques.

As Luke began moving closer to his opponent, the baldheaded man's hands began moving continuously as he stood in a cat stance; Moss's immediate inference was that he was a student of a Southern Shaolin Kung Fu fighting style. There are over 400 styles of Kung Fu; southern styles are characterized by very low stances, low kicks and sophisticated hand techniques. Luke threw an exploratory *Choon Dan Kong Kyuk* (middle punch) to see how his opponent would respond. The punch was met by a stunningly quick palm block followed by one of the continuous fist techniques: punch, tiger claw to the eyes, back fist to the nose—all delivered in a rapid-fire circular motion. Luke whose own reflexes were lightning fast, avoided this attack by instantly retreating into a *Hu Gul Jaseh* (back stance) and defending with a *Hu Gul Ssang Soo Ahneso Pahkuro Mahk Kee* (two fist middle block, back stance).

Baldy was apparently not used to having his sweet moves countered so aptly...his mouth actually dropped opened momentarily in awe. Believing their fingers are more powerful than their fists, Southern Kung Fu practitioners make use of subtle and highly effective techniques with their digits. The man was in the midst of delivering a crane's beak strike to Luke's eye. Unfortunately for him, his brief lapse *in Chung Shin Tong Il* (concentration) was a huge mistake against a seasoned martial artist like Luke Jackson. Before his rigid three fingers could find their target, Luke had launched an *E Dan Dwi Hu Ri Gi* (jumping long back spinning kick) which landed forcefully in his opponent's throat, crushing his Adam's apple and collapsing his windpipe...a fatal injury. Their team had won again. Three down and one to go, assuming that Falcón did not change the rules on them!

CHAPTER 87

Nicolas Falcón had not uttered a word since they were captured and forced into this bizarre series of fights. He spoke now for the first time, "This contrived multi-fight contest of my brother's is wholly unnecessary and serves no real purpose—all Eduard really wants to do is to kick Steve Moss's ass for escaping us in the first place and then surviving his unsuccessful assassins sent to Minnesota. We should dispense with the rest of the fights except for Eduard versus Steve Moss. If Eduard wins, he and I will be permitted to leave in our own helicopter with your personal pledge that we will neither be shot down nor pursued. If Steve Moss wins, you will all immediately be free to leave. Do you agree?"

Avoiding additional and unnecessary conflict seemed like a good idea to Moss. Eduard Falcón had been countermanded by his younger brother, and despite the booing of Falcón's men who wanted to see more fights, Moss quickly agreed.

Eduard Falcón stepped into the center of the ring, a vicious and vindictive sneer on his face. After a deep cleansing breath and a sigh, Moss followed him.

As they stood facing each other in the center of the ring, Eduard said, "Ms. Jackson, you may signal the beginning of the match at your discretion."

Haley raised her arm in the air, but was obviously hesitant to bring it down to begin the match. After nearly 10 seconds had elapsed, Nicolas Falcón shouted impatiently, "For Christ's sake, drop your damn arm and start the match!" Haley did as she was told and the match began.

Neither of them was entirely sure of the other's martial arts skills. They both moved cautiously around the ring. They both tentatively tried some hand

and foot techniques just to gauge the other's response. Eduard Falcón's martial arts approach was a potpourri of Kung Fu, Tae Kwon Do, Okinawan Karate and Kajukenbo. His blocking skills were excellent. Several times he fooled Moss with fake attacks followed by vicious kicks or punches that connected… none of which injured him severely, although they hurt like hell. Moss was getting some licks in of his own, but was unsuccessful in inflicting any real damage.

He had always taught his students that, if what they are doing does not work, try something else. Moss knew that his opponent was expecting him to fight with a fairly standard set of martial arts techniques. Moss surprised him with a simple but highly effective move he had learned from an elementary school bully on the playground. Moss had noticed that when Falcón threw a punch, he did not instantaneously retract it. When Eduard threw his next punch, rather than blocking, Moss dodged it by quickly stepping aside to Eduard's right; he grabbed Eduard's wrist while his arm was still extended. Moss then stepped behind him with his right leg and circled his right arm around Eduard's chest. He forcefully twisted his hips throwing his opponent backwards to the floor.

When he got back up, Eduard angrily attempted to deliver a debilitating strike with a front snap kick in Moss's solar plexus; he had subtly telegraphed his intent when he shifted back in a cat stance in preparation for the kick. Moss stepped back into his own *Hu Gul* (back stance) and grabbed Eduard's extended kicking foot which had missed him by inches. He forcefully twisted Eduard's foot; an audible snap came from his ankle as it broke. Still holding the foot, Moss swept his opponent's other leg and watched him crash to the floor screaming and cursing in agony and anger. "Stay down and concede the match… if you attempt to get up I will kill you," Moss barked.

"Kill them all now, "commanded the defeated Eduard Falcón as he lay on the floor. He reached in to his pocket and pulled out a small device about the size of a garage door opener and pushed a button; there was a thunderous explosion below them as the castle's communications and computer center was destroyed, along with the EMP weapons; the technology behind them would be gone as well. "Shoot them with the crossbows then carve them into little pieces with your swords!"

His command was met with stunned silence and inaction on the part of his men, who had clearly heard Eduard Falcón dictate the rules and terms of the combat contest. Mok Lee finally spoke: "General Moss, you and your comrades have fairly and skillfully won this contest; you and the rest of your people are free to leave now. I am greatly embarrassed by my own performance, and apologize for the dishonor just displayed by our employer."

Nicolas Falcón, with a look of humiliation and frustration, simply nodded his assent. With the help of two of their men, Nicholas Falcón left the room carrying his brother. The rescue team immediately tried to get the hell out of there.

The huge red-haired man who had been Thomas's opponent bellowed, "Screw the notion that they 'fairly and skillfully won this contest'—kill the invading vermin!"

Clearly this man was more of a leader than Mok Lee with this group of men, as they fired their crossbows and came charging at them. Fortunately, the only two of them who were hit, Jeff Florenzano and Scott Wroblewski, were wearing the Kevlar reinforced wetsuits; while it hurt like hell, the arrows did not penetrate the wetsuits. They all quickly ran through the door and slammed it shut behind them. As soon as they were out, Ross Ericson grabbed Jake Jackson by the wrist and hollered to the others, "Run for it... we'll be right behind you!" He simultaneously unzipped the front of his wetsuit and removed what appeared to be two separate five inch square sheets of plastic that were plastered to his chest; he wadded and kneaded the two sheets together and handed them to Jake. "You have 15 seconds to throw a fastball at those assholes chasing us or you will have an exploding fireball in your hand!" Fortunately, the men pursuing them had paused to reload their crossbows. As Jake opened the door, they saw that the men were only 30 feet away and running directly at them. Jake had a déjà vu moment as he hurled the wadded up ball of plastic at the men. Just as it left Jake's hand, a volatile chemical reaction occurred in the combined sheets of "plastic." Ross yanked Jake back and slammed the door—they only had a brief glance at the fireball that enveloped their pursuers.

"What in God's name was that?" Jake asked incredulously.

"That was a brilliant physicist at work... now let's make like geese and get the flock out of here," Ross exclaimed with a huge grin on his face.

CHAPTER 88

Haley pulled out the radio she had concealed and they transmitted that they would be coming shortly with the rest of the patients. They exited the castle and moved as quickly as they could towards the caverns down to the beach. Moss could not quite fully believe that the rescue had been so successful. As they approached the golden brick trail they halted in their tracks; the explosion triggered by Eduard Falcón had caused a massive cave-in. Their escape route was sealed off! Exhausted from running and feeling defeated, they sat down on the castle floor.

A voice rang out behind them: "You've come too far to fail now...please follow me; there is another way out of here." Before them stood their friend Andy, but he looked different; atop his head was a heavily jeweled crown; at his sides were two scabbards holding short swords with jeweled hilts. Andy led them down another rock-strewn convoluted path; they all shouted with glee when they saw light ahead and the sandy beach! Jeff turned to Andy and said, "I think I know the answer to this, but I'll ask the question anyway. Your highness, would you like to come with us?" Andy simply smiled and replied, "This will always be my home; thank you and your comrades for the kindness and friendship you've shown me. Best wishes for a long and healthy life to all of you. You and your friends are noble warriors—and Thomas is a major stud," he added laughingly, "together you vanquished a great evil!" He paused for a moment, winked at Thomas and then proclaimed "Forgive me Thomas, as I delight in playing practical jokes; it was me who wrote in the salt while you were confined in Bogotá. Should you noble warriors require future assistance in battling other evil forces, you alone Jeff have the psychic capabilities to beckon me." He took off his ring which was set with a massive ruby and handed it to Jeff. "When you need me, hold this in your hands and visualize me with your mind's eye and I will come to you. My consciousness is linked to my earthly possessions." Without another word, "Andy" turned and went back the way they had come….as he walked, he seemed to glimmer a bit—then he vanished into thin air.

"Holy shit, Jeff," Chris exclaimed, "Is he the ghost of King Andrew?"

Jeff paused for several seconds before replying. "I'm not sure what he is; perhaps 'ghost' is not the right term. Maybe 'enduring life force' would be more appropriate—we'll never know for sure."

Moss turned to Thomas and said, "Well, we now know who the practical joker was at FHRI!"

To their great surprise, King Andrew suddenly appeared before them. "I have reconsidered your gracious offer to accompany you. If I am to lend future assistance to you, I must travel to your homes to familiarize myself with the details of the physical locations; I can not in the future will my consciousness to any location with which I am unfamiliar. Oh, I would also feel more comfortable if you kept my unusual nature a secret; I would prefer that you simply call me Andy."

As they all swam out to the tender, including Andy, they heard the unmistakable sound of a helicopter taking off just as they climbed aboard. Moss saw a type of helicopter he had never seen before lift off from one of the castle's tall towers; it turned and began heading straight for them.

"Get us to the yacht is fast as you can," Moss barked at the tender's pilot. He got on the radio and called Ian. "Ian, we are on board the tender en route to the Almirante Cochrane. A helicopter unlike any I've seen before just lifted off from the castle and is heading directly for us; take off from the aircraft carrier now and prepare to intercept."

Ian's response was swift: "Roger, General Moss; I will take off from the aircraft carrier shortly and prepare to intercept."

They were heading towards the *Almirante Cochrane* at full throttle. Moss could see the helicopter closing quickly; as it flew directly over them, it matched speeds with the tender and descended until it was flying in parallel with them. Moss now recognized the helicopter, which he had only seen in pictures before. It was aSikorsky X2 helicopter, reputed to be the world's fastest whirlybird.

He could see that Nicolas Falcón was at the controls; his brother Eduard was in the passenger seat next to him. Eduard grinned sadistically and pointed to the missiles mounted on the helicopter, pointed at Moss, and then flipped him the bird. When he was sure that Moss had seen them, he said something to his brother and the helicopter rapidly climbed until Moss lost sight of it in the clouds.

About 15 minutes later they were all safely aboard the *Almirante Cochrane*. Ian McDonald contacted them by radio from his Harrier aircraft to let them know he would be circling above them watching for the return of the helicopter and guarding them from any other airborne threats.

They told Captain Jim Dexter what had transpired at the castle, and about the contrived fights imposed on them by Eduard Falcón (but intentionally omitted the existence and acts of King Andrew); Moss also advised him that Nicolas and Eduard Falcón were somewhere in their vicinity in a missile-equipped helicopter, and that he believed that an attack on the *Almirante Cochrane* was imminent. They next sent encrypted messages to the president and Prime Minister informing them that the rescue mission had been successful and that all the patients were safely aboard the *Almirante Cochrane* en route to Glasgow, but that they were being threatened by a missile equipped helicopter. Suddenly they got a frantic radio transmission from Ian. "My radar indicates an aircraft about 10 km to the east of you approaching at a speed of over 200 knots; I am going to intercept now."

"We can see it on our radar too," responded Captain Jim Dexter. "It appears to be closing rapidly on our position."

Captain Dexter quickly dug out a pair of binoculars and a handheld radio, and then handed them to Moss. Get out on the deck and let me know the second you can see that damned helicopter," he commanded. At sea, the captain of a vessel is the absolute authority, regardless of anybody else's rank. General Moss did as he was ordered.

CHAPTER 89

As soon as Moss was on the deck, he could hear the unmistakable sound of a helicopter in the distance. All the passengers, including Andy, were shown to their quarters.

Moss was momentarily surprised to see a battery of small surface to air missiles (SAMs) rising up from below decks on the bow of the huge yacht. Moss quickly remembered that this was the personal private vessel of the president of the United States of America. Missiles of this type would likely be capable of guidance from the radar aboard the *Almirante Cochrane*. Captain Dexter would not lock the missile guidance radar on a target unless he was absolutely sure that they were under attack.

Moss turned on the radio then scanned the horizon with binoculars. He quickly acquired the helicopter, which was flying low and fast straight towards them. He keyed the mike on the radio and said "Captain Dexter, I have a helicopter in sight now; altitude appears to be less than 1000 feet and it is closing rapidly on our position."

Captain Dexter immediately replied: "I have it on the radar and will attempt to raise them on the international air distress (IAD) frequency. Please come back in here General... I would like for you to try to reason with them."

"This is Captain Dexter aboard the *Almirante Cochrane*. You are rapidly approaching us; declare your intent now, as I have surface to air missiles locked onto you."

A response came a few moments later and the angry voice of Eduard Falcón: "Our intent is to blow your miserable asses out of the water... our missile is locked onto you!"

Captain Dexter wasted no time—he immediately launched his missiles that already had radar locks on the helicopter. Within 15 seconds, they could see a missile launch from the helicopter, which was now within their visual range. They also heard, and then saw Ian's Harrier streaking down directly towards the helicopter. The missiles from *Almirante Cochrane* were within seconds of reaching the helicopter; the missile launched from the helicopter was now less than a kilometer from the *Almirante Cochrane*. It looked like both Falcón brothers and all the souls aboard the *Almirante Cochrane* would soon be goners, barring a miracle.

They watched in stunned silence as their missiles blew the Falcón's helicopter to smithereens. They then watched an act of incredible heroism: Ian McDonald slowed his Harrier and transitioned from forward flight to a hover directly in the path of the oncoming missile; there was an incredible explosion, and the sky was full of smoke and debris falling into the ocean. At first they believed that their dear friend Ian had just sacrificed himself so that they might live. But, as the smoke began to clear, they saw the parachute—Ian had ejected just seconds before the missile hit his Harrier. The AV-8B Harrier is equipped with a version of the Stencel S-III-S ejection seat. This particular seat is designed for fast parachute deployment for the low speed/low altitude portion of this unique aircraft's flight envelope, including the hover which is the most dangerous portion… especially if the aircraft is about to be blown up! Amid the smoke and debris falling from the sky, they did not see the second parachute descending rapidly, which was in tatters and on fire.

CHAPTER 90

B y the time the *Almirante Cochrane* reached Glasgow, all of the patients had been cleared physically for their flight back to the United States. Once back on American soil, they would get an extremely thorough set of medical tests. They would also be debriefed by both the FBI and the CIA before being reunited with their families or permitted to do media interviews.

Andy was introduced as an escaping Falcón maintenance worker. Andy would travel first to Jake's home, then on to Ross Erickson's home, and finally, to Jeff Florenzano's home. No one noticed that he was anything other than a polite and friendly gentleman.

Ocean Centre was descended upon by a small army of Scottish law enforcement personnel. The Falcón organization's security force put up no resistance and surrendered immediately; all of them were arrested. Dale Vandermeer confidentially advised Luke Jackson and Moss that he had secretly copied encrypted files containing details of the Falcón organization's global operations; he had also copied the encrypted files which Dale believed contained all of the knowledge and curative stem cell procedures developed by Dr. Nicolas Falcón and his unethical evil associates, including case records and a list of patients who had died. He had the DVDs stashed beneath a pile of rubble in an unrestored area back at Ocean Centre; he requested Luke and Moss to accompany him in retrieving the DVDs. They granted his request; the next day Ian flew Dale, Luke and Moss back to Ocean Centre in his Bonanza, which was sporting new state-of-the-art avionics.

They were totally unaware that, with Eduard Falcón's apparent death, the devices located at Eduard's six secret caches were now ticking time bombs.

CHAPTER 91

Jake Jackson, Luke Jackson, Haley Jackson, Ross Ericson, Jeff Florenzano, Scott Wroblewski and Moss were all awarded the Presidential Medal of Freedom for their efforts in rescuing the patients and helping to bring down the largest criminal organization in modern times. They realized that the president's motivation in awarding them these high honors was not entirely all altruistic; by doing so, President Paxton was able to bring media attention to his own role (in an election year) in the successful covert rescue operation and the demise of the Falcón organization—a savvy political maneuver. Upon successful completion of the mission, Ross, Chris and Moss had resigned from the military with the president's blessing, and were once again civilians; they agreed to keep secret the existence of King Andrew—the world was not yet ready to comprehend the nature of his existence. Andy paid an extensive visit at Jake's home. He became good friends with Jake, Chris, Haley, Alicia and Moss.

Ian McDonald was given a knighthood for his heroic saving of all who were aboard the *Almirante Cochrane* with a missile strike imminent.

Mike Pellizari, CEO and president of PraxMed, was tried on multiple counts, convicted, and began serving multiple life sentences. A number of other PraxMed executives were under indictment based on the files left by Ted Mallick after his death. PraxMed faced a large number of criminal and civil actions; it eventually went bankrupt.

Some of the Ocean Centre security forces were never prosecuted; it was found that many of them, like Dale Vandermeer, were being coerced in one way or another to work for the Falcón organization. They all believed that a multibillion-dollar fortune in gold and various currencies was being kept in the massive castle vault; everyone was at first greatly surprised when it was found to hold less than $100 million dollars, which was seized by the Scottish government and eventually dispersed to the patients who had been kidnapped.

What had become of the Falcón fortune was finally clarified: Eduard Falcón's attorney had contacted authorities regarding disturbing facts detailed in Eduard's will. His vast fortune was not stored in the castle at all; it had been transported at regular intervals by submarine to six secret secure repositories distributed around the world. These repositories were not banks; they were in unlikely and hidden locations in the midst of highly populated areas. Deliveries to the secret locations had consisted of large sealed containers; in each container was, along with huge amounts of gold and cash, a pressurized cylinder holding enough bio-toxic gas to wipe out an entire city. Each cylinder was equipped with a timing device; they would count down for an entire year, and if not reset with the proper code within that time, then release their deadly contents.

The lawyer had further revealed that the locations of the deadly cylinders were not recorded in the will; it was written in the will that the locations could be found only on the large map tattooed on Eduard's chest. The problem was that Eduard's and Nicolas's bodies had presumably been blown to bits when the missile destroyed their helicopter. Clearly, this was a horrendous problem that would have to be dealt with another day. The information about the existence of the deadly cylinders was promptly classified as top secret.

Haley and Moss tried to return to a semblance of normal lives. They have been living together for a while, and so far it is going well; they are very much in love. Haley went back to teaching. Regarding Moss's alcoholism, he has been sober ever since the day he was kidnapped. With a price no longer on his head, he got his identity as Steve Moss back. He did a nationwide search for a certified physical therapist who was also a Soo Bahk Do master. He found Rose Baker, who fit the bill, and offered her a lucrative salary to join him in opening a Do Jang that specializes in teaching Soo Bahk Do as "advanced physical therapy" to students with a wide range of disabilities. Chris Meyer continued to progress and became a certified Soo Bahk Do instructor. Chris was invited to join Rose and Moss when their new Do Jang opened.

Jake Jackson decided not to seek reelection in the senate and married Sally Peters. He told Moss privately that he is considering a run for the presidency.

Dr. Thomas Hunt married Alicia Jones, who, along with Dale Vandermeer, had received a full pardon from the president. Dale and Laura Berg got married. When Moss learned of Dale's experience in the U.S. Army Criminal Investigation Command, as well as his educational background, he offered him a full partnership in a new private investigations company they would call "Moss and Vandermeer Investigations."

The Hunts moved back east, where Thomas is again practicing medicine. They are adopting a baby, and have asked Haley and Moss to be godparents.

Ocean Centre was seized by the Scottish government and thoroughly searched; once the damage from the explosion triggered by Eduard Falcón had been repaired, it was reopened as a luxury hotel and restaurant; Harriet Beecher and Jane Alexander were hired to manage it, and were permitted to live there as part of their compensation. All profits went to a foundation to support victims of kidnapping.

The knowledge and curative procedures resulting from the Bogotá experiments had come at the price of an untold number of human deaths and incredible suffering. There were those, including the president, who argued that the knowledge and procedures should not be disseminated because of the moral transgressions and unforgivable methods used in their development. Moss could understand that point of view, but he wasn't sure he agreed. No one other than Luke Jackson and Moss knew that Dale had given him secretly copied encrypted files containing details of Nicolas Falcón's experiments and the Falcón organization's global operations. Luke had the NSA decrypt them for Moss; this at first looked impossible, but a successful decryption strategy was finally devised by Sally Peters; she directed an NSA team that, per her scheme, allowed multiple super computers to perform simultaneous parallel decryption algorithms. Several weeks later the decryption of the files was complete. They contained all of the knowledge and curative stem cell procedures developed by Dr. Nicolas Falcón and his unethical evil associates, including case records and a list of patients who had died. Also decrypted was the master list Dale Vandermeer had given them of the Falcón organization's corruption worldwide: corrupted judges, bribed law enforcement and military personnel, operatives, and informants were eventually identified and neutralized.

As Moss sat at his computer loaded with the decrypted files, he composed an anonymous cover letter and attached all the Falcón files relating to the medical cures and stem cell techniques. Thomas had provided him with an extensive mailing list of major medical schools, research centers and hospitals from around the world. Undecided, his finger hovered over the key that would send the files to the mailing list, putting the knowledge and procedures in to the public domain. President Paxton, along with his evangelist brother Mason, citing religious and moral concerns, had insisted that none of the procedures developed by Dr. Falcón in collusion with PraxMed should ever be disseminated.

An inestimable number of lives could be extended and suffering reduced by employing the stem cell knowledge and procedures resulting from the Bogotá experiments. Moss reflected on one of the purposes of Soo Bahk Do which is the extension of life. He decided the ethical decisions regarding the use of the Falcón stem cell procedures should be made by the medical community. Screw the sanctimonious president and his holier -than-thou evangelist brother.

SEND.

CHAPTER 92

PARIS

Paris has a population of over two million; the density of population varies between the different districts of the city. As in all major cities, crime is prevalent, as are organized gangs.

Le Diable de L'armée (The Devil's Army) was the Parisian gang retained by Eduard Falcón to guard his treasure cache in the capitol city of France. This particular group's members were all former military men who dealt in drugs, gambling, prostitution and human trafficking. A large warehouse located in the outskirts of Paris was guarded by at least six members of the gang 24 hours a day.

Le Diable de L'armée had an additional level of security: Barbary apes trained for attack. Imported illegally through Spain, the Barbary apes are known for their powerful limbs, sharp teeth and short tempers; they can be turned into highly effective weapons. They have a bone-crushing bite, and their favored method of attack is to hurl themselves at an adversary's head.

Louis Moro, the leader of the gang, could hardly believe his good luck in landing this lucrative "babysitting" job; *Le Diable de L'armée* was paid ten million dollars in cash by a total stranger each year to simply guard some very large packages, which would arrive sporadically, in their warehouse. He was unaware that these packages contained considerable wealth; he was also unaware that the packages were toxic ticking time bombs—if not reset properly once a year, they would explode and disperse enough biotoxins to wipe out the entire population of Paris.

***

MANHATTAN

The population of Manhattan is over one and a half million. Satan's Militia was the eastern American offshoot of *Le Diable de L'armée*, the Parisian gang retained by Eduard Falcón to guard his treasure cache in the capitol city of France. This particular group's members were also all former military men who dealt in drugs, gambling, prostitution and human trafficking; they also committed arson for the right price. A large office building, located nearly in the center of Manhattan was guarded by at least six members of the militia 24 hours a day.

***

LOS ANGELES

Los Angeles is the 14th largest urban area in the world with a population of over 14.8 million. Beelzebub's Battalion was the western American offshoot of *Le Diable de L'armée*, the Parisian gang retained by Eduard Falcón to guard his treasure cache in the capitol city of France. This particular group's members were also all former military men—many of them bikers—who dealt in a wide spectrum of criminal endeavors, including murder for hire. Their warehouse was near the geographic center of the urban area, and was similarly guarded by at least six members of Beelzebub's Battalion 24 hours a day.

***

MEXICO CITY

With a population exeeding110 million, Mexico City most is the most populous Spanish-speaking country in the world. *El Diablo Ejército* (The Devil's Army) was the Mexican offshoot of *Le Diable de L'armée*, the Parisian gang retained by Eduard Falcón to guard his treasure cache in the capitol city of France. Nearly all of the members of El Diablo Ejército were corrupt police officers whose services could be purchased for the right price.

Their warehouse was on the edge of the urban area, and was similarly guarded by at least six members of El Diablo Ejército 24 hours a day.

***

HONG KONG

Hong Kong has a population of over seven million. The Devil's Army was the Hong Kong offshoot of *Le Diable de L'armée*, the Parisian gang retained by Eduard Falcón to guard his treasure cache in the capitol city of France. This group had connections with the Triad, and engaged in all manner of criminal enterprises.

Their warehouse was on the edge of Kowloon, and was similarly guarded by at least six members of The Devil's Army 24 hours a day.

***

LONDON

Greater London has a population of over seven and a half million. Satan's Servants was the English offshoot of *Le Diable de L'armée*, the Parisian gang retained by Eduard Falcón to guard his treasure cache in the capitol city of France.

This group's members were also all former military men who dealt in drugs, gambling, prostitution and human trafficking; they also engaged in assassinations. A large warehouse, located in Shepherd Market (a small square in the Mayfair area of central London), was guarded by at least six members of Satan's Servants 24 hours a day.

Epilogue

I greatly enjoyed my visit to America. I was the guest of Senator Jake Jackson in his magnificent home on Lake Minnetonka for nearly three months. I became good friends with Jake, Chris, Haley, Alicia and Steve. As a student of life, I have become greatly interested in the martial art called Soo Bahk Do, and asked Steve to explain its history and philosophy; I was greatly impressed! This is what he told me:

Soo Bahk Do, translated means "Hand Striking Way", and is a way to forge a body towards gaining ultimate use of its faculties through intensive physical and mental training. It is an art of self defense and philosophy that's secrets cannot be bought at any price other than serious and rigorous training.

Kwang Jang Nim (Grand Master) Hwang Kee was the founder of the *Moo Duk Kwan* and creator of the Soo Bahk Do *Moo Duk Kwan* ("School of Martial Virtue") system. He passed on his lineage to his son, who is now president and grandmaster of the *Moo Duk Kwan*. The "ten articles of faith" of Soo Bahk Do make great sense to me; my conclusion is that Soo Bahk Do is more than a martial art—it is a philosophy and way of life. Its purpose is unification of the body, mind, and spirit. Its practitioners focus not on besting others in combat, but on bettering themselves in many ways.

Steve invited me to train with him and others in the household...after each class, we would shout "Soo Bahk!"

I am glad I was able to lend some assistance to some deserving and truly noble warriors. While it appears that the evil forces permeating my ancestral home have been vanquished, time bombs are literally ticking in six major population centers around the world; clearly, my work in ending this evil is not yet done. Yesterday I learned that the president has called on Steve to lead the covert investigation in to the locations of the deadly cylinders. Jake and Sally

Jackson, Luke Jackson, Haley Jackson, Ross Ericson, Jeff Florenzano, Scott Wroblewski, Chris Meyer and Dale Vandermeer all agreed to assist. I will forge an alliance with this small band of noble warriors—together, I am sure that we will prevail in ending this threat borne from the stem of evil.

Soo Bahk!.